P9-CCO-983

I'M NOT MISSING

CARRIE FOUNTAIN

FLATIRON
BOOKS
NEW YORK

I'M NOT MISSING. Copyright © 2018 by Carrie Fountain. All rights
reserved. Printed in the United States of America. For information,
address Flatiron Books, 175 Fifth Avenue, New York, N.Y. 10010.

Grateful acknowledgment is made for permission to reproduce
from the following:

W. S. Merwin, excerpt from "Another to Echo" from
The Moon Before Morning. Copyright © 2014 by W. S. Merwin.
Reprinted with the permission of The Permissions Company, Inc.
on behalf of Copper Canyon Press, www.coppercanyonpress.org.

www.flatironbooks.com

Designed by Anna Gorovoy

The Library of Congress Cataloging-in-Publication Data is
available upon request.

ISBN 978-1-250-13251-2 (hardcover)
ISBN 978-1-250-13252-9 (ebook)

Our books may be purchased in bulk for promotional, educational,
or business use. Please contact your local bookseller or the Macmillan
Corporate and Premium Sales Department at 1-800-221-7945, extension 5442, or by email at MacmillanSpecialMarkets@macmillan.com.

First Edition: July 2018

10 9 8 7 6 5 4 3 2 1

For the James Webb Space Telescope,
fearless seeker headed into the mystery,
and the human minds who made it.

And for Susannah, duh.

How beautiful you must be
to have been able to lead me
this far with only
the sound of your going away

—W. S. MERWIN
FROM "ANOTHER TO ECHO"

I

1

"It's not weird." I sat down in the dirt and leaned back against the cold granite of Manny's tombstone. I tried to breathe in the winter air, but really all I could smell was enchiladas. "Why's it suddenly weird?"

"'Cause it's weird," Syd said, without looking up from her phone. "It's always been weird. I just— Now I'm not as tolerant."

"Whatever. I like being here. It's relaxing." I shielded my eyes and looked up at her wild halo of curls, blazing gold in the afternoon sunlight. Earlier, at our Feminism Club's annual fund-raising enchilada supper, a boy tripped and spilled his entire plate on Syd. She'd had to change out of her Feminism Club T-shirt and into one Katelyn Reed found in her car. It was too small for her and looked obscene. Even the rosette of her black lace bra was clearly visible beneath it. Her shirt read, ironically: KINDA DON'T CARE. There were still bright red splotches of enchilada sauce on her jeans.

"This is not relaxing." She shot me a two-second look of disgust. "Don't try to normalize this, Miranda."

"Dang. Why the grumpus?" I asked, though I knew exactly why the grumpus. It'd been two days since colleges were supposed to tell you if you'd been admitted early decision or not, but Syd still hadn't heard a word from Stanford about her application. Not a yes, not a no. It was crickets, and the crickets were becoming deafening with every passing minute.

Syd peeled her eyes away from her phone and plopped down beside me in the dirt, then took the elastic from around her wrist, gathered her mass of curls, and affixed them to the top of her head in a loose, unruly bun. It looked like a messy little cloud hanging over her head. "I'm just sick of sitting in a graveyard for fun. You know? I'm eighteen years old. I could be watching and/or making pornography right now. Legally."

"Whatever," I said. I leaned back against the cool tombstone and tuned my ears to the whoosh of the traffic passing on the interstate. As soon as I closed my eyes, she poked me with her toe.

"And I'm just sad." She wasn't going to let me relax. "I'm very sad." She toed me again, this time harder. "Miranda."

"Stop." I swiped her ankle without opening my eyes. "Why are you sad?"

"I dunno. I guess because our Feminism Club enchilada supper failed for the fourth year in a row to end misogyny and sexism."

"We made five hundred dollars." I tipped my face up to the winter sun. "That's not nothing."

"It's not something." She tossed her phone to the ground. "Seriously, though, you're the writer. This activity—this, like, *metaphor*, sitting among graves—it doesn't strike you as disturbing?"

"No." Without opening my eyes, I knew she'd rolled hers. "I love it."

It was true. The graveyard was probably my favorite place in Las Cruces. I loved the way it made me feel swallowed up. Invisible. I loved the way the tombstones faced the interstate, aligned neatly, like seats in a movie theater, and I liked watching the traffic. Something about it felt sacred.

The graveyard was like my church. Or whatever.

Anyway, it's not like it was a real graveyard. There were no bodies. It was just the dusty corner of the lot behind Syd's, where her dad, Ray, had dumped tombstones that had gone unpaid for, or that he'd screwed up. I REJOICE IN THY SALIVATION read one slab of marble. REST IN PIECE read another. Ray hadn't lasted long in the tombstone business. After a year, he sold his tools and went back to bartending, and Syd and I took over the graveyard.

MANUEL P. MONTOYA, ETERNALLY RESTFUL was my favorite: a black slab of granite with a pair of marble hands clasped in prayer rising from the top. Manny died at 101. I thought of his tombstone as a trophy he'd won for living so long. There was a space the shape of my butt worn into the earth beneath it, so great was my devotion to him. Of course, it was too bad Manny's family wasn't able to pay for the tombstone, and so it ended up here, behind Ray's double-wide, forever separated from Manny's actual eternally restful remains in the San Albino Cemetery a mile away.

Ray was such a loser. "I'm not running a charity here, ma'am," we'd once heard him say on the phone to some grieving widow while we were watching TV. *Asshole*, Syd mouthed, grabbing the remote and cranking the TV up so loud that Ray, scowling under his cowboy hat, had had to take the conversation outside.

Of course, we didn't know it then, but those were actually the good old days. The days before Tonya moved in, when Ray was mostly just gone and we had full rein of the trailer and the acre of dust and junk, each pile of crap further evidence of Ray's lifelong love affair with failure: piles of car parts, a shed full of rotted firewood, a broken-down stable for a horse-breeding business that never materialized beyond one vial of sperm he'd kept in the freezer for over a year. Now he was the assistant manager at Desperados, a bar in a strip mall between a nail place and a tanning salon. The polos Ray wore to work boasted that Desperados was "the hottest spot in Las Cruces." Who'd judged it thus remained uncertain. Syd called it Desperate A-holes.

"They make porn in Las Cruces, I bet. I bet I could be starring in my own porn by eight o'clock tonight if I wanted to. Right?"

"Let's just be quiet for two seconds," I said.

When she was actually quiet for two seconds, I became suspicious and I opened my eyes to find her leaning sideways against the grave next to mine, ISADORA THORNE, BELOVED SISTER AND AUNT. She was staring at me, her arms wrapped around her knees.

"What?" I said.

"Nothing," she said. "I'm just being quiet. I'm just sitting here very quietly, coming up with my porn name."

She put her finger in the air. "*Misty Buckets*. That's it. Yes. That's who I am now."

"Stop." I sat up straight and turned to face her squarely. "Stanford's gonna write. It's gonna happen. And you're gonna get in. And if you don't get into Stanford, you're going to get in somewhere even better with Misty Buckets ful of financial aid and you're gonna get out of here and it's going to be great and someday you'll fly your private helicopter jet over this shit hole of a town and laugh and laugh and laugh. Please. Let's wait five minutes before you commit to a life of porn. Okay?"

She looked at me sternly for a moment, skeptical. "What's a helicopter jet?"

"Shut up—you know what I mean." I didn't know what else to say. I had very little experience giving pep talks to Syd. Syd was usually the one giving them to *me*.

She laid her cheek on her knees, and the little cloud of curls flopped to one side. She looked genuinely worried. "The Plan," I said. When she nodded and looked away, I gave her a little shove. "It's going to work. Misty."

"Okay." She gave me the tiniest of smiles. "Yeah," she said.

Syd's Escape Plan had become legend at Las Cruces High. Her mom was a drunk who'd abandoned her, and her dad was a professional jackass. But Syd was different. She was defying the odds, and people loved it when people defied odds. She'd stockpiled awards and honors. She'd ranked number one in our class three semesters in a row. When, as a junior, she maxed out on AP math and science classes, she started spending half her days down the road at New Mexico State. She'd formed no fewer than four clubs since freshman year, each one earning its own venerated line on the work of art that was her college résumé. STEM Club, Robotics Club, Feminism Club, and, by far her most successful endeavor, College Prep Assembly, which everyone had quickly come to call Life Club and mainly involved Syd coaching other kids on how to properly execute their own escape plans.

She hadn't always been like this. Everything changed the summer before our freshman year, when her mom left the rehab facility where she'd spent two months getting sober and hightailed it to Colorado, surrendering full custody of Syd to Ray. She left Syd without an explanation or an apology or anything. It was baffling. I was wrecked. I stopped sleeping; my panic attacks returned full force. My father went into emergency mode, sending me back to the therapist I'd seen after my own mother had left seven years before.

I made *incremental progress in processing the loss in context of previous traumas*, as I overheard my therapist report to my father.

Syd, on the other hand, made a plan.

She was always smart, but the morning after Patience left, she woke up a genius. And she was hell-bent. That morning, she sat at my laptop with a singular focus, Googling, reading, taking notes. In about thirty minutes she'd put together her Escape Plan. That afternoon we walked to the high school and met with Ms. Yslas, her guidance counselor, who grudgingly changed all of Syd's classes: the easy ones to hard ones and the hard ones to the hardest.

Ms. Yslas was skeptical. Syd took that as a challenge.

A few days later she brought an empty Altoids box and a garden trowel out to the graveyard. She'd printed out a contract. It stated that, because the two of us were now both motherless, we were adopting each other. From now on we were officially the other person's person, and as such we were bound by honor and blood (*And blood?* I'd thought as she read the document aloud) to never stray from the other, and to never go after our mothers. "Our mothers left us," she said, her voice erupting dramatically, like a lawyer's on a TV show. "We won't go begging for scraps."

For me, the part about going after our mothers was pretty immaterial. My mom had been at the Garden over seven years by then. All efforts on the part of my father and my uncle Benny to extract her had been fruitless. My father had set about erasing all evidence of her existence. I'd forgotten what it'd been like when she was around. Patience had been gone a handful of days. For Syd, this strange ritual was a necessary protection. It was an action, and actions were all she had, besides me. And while I really loved the part about us adopting each other, I'd have preferred a milder action, something less blood pact-y. A dorky best-friends-forever necklace from Claire's would've worked just fine for me.

For Syd, only blood would do.

We signed our names with a pen, and then Syd quickly poked her finger with an old pin she'd taken off my backpack. When it was my turn, I couldn't do it. But Syd was dead set. So I handed her the pin and closed my eyes and felt her clasp my hand tightly and then push the point to my index finger.

"There," I heard her say. When I opened my eyes, I found a perfectly spherical drop of dark red blood on the tip of my finger. The graveyard spun. "Don't barf, okay?"

Syd whispered. "Just breathe." I nodded, unable to speak. I pressed my bloody fingerprint to the page next to hers. She folded the paper until it was small enough to fit into the Altoids box. Then she dug a deep, narrow hole between Manny and Isadora, and buried the box.

After that, Syd never mentioned Patience. She focused all her attention on the Plan. Junior year, she decided she wanted to go to Stanford because Stanford was a pipeline to Silicon Valley, and Silicon Valley was where Syd would make her eventual millions—doing what? It didn't matter. She'd figure that out later. Her mind was worth millions. California was her destiny. She talked about it with such specificity and nostalgia, you'd never guess she'd been there exactly zero times.

It was her Goldilocks planet, she'd decided.

We'd learned about Goldilocks planets from my dad, who'd made it his career at the small NASA facility outside town to help in the effort to find one. A Goldilocks planet was a planet like Earth, not too hot and not too cold, just right for sustaining life. To us, though, it'd come to mean more. For us, a Goldilocks planet was a place, definitely away from here, where a person became the person they were meant to be. A place to *live*. I was still looking for mine, though I suspected Las Cruces, New Mexico, was not it. I had lower expectations than Syd. But then again, the entire world had lower expectations than Syd.

And so, seeing as there was nothing else to do but join her when she kicked into high gear, I signed on to the Plan myself. I did all of the extracurriculars. I found cross-country, the one sport that didn't require coordination or even real speed, and I ran, sometimes training with my dad, until actual muscles were cut into my long, scrawny legs. I was the editor of the school paper and had won an award from the New Mexico Press Association for a series of essays I wrote documenting the life of the Future Farmers of America's prizewinning pig, Gracie. All that was only step one. I'd also taken as many AP classes as I could, except math, which I would have failed. Step two. And, by taking less difficult math classes, I'd kept my grade-point average sky-high. Step three. I'd even accomplished step four: after months of tutoring sessions with my dad that he often ended with baffling encouragements like "You *are* the math, Miranda," I'd managed a decent score on the SAT. I was sure my efforts would get me into UNM in Albuquerque, maybe even get me a scholarship. I'd started to think Albuquerque could be my Goldilocks planet. It was far enough away that only a handful of people would know about the Nick Allison Event, but close enough that I could visit my dad. I was happy with that. I was even a little proud.

Of course, Syd had walked away from the SAT with a score so close to perfect, she set a record for the school and they wrote about it in the *Las Cruces Sun-News*. She was unstoppable, an honest-to-god phenomenon, and until two days ago there'd been no doubt in my mind she would achieve the dream: early admission at Stanford. Honestly, I hadn't even considered the possibility the Plan wouldn't work. It hadn't dawned on me to imagine the world handing Syd a *no*.

Now doubt had begun to seep in, and I found the only way to hold it back was to feed Syd a constant stream of assurances, trying hard to deliver them with a disaffected air, even a slight annoyance, so as to indicate a certainty in me so complete, I was getting sick of talking about it.

"Seriously," I said, "stop being an idiot. You're a genius. They're gonna write." I leaned back against Manny again. "Misty Buckets. That's so gross. What's in the buckets?"

A huge, proud smile appeared on her face and I was relieved to see it. "Don't act like you don't know what's in the buckets."

Behind us, I heard the door of the trailer open and smack shut.

"Ugh." Syd's smile disappeared. She swung around and hid behind Isadora. "Devil or spawn?" I turned to see Tonya's son, Tyler, his shaggy red hair flying, running across the lot to us at top speed.

"Spawn," I said, but when Syd turned to see him coming, her face brightened again. "Slow down, mister!" she called.

We'd tried so hard over the last year to hate Tyler, but he was just too cute. We were his heroes. We couldn't help but love him. Syd consoled herself with the fact that Tyler's adoration of her pissed Tonya off big-time.

"Hi." He planted himself directly in front of us, breathing hard through his mouth.

"What up, T-bone?" Syd put out a fist and Tyler bent at the waist and bumped her fist painstakingly with his own.

"My mom said to tell you to stop using her hair dryer."

Syd turned to me, smiling, and shook her head. "*B-I-T-C-H*," she said. "She sent you out here just to say that?" she asked Tyler. He nodded.

"Okay. Tell her okay." She looked at me again. "And tell her I'm really sorry."

"Okay," Tyler said. He turned to run back, hyper-focused on the responsibility of relaying Syd's message, but he stopped again when Syd called his name.

"What?" he said.

"Love you, Ty." It was a rare display of affection for Syd, and it made me feel weird sitting there being witness to it.

"I love you too, Sydney," he said, and then cut off through the dust back to the trailer.

"Oh my god, she's, like, next-level bitch," Syd said, putting both hands on top of her head. "Fucking major league." Her phone received a text and she snatched the phone up and dusted it off.

"Uh-oh."

"What? Who is it?" I had the momentary hope it was Stanford, but then realized that was ridiculous. Stanford wouldn't text. She shoved the phone in my face. She'd received a text from someone she called Medium Hottie.

Party at 10k Poles, the text read. *COME.*

"Who's Medium Hottie?" I asked.

"I can't remember. Joe Moya? Isaac Chavez? I think it's Joe."

"Dude, you need to stop screwing with your contacts. Someone's going to see that someday and get mad."

She cocked her head. "Um, someone like you?"

"No." I looked at the highway. "I know what you call me."

"No, you don't." A smile took over her face, making apples of her rosy cheeks.

"Goody Two-Shoes," I said.

"Not anymore." She saw me eye her phone. I grabbed for it, but she was too fast.

"Whatever. I don't even care," I said, leaning back against Manny.

"Yeah, you definitely don't care."

She typed.

"Wait, if Joe's Medium Hottie, what is Isaac?" I asked.

"Big Boy." She looked at me and lifted her eyebrows. "I think."

"Oh god," I said. "Never mind."

One area of Syd's life that remained a mystery to me could be classified as Sex Stuff with Boys. It wasn't that she kept it off-limits or anything like that. In fact, she talked all the time about her conquests, especially those involving college boys. It was more that she'd done what could be classified as Sex Stuff with Boys, and I'd done only what could be classified as Pathetic Maintenance of Hyper-Virginity. And it wasn't even that I didn't like the idea of sex. Not at all. I did it alone in my room all the time. It was just that I'd never catch up to Syd, especially because the Nick Allison Event had essentially forced me into hiding. The heartache and humiliation of being stood up on prom night by the boy I'd secretly been in love with for three years was bigger than me. It was kicking my ass. And the worst part was I was still totally in love with Nick. I couldn't help it. I got butterflies every single time he walked into French class. It was pathetic.

"So we're going, yes?" Syd held up her phone and gave me a sideways grin. "I kinda wanna make out with him."

"Dude, you don't know who he is."

"So what?"

"So you're lifting the ban on high school boys?" Syd

had made it clear to anyone who wanted to know that she preferred college guys to high school boys. She hadn't gone out with a high school boy in over a year. Even her prom date with Matt Martinez had been platonic.

"No party times for me," I said.

"We'll go for half an hour." It was as if she hadn't heard me.

"I told my dad I'd be home. He's mad I'm never home. And he cooked all those enchiladas."

My father was probably the LCHS Feminism Club's most enthusiastic advocate. Every year he made the enchiladas we sold at the supper, and showed up to serve them, standing tall among the girls in his Feminism Club T-shirt, clearly enjoying that his presence mortified me. Times like these, the fact that my dad and I didn't look like we belonged to each other—him with his light hair and blue eyes and me with my dark skin and unquestionable Latina-ness—didn't bother me. When Lindsay Reynolds was tipped off by my dad calling me Miry today, she looked confused. "That's your dad, Miranda?" I honestly considered answering no.

"Bet I can steal a bottle of wine." Syd was already scheming.

"I can't go," I said plainly.

"I have life problems, Miranda." She gave me big, sad eyes. "I need to take my mind off my life problems."

"But—" I opened my mouth to offer my real protest but then swallowed it. Still, she knew exactly what I was going to say.

"He won't be there," she said.

"How do you know that?"

"'Cause he's a straight-up dork. Who only goes to

house parties. That's a known fact. Nick Allison maxes out at lame-ass house parties with parents in attendance. He's not going to be there. Just text your dad. Tell him you're going to help me organize my closet."

"I don't wanna lie."

"Life problems! Miranda!" She took down her hair and shook out the curls and flung them over her shoulder. "Just organize my closet. It's a freakin' mess. Please?" She sat up and flashed me a big, geeky smile. Then her face fell. "Seriously." She glanced at the trailer. "I so don't want to be here tonight."

I was defeated. "I can't drink. Not a sip. And I have to be home by nine."

She nodded in agreement of my terms. "Text the dad, please and thank you."

I texted the dad. She texted Medium Hottie, whoever he was. I felt bad lying to my dad, especially when the lie was about something as stupid as a Sunday night party at Ten Thousand Poles.

"You're the best," she said, her thumbs flying.

"You're the worst." I put my phone in my pocket and leaned back against Manny and tried to return my attention to the highway and its calming rumble and hiss and the big orange sun beginning to sink into the distant mesa behind it.

"I know." She looked up from her phone.

It seemed like she might say something else, but she didn't.

2

No one knew why the spot was called Ten Thousand Poles. There were no poles. Not even one single pole. In fact, there was nothing out there on the west mesa but barren desert spreading out in all directions, thorny mesquite bushes, and a silty red dirt that had ruined more than one pair of my shoes. I was sure my parents had come here when they were in high school. I guess I could've asked my dad if he knew why it was called Ten Thousand Poles. That was the kind of inane factoid he'd be certain to know and would be so pleased to call up. But then I'd have to admit I knew about Ten Thousand Poles and that I went to parties in the desert, which he'd strictly forbidden. If I ruined my shoes at Ten Thousand Poles, I hid them from my dad. He knew that red dirt.

We drove out of town on the old highway and then turned off onto a dirt road that led to the base of the mesa. We drove down it slowly, searching for the elusive road that would take us to the top. Mesas were weird landforms, like steep hills with their tops sliced off. There was no graceful way to drive up one. Syd and I argued about which path up was the one we needed to take, and which was an arroyo that would lead us out into the darkest heart of the desert and thus to certain death.

I hemmed and hawed until Syd finally lost it. "That's it, dingus!" She pointed to something that looked to me more like a horse path than a drivable road.

"Don't yell at me!" I yelled at her.

"Don't be a dingus! Just go!" When I didn't go, she reached over and laid her hand on the horn. "Goooooo!"

I turned and started up the path and almost immediately, my car started to struggle against the sand. My wheels spun. "This isn't it," I said. "We're going to die now." I braked.

"Yes, it is," she barked. "Go! Don't stop or you'll get stuck. Just go—go forward. Go!" She was having a hard time yelling at me through her laughter.

I kept going, up and up, until it felt like we were completely vertical. At the very top, my tires started spinning again, kicking up a giant cloud of dust. "Okay," I said. "We're going to die now." I pressed my foot all the way down on the accelerator. We jerked forward suddenly and my car bottomed out. We were at the top. We'd made it.

But there was nothing there. I'd been right all along. "This isn't it," I said. I turned to face her. "This isn't it."

"Oh my god, yes, it is." She was losing her mind. "Just. Fucking. Go."

I followed the path as best as I could, inching along, certain it was becoming more faint. Just as I was about to repeat again my certainty that we were going to die, my headlights glinted off the license plate of a car. Then they hit another, and another.

"See, dingus." Syd pointed to a guy standing behind

one of the cars, peeing with his back to us. He squinted over his shoulder, unfazed.

"This isn't it," I said again. We both laughed. I drove a little farther and my lights found a group of kids. I recognized some of them from school. They were standing in a semicircle, staring up at a giant sign that had been planted just beside a circle of charred tires and beer bottles.

"No way." Syd peered out the windshield.

COMING SOON, the sign read in cursive script. ENCHANTED ACRES, ADOBE-STYLE HOMES STARTING IN THE 200s. At the bottom, in big black letters, it read: PRIVATE PROPERTY! NO TRESPASSING!

"Gross," I said. "Did you know they make the houses look adobe-style using Styrofoam?" I edged my car off the road, narrowly avoiding a mesquite bush and making my own parking spot. "Like, at the edges, for the rounded look. My dad told me that." My dad was exceedingly proud we lived in an authentic adobe, tiny though it was and over one hundred years old, with walls so thick I had no cell reception in my bedroom and had to place my phone in the windowsill, like a beacon to the modern world. It'd been the house my mother and her brothers, Benny and Jacob, had grown up in, and my parents had bought it from my grandparents when they retired and moved to Deming. It seemed weird to me, to live in the house where your ex-wife had grown up, the very house from which she'd driven away one morning, never to be seen or heard from again.

"Why does everything always have to be ruined?" Syd opened the door and stepped out. "Enchanted Acres? It's so stupid. It sounds haunted."

Two guys in LCHS WRESTLING shirts started working together, one on each post, trying to maneuver the sign out of the ground. The posts wouldn't give. We walked over to join the crowd. "So much for the middle of nowhere," I said, zipping up my coat against the frigid evening. Syd linked her arm with mine and we stood and watched as the sign began to move incrementally against the dark sky. When two more guys joined in, the posts began to give way. The last heave dislodged them suddenly, and we all had to scramble as the giant sign fell, sending up a plume of dust and ash as it hit the ground.

"That was easy," I said. We looked on as people started stomping on the sign.

"I hate that I love destruction so much," Syd whispered gleefully. "Come on."

Syd brightened as we walked through the crowd, our arms still linked. She was like the Pope, anointing people with her smile. As usual, she looked amazing. She'd showered and changed out of her enchilada-stained jeans and T-shirt into a sweater and leggings and boots. She'd spent half an hour blowing her curls into beautiful, smooth submission. Her makeup was perfect. We'd swung by my house, but I'd only had time to go in and switch T-shirts. And then I just threw on another T-shirt because I didn't want my father to become suspicious. Why would I need to look good to help Syd organize her closet? I felt grungy next to her, and I detected the lingering smell of enchiladas in my hair, which was held back in an ugly French braid. I suddenly regretted having given in to Syd. I could be home right now, watching TV with my dad, studying the future perfect for my French quiz tomorrow.

Syd stopped at a pickup and let down the tailgate and hopped up onto it.

"Whose truck is this?" I asked, joining her.

"I dunno." She pulled a bottle of wine from her bag, along with two small plastic cups. She unscrewed the top, then poured one cup and handed it to me.

"I'm not drinking," I said, taking the cup.

"Fine," she said. "Just to toast." She poured the other cup to the brim and screwed the cap on the wine bottle and put it back into her bag.

I held up my cup. "To what?"

She glanced around the party as if looking for something to celebrate. "I don't know. The future."

"To the future," I repeated. "It's gonna happen," I added under my breath. She locked eyes with me. We tapped our cups. I took a sip of the wine. She downed hers. Then she grabbed mine and poured it into her cup.

"Hello, wino," I said.

"Jealous," she replied, taking a big swig from my cup and holding back a grimace. Syd wasn't a drinker, usually. She was cautious. She wasn't going to allow a clichéd predisposition to alcohol to be the thing that kept her here. She *wasn't* going to become her mother. Tonight, though, she seemed ready to get drunk. "I wanna make out with Medium Hottie," she whispered, singsong. "But I don't know who he is."

"Fabulous," I answered. I regretted even more having agreed to come. What was I going to do while Syd made out with Medium Hottie? Scan the party for Nick Allison and wait it out?

The wrestlers came walking toward us, dragging the

giant sign behind them. They couldn't help but resemble cavemen. "Hey, Syd," someone called from the back of the pack. As he got closer, I saw it was Joe Moya, aka possible Medium Hottie. He must've just arrived. Great.

I was formulating a plan for what I'd do while the two of them made out when, behind Joe, presumably from thin air, Nick's best friend, Tomás, appeared. My heart picked up speed. I noted he was wearing his letterman's jacket and was flanked on both sides by his baseball teammates. The chances were slim that Nick would join Tomás with his baseball friends.

I saw Tomás a second before he saw me and so had the great pleasure of watching his face go from neutral to stink eye.

One of the most mind-boggling aspects of the Nick Allison Event was that it had rendered Tomás and me enemies. I'd known Tomás since kindergarten. He was probably one of the most familiar people in my life—he was there the morning after my mother left, when my father had forced me to go to school. I knew he was dyslexic; he knew I was math-phobic. But for the last eight months, we'd been forced into to this weird routine, arranging our faces into *fuck you* every time we saw each other.

Nick himself didn't even do this. When he saw me in the hall, he simply looked away and, because seeing him hurt my heart, I paid him the same strange courtesy. It was Syd and Tomás who ended up doing our dirty work for us, our glaring and, in Syd's case, our torturing.

In this way, the whole thing was an entirely fifth-grade affair.

I scanned the faces of the pack of boys, but I knew before I was done that Nick wasn't among them. Nick would've towered over them in the most frustratingly awkward and adorable way.

Still, if this was the kind of party Tomás would attend, it was one Nick might attend too, theoretically.

"Hey, Joe," Syd said, elbowing me in the ribs. "You text me?"

"Nah," Joe called back. "What you want to text, bae?"

I fake puked. Joe's friends whooped.

"Aw, big boy," Syd said. She couldn't possibly be drunk yet, though she was acting a little like she was.

"Mystery solved," I said. "Where's Isaac?" I looked around, happy to have an excuse to scan the rest of the party for Nick. There weren't many people, and many of the faces I didn't know. They must've been kids from Mayfield or Oñate.

There was no Nick, thank god. But also no Isaac.

"He'll show." Syd sipped the wine. She was confident now that Isaac was Medium Hottie. I always had a feeling Syd knew exactly who everyone was in her contacts. She wasn't the type to actually mistake anyone—or anything. Ever. Mistakes were not her jam. More likely, to her, Joe and Isaac were simply interchangeable beings, lowly high school boys she'd make out with only when college boys weren't immediately available. I suspected it was this very quality in Syd—the *don't call me, I'll call you* vibe she put out—that made boys crazy about her.

"What're you going to do with that?" Syd called out to the guys with the sign.

"Burn it, I guess," Joe said. The crowd thought that was a great idea. In no time, the whole party was yelling, "Burn it, burn it."

"You can't just burn it like that," Syd called out. "Guys." She hopped down from the tailgate. "Seriously. You're gonna start a wildfire."

Joe shrugged as if to indicate things were out of his hands. No one, in fact, seemed to care for Syd's opinions at that moment. People had produced lighters and started gathering kindling.

"You need to cut the posts into smaller pieces. You can't burn it like that."

"Well, what are we supposed to do, Smokey the Bear?" Joe asked playfully.

"You guys are idiots," she said, her sudden rudeness leaving a tense silence.

"Day-um," Joe said. A few people oohed. "Just 'cause you broke the SAT, doesn't mean the rest of us are idiots." Syd shook her head and took a sip of wine.

"Syd," I whisper-called to her. "Come here." She swung around and walked back to the tailgate, incensed.

"I didn't break the SAT," she said loudly as she walked, raising her voice even more. "Just because I'm not a moron."

Joe shook his head and gave his attention back to the posts and the sign, perhaps realizing Syd was right: they couldn't burn the ten-foot posts the way they were. If he agreed, though, he gave no indication. The charged silence was obliterated when someone put on country music in their car and blasted it out of the open windows.

This officially became the lamest party I'd ever been to.

"Whatever." Syd leaned on the tailgate beside me, took out her phone, and disappeared into it once again, leaving me completely alone. Why had I even come?

"Dude," I said finally, a sharpness in my voice. She looked up. "Come on. What are you doing? Who are you texting? What's the deal?"

"Nothing," she said. "Sorry." She made a big show of turning her phone dark. She looked around. "I don't even know any of these people," she said flatly.

"Me neither," I answered.

Her phone dinged loudly in her hand. Of course. We locked eyes.

"Just wait." She swiped her phone and read the text.

"Fine." I hopped off the tailgate. I wanted to get away from Syd, but I had no one I could talk to at the party. The only person I really knew was Anna Oliver, one of the other staff writers for the newspaper. Anna had a dumb tattoo of a human heart on her forearm and a penchant for dangling modifiers and, at the moment, seemed to be on the verge of a make-out session with a guy from Mayfield. I turned. "I'm gonna sit in the car," I said, huffy. "It's freezing."

"Wait," she said. She turned her phone dark again and pushed off from the tailgate. Then her face lit up with an idea. I dreaded hearing it. All I wanted was to go home, really. "Wanna go get tacos? At La Posta? My treat?"

Tacos actually sounded good, I had to admit. I'd passed on the leftover enchiladas my dad was eating for dinner and I was hungry. "That place is gonna be packed right now."

"We'll be fine, Granny. It'll be fun. More fun than this."

"What about Isaac?"

"Over it," she said, shoving her phone into her bag. I'd guessed it was him she'd been texting. I wondered what he'd said to make her mad, but she clearly didn't feel like sharing and I didn't care enough to ask.

"Will you put your phone on silent, at least?"

She rolled her eyes. "Yes, Mom," she said. She finished the last sip of her wine and shoved the half-empty bottle back into her bag.

Joe and the others had given up on the posts and were starting a fire with a couple tires someone had brought out from the bed of their truck and tossed into the pit.

"See!" Syd called out. "Told you." No one but Tomás looked over. He shook his head and gave a halfhearted glare. She locked her arm with mine again and we walked back to my car, using the flashlight from my phone to look out for rattlesnakes.

It was a relief to get in the car and close the door and suddenly mute the music's shrill, swollen guitars. With thorny mesquite everywhere, it took forever to turn my car around. Syd barked advice the whole time.

"This isn't it," she said when we finally got onto the paved road that led back into town. We laughed.

La Posta was packed. When the hostess told us it could be a half-hour wait, I suggested we go to Napolito's, but Syd insisted. "It's only seven," she said. "We can wait." The *Granny* was implied in her tone. We sat on a bench and I was beginning to feel grumpy when the hostess came with our menus much sooner than a half an hour and showed us to our table in the back of the restaurant.

La Posta was the one of the oldest restaurants in town. It was a tourist trap, for sure, dripping with piñatas and (probably fake) Mexican folk art. The waitstaff wore weird uniforms that made them look like a cross between a bullfighter and a pirate, with bolero vests and red sashes around their waists. But it was true: La Posta did have the best tacos in town.

Syd was in a better mood as we sat down at our booth and dove into our chips and salsa. When our waiter came to take our order, she sized him up and immediately started flirting. He was college-aged, maybe a little older, and nervous.

"My name is Justin. I'll be your waiter." He leaned much more toward the pirate than the bullfighter. I felt for him immediately.

"Well, my name is Syd and I'll be your customer." She slung her hair over her shoulder and gazed up at him. As soon as Syd had him in her crosshairs, the poor guy's nervousness multiplied exponentially.

It was a pastime of Syd's, this weird, shameless flirting. Some guys liked it—most guys, I guessed. But others, like poor Justin, seemed to understand right away that Syd was far out of their league and was, in the best-case scenario, simply flirting to flirt. In the worst-case scenario, she was being cruel. It was one of Syd's blind spots. It never occurred to her that the receiver of her attentions might not actually want them.

Justin took our drink order and hurried off.

"Leave this poor guy alone," I said.

"What does that mean?" Syd snapped. "Fine," she added before I could tell her what I meant. But when he returned with our sodas, she went right back to it, complimenting his embarrassing oversized red sash.

"So, are you two sisters?" he bumbled nervously, spilling a little of my Sprite as he placed it on the table. I swiped the spill away with my napkin and smiled kindly. It was quite obvious Syd and I weren't sisters.

"Nope," I offered, beating Syd to the punch. "We're just super-close friends. We might as well be sisters." I thought I might've staved off an assault, but when she looked at me and widened her eyes, I knew Justin was in for the full Syd.

"Yeah, we're just, like, super-close." She put a hand on her heart. "This woman gave me a kidney."

"Whoa. Really?" He looked at me for help.

"Yes," Syd said. "When I was a baby. I was a very sick baby."

"Wow." Justin had walked right into Syd's trap. I'd tried to help him, but if the guy was this easy a target, there was nothing I could to do.

"I owe her my life." Syd reached across the table for my hand, which I pulled away.

"Wait." Justin looked at me again. "Weren't you a baby too?"

"She was a very generous baby," Syd said.

"She's screwing with you." I ended the poor guy's misery. Syd scowled at me. I'd ruined her fun. "I'm sorry. She's not a stable person."

Justin laughed. After that, he avoided looking at Syd, glancing over only once as he took her order before rushing off again.

"Why do you do that?" I asked her. "He's gonna spit in our food."

"That was just fun. He knew it was fun. You're the one who ruined it."

"Whatever," I said. I wasn't up for a fight. "So what happened with Isaac?"

"I dunno." She reached for a chip.

"Maybe he died," I said.

"Better have," she answered halfheartedly. "Still. I'm going back to my high school boys."

"Yeah?"

"I'm done with these stupid college guys. They think it's like charity to touch my boobs. I need to sink my teeth into some good, old-fashioned high school boy."

"Yum," I said, shoving a chip full of salsa into my mouth.

"Sophomores," she said in a perfect Cookie Monster voice, digging her hand into the bowl of chips and stuffing a small handful into her mouth. She laughed and then choked, spraying the table with half-eaten chips. People at the next table looked over.

"Dude. You're so gross."

She smirked and sat up straighter. "What about you?" she asked. "Who's your Medium Hottie?"

"Ugh." I put a chip into my mouth to buy some time. "I dunno."

Of course I knew. And I knew she knew. But she'd basically forbidden the mention of Nick's name. "He's trash," she'd declared the morning after prom. She'd stayed the night and was administering triage. I didn't want to get out of bed. I stayed curled in a ball under the covers and she sat at my feet, trying to make me laugh and planning out her offensive. It was hard to judge what punishment he deserved for standing me up on prom night. It was an unusually heartless thing to have done. But she'd think of something. "Nick Asshole-son has fucked with the wrong best friend-hole-son." When I laughed at that, she lit up, relieved. She stood and spanked me hard on the butt. "Come on. Your dad's making pancakes and having a nervous breakdown. Get your ass out of bed."

She'd started small. She pranked Nick's phone. The first time, it was funny, but I came to hate it very quickly. For some reason, he always answered, even though he had to know it was Syd—Syd whispering expletives, threatening him, calling him all manner of ridiculously offensive names: white boy ass slime, shitbrains dickface, dorky dorkalicious. When Syd got bored with calling him, she moved on to texting him images of dog poop, three a day, at mealtimes. If we were in the cafeteria and had a view of him, she'd watch him check his phone and receive his lunchtime serving. He never looked over. He never acknowledged us. He simply checked his phone and put it away and returned to his conversation with his small group of friends. Tomás would sometimes glare over at us, and Nick would ignore it. It was then I realized something Syd never seemed to: Nick was pranking her back, denying her the reaction she desired. When she called to harass him, he never hung up first. She had to do it. Syd's pride didn't allow her to see that she was the one being owned. She thought he was just stupid. An idiot, like the rest of the idiots she'd been forced into the midst of all her life, one of the first people she'd forget about as soon as she made it out of town.

When eventually she seemed to be moving in the direction of physical harm, after she covered his entire locker with maxi-pads, I told her to stop. I just wanted to forget about the whole Event. And that was true, of course. I did want to forget. But I also couldn't stand to think of Nick being publicly humiliated. Nick was super-shy. In

French class he often seemed caught off guard and would blush when called on to speak, even if he'd had his hand up. In fact, aside from having done the meanest thing anyone had ever done to me, he'd always been a genuinely nice guy. That made everything about the Event so much worse, so much more baffling and painful. The graceful way he'd handled Syd's vengeance only twisted up my already twisted feelings. Nick and I had been in French together for three years. I'd been pining for him for three years before the Event, carefully working on a friendship I hoped would turn into something more. Even after the Event, I imagined there might come a time in the future when Nick and I could return to talking, maybe even to being friends again.

I couldn't help it. I missed talking to him, joking around in French, saying hi in the halls. I liked Nick, just as much as I loved him, and just as much as I hated him. It was an impossible situation.

Syd didn't realize this, or else she didn't care. She'd never liked someone the way I liked Nick. She got obsessed with her hatred. That he wouldn't succumb to it drove her bonkers. When he walked up behind us later outside the cafeteria and surprised Syd by sticking one of the maxi-pads to her shoulder, she was baffled. Then she filled with rage. I don't think I'd ever seen her so angry before. Nick, on the other hand, was utterly composed. He even seemed sympathetic. "Maxi-pads are kinda cliché," he said, "but this was pretty funny." His shoulders slumped beautifully. His brown curls sat with perfect obedience on top of his head. I thought of him walking all the way from his locker to the cafeteria holding a maxi-pad and had to suppress a groan of actual pain. He glanced to me before he walked ahead of us and into the cafeteria. I could've sworn there was a little something there—a little apology, a little sadness. Something. The knot inside me tightened. Syd yanked the giant maxi-pad off her shirt and attempted to throw it in the trash, but it stuck stubbornly to her fingertips. "God, I hate him," I said. It was the worst lie I'd ever told.

"Maybe I need a Medium Hottie." I sipped my Sprite.

"I recommend the Medium Hottie," she said.

"You literally don't know who he is."

"Exactly," she said. We both cracked up.

"Whatever. I'll meet someone. In college," I said. "Or in jail."

Syd looked up at me, her face suddenly urgent, as if something wonderful had just occurred to her. Her blue eyes shone under her perfect eye makeup.

"What?" I said.

She blinked. She looked away. "Nothing," she said finally. I couldn't decide if she was still tipsy or if there was something she wasn't telling me.

"*What?*" I asked again.

She inhaled. But she didn't say anything. She dropped her head and started laughing.

"You're such a freak," I said.

She bolted upright. "But I'm your freak." She reached over and laid her hand on mine. "Forevah?"

"Keep your hands to yourself, mister." I slapped her wrist.

We scarfed our tacos. They were delicious. I checked the time on my phone and realized it was getting late.

"You can check your phone if you want," I said to Syd.

"Oh no. A promise is a promise, Gran."

We paid the check and got up to leave. Syd sauntered through the dining room, looking like a celebrity, and I followed behind her, head down, feeling like a bum. When she stopped suddenly, I nearly walked into her back.

She turned to face me. Her eyes were huge.

"What?" I asked.

"Corner table, corner table," she said, thrusting her chin to the left. I followed it and nearly died.

It was Nick Allison. He was sitting right there, looking perfect, eating a combo plate with his parents. It was uncanny, seeing him, because I'd just been thinking about him. But then again, any time I laid eyes on Nick it felt uncanny, because I'd pretty much always just been thinking about him. This time, however, felt actually weird. If Syd hadn't been the one who'd pointed him out I might have thought I was hallucinating.

"Oh my god, go," I said. "Go!" I pushed her forward forcefully, toward the long, piñata-strewn hallway that would lead us to the door, to the outside, to my escape from humiliation. But she wouldn't budge.

"Oh, no." She had fire in her eyes and it terrified me. "We're doing this." She turned sharply and started over to the table, grabbing me by my wrist and dragging me behind her.

"Syd, stop," I whispered. I felt like I was being dragged into a bad dream. "Please." I tried to wriggle free, but she tightened her grip on my wrist until it hurt. "What are you doing?"

"Just watch," she said. "This'll be good."

A few agonizing steps later and we were standing directly behind Nick. His hair was so close that I could see the auburn highlights winding through his curls. His mother and father looked up at us with curiosity. We must've looked like a couple of Nick's friends, just stopping by to say hey. But when Nick turned and looked up to see Syd standing behind him, and me cowering behind her, his face went completely blank. He was stunned. It was terrible. For my part, I was sure I looked like I was being eaten from the inside out, my organs liquefying.

Almost immediately, though, Nick seemed to understand what Syd was up to. His mouth went from a hard, straight line of terror to a small, grudging smile.

"Hey, guys," Nick said to Syd, not even daring to look at me.

"Hey," Syd said. "Nick-o." She'd been caught off guard. He'd said hi first and she hadn't expected that. She raised the ante and put a hand on his shoulder. He froze up but then absorbed the shock and relaxed.

"I'm Syd," Syd said, offering a handshake across the table to no one in particular. She surprised his parents with her weird friendliness and they looked at each other, deciding which of them should shake her hand. Nick's mom went for it.

"Hi," she said, taking Syd's hand. "I'm Maggie. I'm Nick's mom. You go to school with Nick?" I was trying not to stare at her, but it was hard not to. Besides being beautiful and radiant and looking a strange lot like the boy I loved, Nick's mom was *young*. Or maybe she wasn't that young. Maybe it was that Nick's dad was so *old*. He looked to be at least twenty years older. I guess you could say he was handsome, though, in an austere, professorial way. He had striking blue eyes and his wavy hair was gray-ing at the temples.

"Yes," Syd said. "We're friends." As soon as she'd ex-tracted her hand from his mother's, she held it out to his father. "Sydney Miller," she said when his father rose halfway and took her hand.

"Nice to meet you, Sydney," his dad said.

"We've met before, Professor Allison," Syd said, still shaking his hand vigorously. "I was in Dr. Freemont's calculus class last year. You came to guest-lecture—on computable model theory. It was such a great lecture. You really blew my mind. I introduced myself after class. You probably don't remember me." She finally let go of his hand, rather suddenly, and he seemed to lose his balance before sitting back down and looking to his wife, stunned.

"I'm sorry—no. That was a while ago. But yes, sure. I remember you. Sydney. Yes." He nodded like a fool. Only Syd could turn a distinguished math professor into a bumbling idiot with one handshake.

"So you guys just out to eat on a Sunday night, huh?"

"Yep." Nick jumped in to save his parents. He'd gained a bit of composure. Just as he'd done when she'd called all those times to cuss him out, he'd go along with this lunatic visit she was forcing upon his table in order to win the upper hand. He shot me a look. "Hey," he said.

It was the first time he'd spoken words to me in eight months. It was only one word, but it was enough to stun me, deer-in-headlights style. I stared at him. "Hi," I said finally. I focused all my attention on staying upright. I couldn't believe what was happening. It truly did feel like a bad dream, one where I was paralyzed while some terrible beast approached. I was able to observe everything, but unable to run or move or even make words come out of my mouth.

"That looks so good." Syd pointed at Nick's mom's half-eaten chile relleno. "Doesn't it?" She turned to me. She was a time bomb. I didn't know what she was going to say or do next. All I wanted to do was leave, to escape. I twisted my wrist out of her grip and took a big step back.

"It's very good," Nick's mom said politely. "So you girls go to Cruces?" She powered forward, trying to regain a sense of normalcy. She looked to me as if to ask that I take over here.

"We do," Syd shot back. "I take half my classes at the university. But yeah, we're friends with Nick. And Mir has French with him." She yanked me forward so I was standing next to her. "Right? Mir?"

"Yes." I couldn't sound normal or act normal or breathe normally. Nick's mom gave me a sympathetic look, as if maybe I was slow. Why else would I hang around with a lunatic like the one standing beside me?

"Super meeting you two," Syd said. "Nick's always talking about you guys."

The weirdness level had reached a peak. We'd bottomed out on the mesa of this interaction. Because Syd was having trouble using her inside voice, people at other tables were beginning to shoot us looks.

Nick cleared his throat. He lifted his head and placed his fork beside his plate and turned in his seat to look us both right in our faces, first Syd's, then mine. "Cool seeing you guys." He was calm and friendly. He was doing it again, beating Syd at her own game, trouncing her. Given that I hated her guts for dragging me into this situation,

I sided with him on this one. "See you tomorrow, Miranda."

"Yeah." I was looking him in the eyes for the first time in eight months. It felt so good, being friendly with Nick, even for just a moment, even if it was a sham. It was as if we'd stepped back in time to a year ago. "Hey," I tossed in. "Remember, we have that quiz tomorrow. Future perfect."

"Oh yeah," Nick said. "Future perfect." He turned to his parents and shrugged. "A quiz on a Monday."

Syd looked at me and furrowed her brow as if to ask what the hell I was doing.

"Oh—wait." Nick's mom looked from Nick to me then back to Nick again. "Miranda? This isn't Miranda?"

Nick shot me the briefest of desperate looks before his eyes fell to his half-eaten tamale. "Oh yeah. This is Miranda."

Nick's mom looked at me, and a big sympathetic smile bloomed on her face. She put down her napkin and rose from the table, walked around Nick, and edged Syd out of the way. Then she opened her arms. Not having a clue what else I should do, I opened my own.

All of a sudden, we were hugging. It was totally insane.

"Oh, Miranda, it's so nice to finally meet you. We were so sorry to hear about your ordeal on prom night." I looked to Nick in disbelief—he'd told his parents about standing me up on prom night? My *ordeal*? He refused to return my gaze. I was speechless. When I disengaged from the hug and stood back, I turned to Syd, actually hoping she might do something crazy just to distract everyone, to make this horrible moment pass more quickly. But Syd wasn't there. I turned to see the back of her perfectly smooth hair as she slunk down the hall of piñatas and out of sight.

She'd left me there all alone with Nick Allison and his weird mismatched parents, who seemed strangely fine with their son having put me through a prom night ordeal.

"Thanks," I said to his mom. I looked at the back of Nick's head. "It was terrible." Nick offered me his eyes and I tried to shoot daggers out of mine. "It was the worst."

"Yes," she said, taking a step back. She was suddenly self-conscious. "So sorry—to accost you. Look at me." She turned to Nick, then back to me. "Nick's said such nice things about you. We were so sad—about everything. Anyway." She clasped her hands in front of herself nervously. It was a familiar gesture, something Nick would do. One of the millions of things I loved about Nick was that he very rarely seemed to know what to do with his hands. He was always shoving them in his pockets or putting them behind his back.

"It was nice to meet you," I said. I gave a nod to Nick's father, who still looked stunned and confused, a flank of hair hanging out of place on his forehead. I avoided looking at Nick.

I turned and walked away from the table.

I was so furious, I thought I might burst out into newborn-baby-style tears as I stormed down the hall of piñatas, past the pirate-y hostess, through the crowd of waiting patrons, and out the door, into the stark, frigid night and across the street to the lot where I'd parked my car.

Syd was leaning against the passenger-side door, her back to me. I got in the driver's seat and put on my seat belt and turned on the engine. My hands were shaking.

I threw the car in reverse. A moment later Syd slunk in. We sat there, breathing cold air.

"Sorry," she said meekly.

"What the fuck is wrong with you, Syd?" I'd hardly let her get through her apology. I'd never yelled at Syd before—I'd endured a lot of ridiculous stuff, and I'd mediated a lot of situations like the one with the waiter, but she'd never done something like this to me. I'd never felt this much anger toward her. Never.

"Jeez." She blinked a few big blinks. "Chill. It was just a joke."

"No, it wasn't. That was mean." She tried to insert a response, a denial, but I ran right over it. "And no, I don't mean to Nick—I don't care about Nick. It was mean to do that to me. What were you even thinking?"

"I just wanted to screw with him."

"Of course! Exactly! Because it's always what you want to do!" I threw my car back into park and gripped the steering wheel. I couldn't drive. I couldn't even see straight. So I just sat there, staring forward. I tried for my slowest, calmest voice. "As unbelievable as it may be to you, Syd, not every single fucking thing in this world is about you."

"Damn," she said. I'd gone straight for her weakness and I'd slashed. I'd wounded her. And I wasn't sorry.

"Yeah, damn! Dude! That sucked. You suck for doing that."

"Okay. I get it!" she shouted back. "I'm sorry."

"Are you though?" I turned to her. She was looking out her window into the parking lot. When she finally turned to face me, she was holding back tears.

"I'm sorry," she said quietly. "That was stupid. And it was mean. To you." She took a big, ragged breath. "And— I'm sorry. I'm really sorry."

I loosened my grip on the steering wheel a little. "Just leave Nick alone," I said. "Leave him alone. He's my enemy. Okay? At least let me have my own enemies."

"Okay," she said. She looked exhausted. The eyeliner she'd applied so meticulously to her bottom lids had begun to run. Her hair was limp. The two of us sat there silently for a moment. "I'm sorry," she said again.

"Okay." I shook my head. I tried to will myself to cool down, to allow her apology into my overheated brain, but I was struggling. "All right." I carefully backed out of the space, still shaking.

We didn't speak the whole way to her house. I glanced over at her a couple of times. She was lost in thought, a million miles away. She was probably thinking about Stanford again. She'd gone back to fretting. Or she was thinking about Medium Hottie. Whatever.

"Just check your phone." I finally broke the silence.

"I don't need to check my phone," she said flatly. "I know everything I need to know." She stared out the window and into the darkness. I had no idea what she meant by that, and I was too mad and too exhausted to care, so I didn't say anything.

When we got to her house, she got out of the car and turned and looked in at me. I could hardly return her gaze.

"Bye," she said.

"See you tomorrow." I only gave her half my voice.

She closed the door and walked halfway to the trailer. Then, just as I was about to pull forward and turn around, she stopped and walked back to the car. She came around to my side and I rolled down the window.

"I'm really sorry," she said again.

"Okay," I said. I just wanted her to walk away. I was done with her and her thousand *sorry*s. Somehow they didn't quite add up to one genuine one.

But then she just stood there. "You're a really good friend, Miranda. The best. Really. And I don't deserve you." Her face hung above me, obscured by shadow. I was disoriented by her earnestness but also pretty annoyed by it. "I love you," she said. And then very quickly—so quickly I wasn't even sure it happened—she leaned her head into the car and kissed me on the forehead.

I was still sitting there, stunned, with the window down, when she walked away, up the steps, and into the trailer.

Her show of affection dulled but did not extinguish my anger.

I pulled forward and turned around and drove away the second she opened the door, before she'd even stepped inside.

3

I was still wound up when I got home. I kept replaying the scene in the restaurant. Nick's mom hugging me. His dad looking confused. Syd and her unhinged performance, so caught up in her one-woman show that she hadn't even bothered to notice she was using me as her prop.

I got into bed and closed my eyes and tried to pray.

I tried to pray like I always did, the way my mother had taught me.

My strongest memories of my mother were of watching her in church. She'd kneel and plant her elbows on the pew in front of her and lean into it, letting her long black hair fall forward, holding her hands up to her temples and planting her palms there, as if thinking hard or peering into a dark window. Her hands made a shield. She blocked out the world. My mother was a self-conscious person. She didn't like to be looked at or complimented. When she prayed, though, she did it with her whole body, her whole self. She disappeared into it. And when she did, I could look at her. I could observe her freely.

I didn't really like church, and was never confirmed Catholic, but I'd go to mass sometimes simply to watch my mother pray. Looking back, I guess it should've been a sign of warning, the way she could vanish so easily, before my very eyes.

I asked her how to do it once. I told her I wanted to try. I remember being nervous asking. I guess I thought it was something very private, or very difficult. She answered with strange authority: "Close your eyes and listen. When God says, 'Go,' start." That was it. That was the extent of her spiritual guidance.

Prayer was a phone call. Dial and wait. When God picks up, start talking.

I took her brief instructions and tried. Lo and behold, it worked. Only I didn't really know what God was supposed to look like, so I didn't know what to imagine when God picked up the phone.

When I closed my eyes and listened, what came to me was the Milky Way. I don't know why. I'd only seen the Milky Way once, when my father had driven us out to the dark desert behind my uncle Benny's house in Española. It was definitely the biggest, most Godlike thing I'd ever seen. And it looked so close and so inviting, as if I could reach up from the hood of my dad's car and run my hand through those billions of planets like sand. I asked my dad how far away it was. "That's the crazy thing. We're looking at it from the inside. The Milky Way is right here." He'd smacked the hood of his car for emphasis.

It was kind of perfect, the way my mother's religiosity and my father's science-minded rationalism canceled each other out inside me. She showed me how to pray. He directed the call to the Milky Way.

Inside me, God was a math problem that always came up *zero.*

And though my methods were untraditional, I knew God wouldn't mind being the Milky Way, because God *was* the Milky Way, just exactly as much as God was everything else and just exactly as much as God was nothing at all. *Zero.* Right?

For as long as it lasted, my belief in God balanced on that *Right?*

But when my mother left, everything fell apart. I'd close my eyes and dial, but no one picked up. Not God, not the Milky Way. Nothing. And there was a big difference between zero and nothing.

Then, one day, seemingly out of nowhere, I started reciting the Gettysburg Address instead of praying. I happened to be memorizing it for a presentation at school. It'd lodged in my brain. After that, whenever I closed my eyes and dialed, I got Abraham Lincoln, standing on the battlefield, pulling from his coat pocket a piece of paper with those 272 words written on it.

It wasn't the same. I guessed it would never be the same. But it worked in a pinch. It worked better than all the breathing exercises I'd learned from all the therapists my father had sent me to in the year after my mom left, all those dumb visualizations and affirmations and behavior modifications. It felt like praying, even if it wasn't praying. I'd take what I could get. I told no one about this, of course, not even Syd. It was mortifying. I avoided Googling it. I was sure I'd find I was suffering from some obscure form of obsessive-compulsive disorder. *Lincolnism.*

Eventually, as my father had gotten rid of all my

mother's stuff, the Gettysburg Address was all I had left. Of her. Of God. But then, when I was thirteen, I found a copy of *Lives of the Saints* that had fallen behind a stack of books on a shelf in the guest room—it'd been there for years, I guessed—and I opened it to find my mother's handwriting on nearly every page. I was thrilled and dumbfounded. This oversight of my father's was close to a miracle.

I snuck the book into my room and set about reading everything, every passage she'd underlined, every note she'd dashed off in the margins. She liked the gruesome stories most: saints who'd endured nauseating wounds that bled for years on end, or who'd been martyred by beheading. She liked penitents who starved themselves and wore hair shirts and went off to the desert to pray themselves to death in a cave. She had a soft spot for stigmatists, especially those who were the only ones who could see their own wounds (*can you imagine? Absolute torture*), and for those who heard voices (*how do you know the difference between hearing God and LOSING YOUR MIND???*). Saint Jude's was the page on which the spine of the book had broken. In the illustration, Jude's face was pure serenity. He looked almost exactly like Ryan Gosling. Saint Jude was the patron saint of lost causes, disasters, and hopeless situations. *Patron saint of the IMPOSSIBLE!* She'd drawn little stars around this, and motion lines, so it looked like it was a comet flying through space. I didn't know for sure, but by investigating the changes in handwriting, I figured she'd begun her annotations as a kid and had been making them right up until she left, or at least until after I was born. I knew this because on the page of Saint Bridget, she'd circled the feast day, July 23, and had written at the bottom of the page in small, stiff writing: *Our Miranda born this day. It's been one week. Peter already better at this than I am. Looking to God for guidance.*

My mother was twenty years old when she'd written that.

I started reading because I found my mother's notes interesting. She was a mystery. I was going to solve her. But then, after a while, I read it just because. Because it was one of the only things left in our house that had belonged to her. Because it helped me sleep at night. Because now it was mine.

I calmed down after a few Gettysburg Addresses and considered texting Syd to say I was sorry. But why was I sorry? For being a human being with feelings? I decided I'd wait until morning. We could talk it out on the way to school.

I slipped the tattered book out from where I kept it in my bedside table and flipped through to Saint Francis, one of my personal favorites, the son of a rich silk merchant whose father disowned him when he joined the church. I intended to read the entire entry and all my mother's notes (*often pictured w STIGMATA; patron of ecologists*), but I must've fallen asleep before I'd even made it through his freewheeling youth, the time before he went pious, when he was just some rich dude's son, living large in Assisi, not knowing what unexpected turn his life was about to take.

4

I heard church bells in my dream. I opened my eyes to see *Lives of the Saints* open beside me on the bed. I'd dreamed about my mother, as I often did when I read from the book, but the dream was too distant to recall. But the bells—the bells wouldn't stop. I sat up and realized it was my phone, up on its perch in my windowsill. Someone was calling.

Someone was calling? I scrambled out of bed and grabbed the phone, but before I could answer the call, I heard pounding on the front door. I stumbled out into the hall, disoriented, and my father swept past me to the front door, looking bewildered, pulling on a T-shirt, his eyes slits. He gave me a look that said, *Stand back*. I registered that the T-shirt he'd put on was his Feminism Club T-shirt from yesterday. I stood back.

Because I'd only ever heard knocking like that in crime shows, I assumed we'd find two police officers standing there, flashing us their badges, informing us of a murderer on the loose. But when my dad opened the door, it was Ray standing there under his giant cowboy hat and

Tonya skulking behind him. Ray had his phone to his face. When he saw me standing behind my father, he ended the call and my own phone went silent in my hand.

"Where's Syd?" He looked past my father to where I stood in the hall.

"What's going on?" My voice sounded strange, like it belonged to someone else. I took a step forward, and my dad turned and put his hand to my shoulder to stop me.

"What's going on?" my dad repeated. He sounded groggy but forceful.

"What's going on is that Syd's gone."

"She took her car," Tonya added. "God knows what else."

"What?" My brain wasn't working. It must not have been, since what they were saying was ludicrous. I'd seen Syd last night. I'd dropped her off and she'd kissed my forehead after our epic fight.

"Syd ran away. She's gone," Tonya said.

"She probably just went to school early," I said. I looked at my phone. It was 5:57 A.M. It was totally unrealistic that Syd had gone to school this early. In reality she'd probably just snuck out. Maybe she'd finally gotten ahold of Isaac. Or she sometimes snuck out just to go for drives. She said driving cleared her head. It was a weird time to be out, but Syd had done weirder things. Last night was a good example.

"No. You don't understand. She's gone," Ray said. He was such a dumbass. He looked like a cartoon character in his cowboy hat. Syd said he wore it because his hair was thinning. I'd never seen him without it on.

"What do you mean?" I was fully awake and getting

angry with the two of them. They'd showed up on our doorstep like a couple of bullies.

"What part of *she's gone* don't you understand?" Tonya snapped. Her highlighted hair blazed in the porch light. Her eyes darted to my father.

"Let's calm down, Tonya." My father stepped forward and stood in the doorway. He was standing so close to Tonya that she took a step back. "Let's speak to each other with a little respect. My daughter's done nothing wrong. It's six o'clock in the morning for Christ's sake." The lump in my throat grew. Tonya looked offended and confused and she glanced at Ray for backup. When Ray did nothing, she shrunk back.

"She left a note," Ray said.

My brain finally caught up. A note? I turned to my dad. "Oh my god."

He nodded to me. His face said everything was going to be fine. I didn't believe his face.

"What did the note say?" My dad put his hands on his hips. He was trying to look imposing in his basketball shorts and yellow Feminism Club T-shirt.

"It said—What did it say, Ton?"

"*I'm gone. I'm not missing.* That's all it said."

"We called the police," Ray said.

"They can't do crap," Tonya barked. Ray shot her a look and she rolled her eyes and threw up her hands.

"They can only do a runaway report. 'Cause she left a note. If she was just missing, we could file a missing persons report and they'd have to help us."

"She obviously looked it all up on the internet." Tonya said the word *internet* as if it were a curse word. I noted she'd done her hair this morning. Definitely. When had she done that? While Ray was talking to the police? "She's a selfish, stuck-up brat." Tonya couldn't help herself. Her hatred of Syd went so deep. But hearing her say those things about Syd didn't even make me angry at her. They made me angry at Ray. Who would let someone say those things about his own daughter? What kind of a father would allow that? I was unable to speak. I was just standing there in my pajamas, staring at them as if they were a movie. When would it end? And how?

My father, on the other hand, was done. "I'm sorry about Syd," he said, gripping the door and beginning to inch it closed. "Miranda obviously has no information about this. I've got to get to work and Mir has to get to school." As if on cue, my father's alarm clock started beeping from his bedroom down the hall. I saw his hand become a fist in frustration and I thought for a second he might punch Ray. But no—my father would never do that. My father was the most rational person on earth.

Ray shoved a business card into my dad's hand and my dad passed it back to me. I looked down at it.

Ray Miller, Manager
Desperados Nightclub
"The hottest spot in Cruces"
575-555-5219

"She'll come back." I don't know why I said it. I had no confidence it was true. If I knew anything, it was that Syd never changed her mind. She didn't make mistakes. That was her whole deal. But then again, why would she run away? The Plan was about to come to fruition. It was all about to happen for her. It didn't make any sense.

"I'm glad to hear you say that." Ray looked down. Maybe he knew what a failure he was as a father. Maybe he was full of guilt and shame. I hoped so.

"And"—I swallowed hard and inched closer to my dad's shoulder and looked Tonya right in the face—"you shouldn't say those things about Syd."

Tonya was so stunned, she had no response.

"What about Patience?" I thought to ask.

Ray looked surprised I'd spoken directly to Tonya, but he didn't seem angry. Maybe he was just scared because my father was at least a foot taller than him and happened to be holding his hand in a fist. "Well, um," Ray stuttered. "She doesn't have a phone. I'll write her. I guess."

Tonya rolled her eyes. My blood boiled with hatred.

"I'll write to her," I said. "I'll get in touch with Patience. Just let me do that, okay?" I knew Ray wouldn't write Patience. He probably didn't even have her address. I did only because I'd kept a couple of the greeting cards Patience had sent over the last few years. A Halloween card, a valentine, a birthday card that had come two weeks late. Syd threw them away without opening them. And I snuck them out of trash can and opened them and read Patience's shaky handwriting. Never an apology. Never a reason. Just some generic note. *Wish I could be with you, my valentine.* Because the gesture was more than my own mother had ever made, I'd kept them, thinking Syd might want them someday.

"All right." Ray nodded. The anger had drained out of him. He looked puny under his dumb cowboy hat. It was so rude that he hadn't taken it off when we opened the door, as any self-respecting actual cowboy would've done immediately.

"Very sorry, Ray," my father said. That his alarm was still blaring down the hall seemed appropriate. He held up his palm. It looked more like *stop* than *good-bye*. Finally Tonya turned and huffed away and Ray followed her across the gravel to his pickup. Not until Ray turned on the engine did I notice Tyler in the cab, strapped into his booster seat. He saw me see him—he'd been waiting for me to see him—and he waved wildly. He looked worried. It broke my heart. Tyler was the only one of the three of them who liked Syd.

I thought of what I'd said last night, about how Syd wasn't the only person on Earth. I wished so much that I could go back now and unsay it.

Tonya climbed into the cab and slammed her door shut and Ray shut his, and then he eased back down the driveway and onto the road. Tyler never stopped waving at me, even after Tonya turned around and scolded him.

"Those people are insane." My father closed the door then locked it.

"Oh god, Dad." That was all I could get out.

"I know," my dad said.

"What if she doesn't come back?"

"Well, wait. We don't know that yet. We don't know anything."

"What are we going to do?" Panic, like a heavier air, flooded my lungs.

"Okay, well." For a second it seemed like he'd gone back to sleep. His long arms hung at his sides.

"What are we going to do?" I barked.

"I don't know right this second!" He turned and stormed

down the hall. His alarm stopped blaring. "Jesus." He returned to the hallway and took a deep breath. "Syd is a smart person," he said. "Let's remember that first and foremost." I was staring at him, wide-eyed. He must've mistaken my numb panic for some kind of dawning revelation. "Is there something to tell me, Miranda? Is something going on?"

"No," I said. "No!" I pressed my palms to my eyes for a moment. "She's still waiting to hear from Stanford about early admission. They're late, but, I mean, a day late. Why would she run away? This cannot be happening."

"Okay, then." My father and I stood looking at each other another long moment. "I need coffee." He shuffled past me into the kitchen and became a whirlwind of activity, setting the kettle on the stove and pouring coffee beans into the grinder. I stood in the hallway, clutching Ray's wilted business card. I thought of Syd sitting in my car last night, staring out into the parking lot while I screamed my head off. I'd driven her home hardly saying a word. Then she'd done that weird thing, making a point to come back and tell me she loved me. She'd kissed me on the forehead. I'd watched her climb the steps to the trailer. I'd waited only until she'd opened the door before driving off. Had I pulled out too eagerly? Had my car tires kicked up dust?

Was that curt good-bye the last thing I'd ever say to Syd?

She's gone. The idea formed around my body like a big glassy bubble, ready to burst and shred my life to pieces. It was like what they say happens in a car accident. Everything slowed down. I was suddenly standing next to myself, examining the weird little details that made up my life. There, tucked into the mirror above the hall table was a photo of my dad with his arm around my uncle Benny. I'd taken the photo a few years ago, the morning the three of us had hiked Baylor Canyon. After the hike, we'd gone to eat at La Cocina, and the woman behind the counter asked Benny how old his girl was. I'd turned to Benny in confusion, and it'd been my father who'd corrected her. "This is Maria's daughter," he'd said, putting his hands on my shoulders. "She's mine." And the woman had looked away at the mention of my mother's name—Maria, the sheep who'd left the flock—and my father pulled me away and hustled me to a table in the back. "This town is too small," he'd said. Below the mirror, on the table, were my dad's keys and his NASA ID badge, placed neatly in the wooden bowl where he placed them each day after work, and my backpack, slung open on the floor, and the hairline crack in the wall that started above my bedroom door and traveled all the way to the vigas. About once a year, my father noticed that crack and would say he needed to fix it, but he never did.

I closed my eyes. It felt like I was seeing too much, like I was glimpsing reality from another place, and it freaked me out to see so clearly my little life in this little house where I'd lived for nearly ten years alone with my father. We'd been left before, the two of us. Was I being left again? Was it even possible I'd survive if it were true—if Syd was gone? I turned to my father in the kitchen. I wanted to tell him: I can see everything and nothing at once. Is that normal? But just as I opened my mouth, the bubble crashed down on me and I was back in the same old hallway, Ray's business card in my sweaty palm.

"Miranda." My father's voice sliced through me. He was pouring hot water into his French press. "Let's talk."

"What do we do?" I rushed into the kitchen.

"Well. You have any sense of where she'd go? Did she say anything? You guys were together all day yesterday."

"No. Nothing." Of course, Syd said she was sad, but she wasn't really sad, she wasn't really depressed, she wasn't really going to run off and become Misty Buckets.

"Has she been having problems? With boys or anything like that?"

"Why would you even ask that?" I shot back.

"I'm just trying to think!" he shouted.

"Well—okay!" I said.

"Would she go to her mom's?" he asked.

"No. She wouldn't go there." It was one thing I knew for sure.

"Okay." He took his coffee to the table. "Okay. Come here and sit down."

I sat across the table from him. The sky outside was lightening. Time was passing, it had to be, though I couldn't feel it. My dad locked eyes with me. "Miranda." He was very serious. "I need you to be truthful with me. Okay?"

"I don't know where she is. I swear to God."

"I know." He looked down at the table. "But you need to stay honest with me. I can't help unless you tell me the truth."

"I'm telling you the truth," I said, getting angry.

"You just need to tell me. Everything. We need to stick together."

I finally understood. My father was more worried about me than he was about Syd. He couldn't help it. He had to be. I couldn't hate him for it, though I wanted to.

"This really sucks." He checked the time on the stove. He got up. "I have to get in the shower. I have a damn Skype call with Goddard at seven thirty."

"What? Wait," I said, the drum of my heart pounding in my ears.

"I have to go to work, Miranda. And you have to go to school."

"No! Syd's missing. We need to do something."

"What can we do?" my father said from the doorway.

"I don't know." It was the worst kind of truth.

"Keep your phone on. Call if you hear anything. We'll reconvene tonight."

My phone! I'd been holding it in my hand this whole time and hadn't even thought to look at it.

I had no new texts or anything. I had one missed call, but that was from Ray.

"Nothing," I said, answering the question on my father's face.

"We've just got to hang in there today. I'll see if I can't talk to someone—I'll call Letty. Or you call her. I can't imagine there isn't something we can do." My uncle Benny's wife, Letty, was a social worker in Santa Fe. She was actually the very person you'd want to call for advice if a friend went missing. Letty and Benny had lived in Cruces until right after my mother left. Sometimes I missed them more than I missed my mom. One of the main reasons I wanted to go to UNM was to be closer to them. They were all the family I had, besides my dad.

"Okay," I said. The idea of Letty getting involved gave me an inkling of hope.

"Okay," he said. "It's going to be okay, okay?"

"Okay," I said.

He walked down the hall. I heard his shower turn on.

I swiped my phone on again and went to my messages. *WHERE ARE YOU?* I wrote to Syd. *WHAT THE HELL IS GOING ON?* I pressed send. The text was delivered. That meant, at least, that Syd's phone was turned on. I watched the text thread for a long time, but she didn't respond. Then I looked at the clock. I'd be late if I didn't get going. I went to my room and got dressed, smoothed my hair into a ponytail, and put on lip balm. I brushed my teeth. It was the best I could do.

I checked my face in the mirror in the hall to see if I looked like I felt: awful. But I didn't. I looked just the same as I always did. I glanced again at the photo of my dad and Benny. The lady at La Cocina was right. There was no denying I looked more like my uncle's kid than my father's. If my parents had had more kids, I might've had siblings who looked more like my dad. Our family could've made a little spectrum of skin tones. But without my mom, my father and I didn't make sense to the world. People felt free to comment on it all the time. A border patrol agent stopped us at the El Paso Airport once, asking me in Spanish to produce an ID. "This is my biological daughter!" my dad shouted. "I'm sorry, sir," the agent said. "With young girls, we're extra careful. We've seen bad things come through here." My father shuddered, and the two of us walked to baggage claim and never mentioned it again. Another time, when I was babysitting my cousin Luciana, reading her *Curious George*, she looked up from the page and said, "This is like you and Uncle Peter. You're George and he's the Man with the Yellow Hat."

I'd thought of that comparison a lot over the years, giving it much more consideration than I probably should've. I'd never mentioned it to my dad, because I thought it might make him sad, but something about it rang so true.

"I guess I'm going to school now!" I called down the hall.

I couldn't believe I was going to school, and it wasn't lost on me—and I hoped it wasn't lost on my father—that he'd forced me to go to school the day after my mother left. To maintain normalcy. I hadn't even gotten one day off.

I slung my backpack over my shoulder and checked to make sure my ringer was on its loudest setting before I shoved my phone in my pocket.

My dad hurried out of his room in a crisp shirt and tie, his hair still wet. He slung his name tag around his neck. "Call me if you hear anything. I'll check on you today. A lot." He stood before me suddenly and took me by my shoulders. It was something he'd done since I was a child, a very straightforward, sometimes very annoying way of getting my full attention. "Deep breaths," he said. He squeezed my shoulders. He smelled like aftershave and toothpaste and coffee. Beneath everything, my father always smelled like coffee. I thought of mentioning how dreadfully similar things felt this morning to the morning after my mother left. It was all fear and not knowing. But I couldn't find a way to do it.

My mother was simply not a subject either of us knew how to bring up.

"Deep breaths," I echoed halfheartedly.

I drove to school in a daze. When I reached the stop sign at Highway 28, I had to tell myself not to turn left and drive to Syd's to pick her up. I took out my phone. *PLEASE JUST LET ME KNOW YOU'RE OKAY. I AM FREAKING OUT.* I pressed send. I imagined Syd's phone dinging beside her on the passenger seat of her car. She was going somewhere; she was getting farther and farther away every minute. Or she wasn't—maybe she was in Cruces somewhere. Holed up with one of her college boys. Maybe she was doing all this simply to make me feel awful for screaming at her last night.

Almost immediately my phone dinged in my hand. My heart nearly hit the roof, I was so relieved. But when I looked, it wasn't Syd. It was my dad. *Love you. Skype postponed, of course. I'm going to spend some time now trying to figure out what we can do. Everything's going to be okay. Text me a lot today, please.* That my dad was genuinely worried made everything feel exponentially shittier. I was staring at his text when the person in the car behind me tapped on their horn. Who knows how long I'd been sitting at the stop sign? For a millisecond I allowed myself to imagine I'd look in my rearview mirror and see Syd in her crappy blue Ford Fiesta, giving me the finger.

I got you so good, her face would say.

But when I looked, it was a guy in a truck wearing a ball cap, with a still-asleep face and somewhere to be.

I tossed up my hand in apology and pulled forward.

5

School was the worst idea I'd ever been talked into. I hated my father for making me come here. When I pushed through the heavy doors into the main breezeway, I was sickened by the smell of it: bodies and cologne and some vague, yeasty smell that could only be found in the halls of Cruces High. I froze. As people pushed past me, I recognized a basic truth about my life: I'd only made it through high school, especially the last eight months of it, because Syd had been beside me, exuding confidence, shining her superstar light so blindingly that I was rendered practically invisible in its glare.

Now I was visible. Entirely. Excruciatingly. I'd pushed through the gates of hell, and I didn't know what to do or how to be or even what to look at. I put my head down, glued my eyes to the linoleum, and plowed through the crowd to the locker we shared. It took me a while to remember the combination. Syd was usually the one to open it every morning. My brain was a ball of fuzz. Somehow I could still hear my father's alarm clock blaring down the hallway of my mind. When I finally opened the locker and saw the photo Syd had stuck there with a piece of chewed gum, a shot of the two of us at a football game that had appeared in the school newspaper (she looked great; I looked not great), my heart fell out of my body, plunking onto the floor like a dead fruit.

This wasn't going to happen. It couldn't. I had to escape this day right now.

I slammed the locker and wheeled around only to find myself staring at Erin Harris. "Where's Syd?" she asked before I could even think.

I didn't know how to answer. I didn't know if I should tell her the truth or if I should lie. I didn't even know how to speak English. "I don't know," I said.

"She's got our notes. I need to type them or Jones will give us an automatic C on our lab. I've been calling her all morning."

"She's not here." I knew I shouldn't lie and say she was sick. Erin was so concerned about grades, she'd probably drive to Syd's house if I told her she was home, puking her guts out.

"She's not coming?"

"I don't know."

"Crap," she said. "She's not returning my texts."

"I know." I stopped myself before I said more. Erin narrowed her eyes and gave me a look that indicated she knew I wasn't telling the whole truth and for this, as well as for the automatic C, I should curl up like a dog and die.

The warning bell rang and the breezeway began to clear.

"When you see her, tell her she needs to get me the notes."

"Okay," I said.

Erin huffed off, her ponytail whooshing behind her.

Strangely, talking to Erin made me feel a little better. I'd done something impossible—I'd spoken words—and I hadn't died. Maybe going to French would be good after all. At least I'd be distracted. I could stare at the back of Nick's head for fifty minutes, loving and hating him in silence. I psyched myself up, grabbed my French book, and made my way to the languages wing.

But when I turned down the hall, I saw Nick heading to class from the opposite direction. He looked up at me and I stopped. I panicked. I spun around and headed back to the breezeway and made a beeline for the door to the parking lot. I was about to push through the doors when I saw the vice principal talking to the tennis coach on the sidewalk. There was no way I was getting past them and to my car and off campus. I turned and jogged back down the now empty breezeway and swung down the hall toward French.

But there was Nick again, standing by himself outside class. He didn't have his backpack or his books. He must've gone into class and dropped them off and come back out. In classic Nick style, he had his hands pushed deeply into his pockets. He looked up, again, straight at me.

I did another 180, but this time smacked into Will Carey, who sat in the seat in front of me in French and, because I was one of the few people he talked to at school, was forever turning around in class to offer me unsolicited observations and advice. Because I'd once mentioned to him that I loved Harry Potter, he often regaled me with the impossible-to-keep-up-with amendments he'd made the night before to the pairings in his fan fiction. I felt for Will. His fan fic was more real and more precious to him than the entire rest of his life in Las Cruces. His family was hardcore Christian. His mom was always posting articles online about the "scientific proof" that some ass-backward conversion therapy cured the sin of homosexuality. Will was resigned to his world of fantasy, biding his time until the ongoing humiliation of high school in a small town was over and he could move far away from here.

"Oh!" we both cried at the same time. He was exactly as tall as I was, so when we smacked, we were staring each other directly in the face. I could see the sprinkle of freckles across the bridge of his nose.

"Oh!" I stepped out of his way, to the right, just as he stepped in the same direction. Then, of course, we did it again, to the left. This was the type of situation where my father would take pleasure in saying something dorky like *Nice dancing with you.*

"Oh my god, stop!" Will laughed.

"Sorry, I forgot my book." I fought the urge to push him out the way, so strong was my desire to escape.

He looked down at the French book in the crook of my arm. "No, you didn't," he said helpfully. He smiled at having solved my problem for me.

"My other book." I glanced back to see Nick still standing there. He'd witnessed the whole awkward dance. "See you in two seconds," I said to Will, and flew past him, back to the breezeway. It was entirely empty now. The final bell would ring any second. I only had one option left. I bolted across the breezeway and down the unbearably long math wing and slipped out the back doors of the building. To the left was the agricultural complex with its rambling array of greenhouses and sheds and the constant, lingering smell of cow manure. To the right was the tall, austere theater building. Between the two buildings, a narrow footpath led to an irrigation ditch behind the school that fed water from the Rio Grande to a field of crops cultivated by the 4-H Club. The Magic Ditch marked the edge of campus. It was called the Magic Ditch because when you walked down the path and crossed a footbridge over the water and sat down on the other side facing the fields, you disappeared from view. Poof. Magic.

It was also called the Stoner's Ditch, for obvious reasons.

I huffed down the path and wobbled over the footbridge and threw myself down against the far slope of the ditch without even taking off my backpack.

I'd never come to the ditch before. I'd never even skipped a class before. I closed my eyes and braced myself, assuming a hand would appear from behind and yank me by the ear to the principal's office.

But no. I opened my eyes and found I was alone. I'd made it. The last bell rang. Class had started. There was no going back.

Deep breaths, I heard my father say.

I yanked my phone out of my pocket. *ARE YOU OKAY?* Again, I waited. Again, I got no reply. I called but got her voice mail and hung up. It occurred to me then to check her Instagram. Syd curated her Instagram like a pro. She had thousands of followers. She could be documenting her gone-ness there now in pristinely filtered detail.

But I couldn't find her. She'd vanished. The only Syd Miller I found was a middle-aged woman from Ann Arbor, Michigan, who had a page full of #kitty photos. I checked. Every one of her accounts was gone. It was as if Syd had never existed online. She'd vanished herself. Poof. Magic.

Gone, not missing.

Deep breaths.

I put my phone down and slipped off my backpack. I looked out over the fields. The air was thick and loamy with fertilizer, even in winter. I wanted to stand, but I remembered the one rule of the ditch. Once you got there, you had to stay sitting. If you stood up, you were visible. If you were visible, you were caught. I'd learned the ditch rules from Syd, who'd maintained a 4.0 GPA even while occasionally skipping class to come here and make out with boys. Imagining her here, sucking face, made me feel more alone than I already did.

Knowing I'd have to sit for a whole class period made me feel like a caged animal. I could feel my heart racing ahead of me. It was chasing Syd. I tried to calm down. I closed my eyes and put my head between my knees and started reciting the Gettysburg Address. *Four score and seven years ago . . .* It was a relief to escape into those worn-in words. Syd would come home. The Civil War would end. The Union would be preserved. Stanford would say yes. Dreams would come true. Everything would be okay. *Four score and seven years ago our fathers brought forth on this continent, a new nation, conceived in liberty . . .*

The Gettysburg Address was short. That was part of its charm. I could head right into the next recitation without pausing to remember how it started. I was on my third one when I felt a presence. It wasn't a divine presence. It was a person presence. I didn't know when they'd gotten there, but I knew when I extracted my head from between my knees, I'd have to explain to whichever stoner had joined me why I'd been reciting the Gettysburg Address to my crotch.

I opened my eyes and turned my head. And it was Nick. He was sitting next to me, looking totally horrified, as if my head was about to explode and he was going to have to be the one to deal with it.

"Are you all right?" he asked.

Again, it was a shock to hear him speak to me. It simply didn't happen, though we saw each other every day in French. I hadn't even said *merci* last month when my pen fell from my desk and rolled up the aisle to his. He'd picked it up and handed it to me and I'd snatched it back and stared straight ahead.

"Yes." I sat up and tried to look sane. I wanted to jump up and run for it, but I remembered the ditch rule.

"That was the Gettysburg Address," he said, as if I hadn't noticed.

"Yes, it was. So what?" I sounded so rude, it was embarrassing. I tried not to look at him, but that was impossible. A stray piece of hair fell into his face and he lifted a finger and tucked the hair behind his ear. It'd taken eight months for his hair to grow to the length it was now. I knew it'd been eight months because I knew everything about Nick. The last haircut he'd gotten had been a week before prom and he hadn't had one since. I knew when Nick washed his car, when he got new shoes, and when he'd run out of his assortment of preferred gray, brown, or dark green T-shirts and so wore the one that read IT'S A STEM THING—YOU WOULDN'T UNDERSTAND. And I knew it was only in the last two weeks that his hair had gotten long enough to pull back into a stubby ponytail. I never thought I'd love a boy with a ponytail, but then Nick walked into French one morning with the nape of his neck exposed, and I had no choice.

"I'm memorizing it for a class," I said after a monumentally long pause.

"Oh," he said.

"I thought I was alone."

"Oh." He offered nothing else.

"Why are you here?" I felt awful. It was so hard loving someone and hating them at the same time. It took so much work, so much effort and precision.

"I need to talk to you."

"Oh, about my ordeal?" I shot him a scowl.

"Yes, there's that," he said. "But this is about Syd."

The look I gave him must've conveyed perfectly the emotion I was feeling: utter confusion and shock that could at any moment turn to disgust, violent anger, or perhaps perfect blankness, a sudden coma, brain death, etc.

"I know," he said before I had a chance to yell/say anything else. "This is weird. But Syd came to my house last night. I think there's something going on."

"She went to your house? What did she say?"

"I didn't see her. She left a note on my car. Here." He opened his palm to reveal a tiny piece of paper folded in half. It was a sticky note in the shape of a hot dog. I'd seen the pad in Syd's car. I could tell Nick was embarrassed by whatever it said. He held it out to me. "Here," he said again, a little more urgently.

"Is it awful?" I looked at him. "Just tell me if it's something awful."

"No. I don't know. I don't think so."

I reached over and took it from him. My fingertips touching his palm was enough to make me blush. I unfolded the note and read it.

Talk to Miranda.

She likes you.

Just tell her the truth.

Before thinking, I crumpled the note in my hand and held it inside my fist as if it were an insect that could get away. It took all I had not to pop the thing in my mouth and swallow it whole. *She likes you.* Jesus. Are you kidding me? Every instinct in my body said *run*. But I was stuck there. I looked at the fallow field before us. An excruciating silence descended.

"I don't like you," I blurted out.

"I know that," he answered, defensive. "I just thought you'd want to see it since it's kind of dramatic. I mean, what, is Syd going to kill herself or something?"

A pulse of alarm traveled up my spine. Was it possible Syd could kill herself?

"No." Saying it aloud helped me know it was true. Syd would consider suicide a personal failing, like getting an F in living. She'd never do that.

A cool breeze picked up. "Wait." I turned to him. "Did you follow me here?"

"Yeah," he said. I saw his Adam's apple rise when he swallowed. "I thought you'd want to see this. You looked freaked out in the hall."

"I don't know why Syd left you that note." I looked away. "I don't know what's going on. But you don't need to follow me around. You've done enough already."

Nick exhaled sharply and looked down. I expected him to get up and walk away. I hoped he would. But he stayed where he was. He shook his head. The silence grew painful. When I began to squirm, he spoke.

"I can't leave or I'll get caught skipping and I can't get caught skipping or my mom will kill me. And my parents are already mad because Syd let the air out of their tires."

"No way." It was such a Syd move. Revenge, served about as cold as it could get. One last achievement in advanced bitchiness, undertaken almost immediately after I told her to leave Nick alone.

"Yes way." Nick looked serious and angry, but then he cracked a tiny smile. "I mean, I guess—it was pretty funny. I had to drive my parents to work this morning. I sort of liked seeing my dad sitting in the backseat of my car like a kid. He deserves it."

"He deserves it?" This was something new. I didn't know this about Nick. He didn't get along with his dad? I filed it away.

"My dad's sort of . . . Whatever. It's complicated." He made a vague sound, like someone with a toothache, and looked away.

I wanted to relish having made him uncomfortable, especially after what happened last night. I wanted to feel entirely uncompelled to smooth out the little wrinkle between us as soon as it'd formed. This was something Syd was forever chiding me about. *God, you're such a people pleaser!* I imagined her glaring at me and I tried to keep my mouth shut. But I couldn't do it.

"Well. My mom joined a religious cult when I was eight and I never saw her again. Like, literally, never. Not a phone call or a letter or anything. And I'm kinda pretty sure she lost her marbles—heard voices, whatever—but I can't talk to my dad about it because he kinda refuses to acknowledge she ever existed on this earthly plane. And he's looking for life on other planets. Which just feels a little, you know—tragic. Or something." I'd said all this to the barren field. I turned to him. "So I get 'complicated.'"

He turned to me. "A religious cult? Like a Jesus freak?"

"No. She was super into Jesus before. Uber Catholic. I guess Jesus stopped doing it for her." Nick smiled. "The Garden—it's like enlightenment slash meditation slash fake Buddhism. But it's a real cult. If you google it. It's got a guru. His name's Solomon. Bad guy. My dad and my uncle tried to get her to come home. But she never did. And then the Garden made it so they couldn't really even communicate with her. She's been there, oh, I'm going to say ten years, three months, and four days—no, five."

"That's crazy." Nick gave me a sideways glance. "I'm sorry. That's—sucky."

"Well. At least the lady's committed, you know?" I thought he might laugh at my dumb joke, but when I looked, his eyes were full of empathy and I had to look away or risk falling into them headfirst. I tried to put my guard back up. "Yes. It's sucky. I'm sure you knew. Everyone knows everything about everyone in this town."

"I didn't."

"Oh." This could be true, I guessed. By the time Nick

came here at the beginning of freshman year, my mom was old news. Even the little Catholic ladies, the *viejitas* like the one at La Cocina, had stopped genuflecting at the mention of her name as if she were the devil incarnate. It was refreshing to think there was one person in town I could reveal this story to myself, one person who didn't already know all the gory details. "Well, now you know."

Nick looked suddenly pained. He shut his eyes tightly. "Okay, never mind. I knew. Tomás told me. I don't know why I said I didn't."

"What?" I felt like an idiot. Here I was spilling my guts, and he was playing some stupid game. "God. Who does that? Why did you do that?"

"I don't know." His eyes searched the ground. "I was embarrassed."

"You were embarrassed? For me?"

"No." His eyes settled on his shoes.

"I'm not embarrassed," I fired back. "Anyway, everyone's got something a little weird about them, right? Hmm? Like how your mom looks closer to your age than she does to your dad's. How *embarrassing*. I'm so *embarrassed* for you."

I looked straight ahead and fumed. He was silent and still beside me. When I ventured a glance from my periphery, I was sure he'd be fuming too. I hoped, even. (Syd would be so proud. *A+ bitch! That's my girl!*)

But instead his eyes were narrowed. He was thinking.

"Whoa." He looked at me and grinned. "You're right. I just did the math. She is closer to my age. That is actually totally embarrassing."

Against my better judgment, I smiled. I imagined Syd shaking her head, changing my A+ to an F-.

"For the record," Nick said, the characteristic earnestness returning to his face and voice. "I'm embarrassed all the time. That's baseline for me. Weird and embarrassed. That's all I meant."

"Okay," I said.

"I wasn't embarrassed for you."

"Okay. Yes. I get it." I watched a crow hop from one greenhouse onto another, higher one, scanning the empty field with its glassy eye. "So he's a teacher? Your dad?"

"Old-ass math professor, yeah. He teaches calculus, stuff like that. But he's an expert in a field called computable model theory. He's one of the smartest dudes in the country, in his field. There are, like, seven people who get what he's talking about when he talks about his stuff."

"That's depressing."

"Nah, it's cool actually, pure math."

"Ew. What's pure math? Sounds even worse than actual math."

"It's not even math, really. It's, like—ideas, almost like metaphors. It's not like algebra, doing equations. It's not even really numbers. It's like what's underneath numbers. Like the ideas that numbers represent."

"Huh. Trippy." I hated math so much, I'd never imagined numbers represented anything but torture. But what Nick just described was beautiful. It almost sounded like praying. Going below the surface, seeking the great, holy *zero* I'd found as a child and then lost. Maybe there were only seven people in the world who really knew how to talk to God. Maybe the rest of us were just plodding along, working equations, unworthy of the bigger truths that lay beneath. Maybe I simply wasn't smart enough. Maybe my whole problem was that I didn't like math.

"Not to be rude, but if your dad's one of the smartest people in the world, why's he at NMSU?"

"Yeah," Nick said. "Well. It's complicated." He smiled. "He started at Berkeley. Got his Ph.D. and taught there. That's where my brother and I were born. And then we moved to Chicago. He taught at the University of Chicago." He shrugged. "He didn't get tenure. So we moved. Here. But he's looking for another job now."

"You're moving?" I was mortified by the quake of distress in my voice.

"Oh, no. Not before graduation. But I guess. For college." He glanced at me. "Are you moving away for college?" I thought I heard the same distress in his voice, but I knew in the same moment I'd only imagined it.

"Probably. Just to Albuquerque. UNM."

"Cool," Nick said.

"Yeah," I said. "No big plans for me."

I refused to ask where he was headed for college. *Refused.* The world was Nick's freaking oyster. It sucked. I felt the air being squeezed from my lungs when I thought of no longer being able to stare at the back of his head in French or catch him smiling or laughing in the hall. The pathetic truth was, I'd miss everything, even my ongoing failed attempts at hating his guts. In college, I'd have to rely on social media to keep up with him, and he was terrible on social media. He'd never once posted a photo of himself on Instagram. He'd had his account for seven years and all he'd posted were a few exceptional sunsets. A couple majestic canyons. It was crap.

I knew a year from now I'd be nothing more than a

story Nick Allison could tell his Ivy League friends. This Girl I Stood Up on Prom Night. It was crushing. And there was nothing I could do to stop it. In a matter of months, I'd lose Nick to the world, just as I'd lose Syd— or as I possibly already had as of this unreal, god-awful morning.

"So what happened? With Syd? She was unusually insane last night."

"Yeah." I resisted the impulse to apologize on her behalf for humiliating both of us in front of his parents. "I don't know," I said. "She left. She didn't tell me anything. We got in a fight—after what happened. In the restaurant. This morning she was gone."

I pinned my eyes to the far end of the field, to a pump house with the words *LCHS Agriculture* painted in red but faded to pink. I could feel Nick looking at me, yet he wasn't saying anything. It was unnerving.

"What?" I said, turning to him finally.

"I'm sorry, Miranda," he said.

Hearing my name in his mouth was pure electricity. "Oh. It's all right," I said.

"I mean for everything. I'm sorry about last night. My mom. And I'm sorry about—everything." He made the gesture again of tucking hair behind his ear, though this time there was no loose hair to tuck.

I returned my eyes to the pump house, its corrugated metal roof glinting in the bright morning sunlight. "It's all right."

It's all right?! In my wildest dreams, I never imagined I'd let Nick off so easy. In fact, in many of the elaborate fantasies I'd been having for the last eight months, he'd utter those exact words and I'd slap him. Hard. Or I'd say something so perfectly mean, he'd wither. In most of the fantasies, though, apologizing was only the first step. Then the slap. And then, after that, he'd give some really decent reason for having done what he'd done. Then I'd accept his apology. Then we'd kiss.

The kiss was by far the most common ending to the fantasy.

Sometimes he'd ask me to give him another chance. He'd beg me to go out with him—maybe even ask me to prom again. I'd say no. *Don't be an idiot.* But I'd soften. And just as he was walking away, all dejected and sad, I'd call after him: *Hey.* He'd turn, looking chastened, and I'd say: *Whatever. Okay. I'll go.* And he'd break out one of his perfect all-lip, no-teeth smiles.

Then we'd kiss.

But the fantasies were always ruined by one thorny detail. I'd been trying for eight months to think of a really decent reason he could give for having done what he'd done. In eight months I hadn't found a single one.

The bell rang and I jumped a little. In the handful of seconds between the sound of the bell and the sound of people beginning to pour out of the building, Nick and I just sat there, looking at each other. It was painful and glorious and totally ill-advised, like looking at a solar eclipse.

"I gotta go." He broke the silence.

"Me too," I said. We both stood.

"We missed the quiz," he said.

"Oh crap." I hadn't thought about French.

"Madame Spencer said she's giving extra credit for seeing a movie at the Fountain Theatre." I looked up at him. "Didn't she say that?" He pursed his lips. "We could go. To that."

"You mean, together?" I asked, too bewildered to be embarrassed for asking.

"Okay." Nick smiled. It was, I noted, all-lip, no teeth. "I was thinking of going Friday night."

"Friday night?"

"Yeah," he said.

Maybe it was the fantasies, all those kisses full of longing and apology. This weird half-invitation to see a movie for extra credit was somehow worse than nothing at all.

"Yeah, no," I said.

"Oh." He fiddled with his backpack strap.

"I don't think we go back to being French class buddies. You know?" It broke my heart to say it, but it was true. I knew I couldn't survive another blow.

"Yeah," he said. "I get it."

"Do you though?" I bit my lips together to try to stop myself, but it didn't work. "Do you know how much this year has sucked for me?"

He heaved the backpack onto his shoulders. "Yeah," he said. "Actually, I think I do." That pissed me off. Had he suffered in the last year? No way. In the gross and distorted social economy of our small-town high school, his standing me up on prom night had only raised his status, elevating him from the fringes of lame (Instagram sunsets, Academic Decathlon, *It's a STEM thing*) to low-level cool.

"I shouldn't have asked." He tucked another phantom piece of hair behind his ear. "See you later." He turned and hiked up the slope of the ditch into the bright sunlight.

"Hey," I called to him, just like I had in all those fantasies. But when he turned and looked down at me, I didn't say, *Whatever. Okay. I'll go.* I shielded my eyes from the sun bursting over his shoulder. "What did Syd mean? About telling me the truth?"

He looked out over the field for a long moment. Then he shrugged. "Who knows?" He hooked his fingers around the straps of his backpack. "Your friend's a mystery to me."

Then he turned and was gone, over the footbridge and down the other side of the ditch, lost in the swarm of bodies moving in and out of the math wing. My heart popped in my chest, a stuck balloon. I stood and waited for the pain to recede. Then I smoothed out the note on my palm and looked at it. *She likes you.* I took out my phone and sent another text.

NICK ALLISON???? WTF????

I hiked up the ditch and over the footbridge. From up high, I looked again to see if I could find Nick's head in the crowd. But I couldn't.

It was for the best, I told myself. I put my head down and insinuated myself into the crowd, adding one more anonymous body to the sea of bodies, making my way to whatever disaster was waiting for me next.

6

At lunch I bought a burrito at the canteen and went out to hide in my car and eat it. I called Letty at her office at Child Protective Services in Santa Fe. It was good to hear her voice, though she didn't have anything hopeful to say. Syd was over eighteen. She wasn't a minor. She wasn't missing. Legally, she'd run away. And in New Mexico it wasn't illegal to run away. The authorities weren't going to be much help. Like Tonya, Letty was sure Syd had done research.

"She planned this, Miry," she said. "She put the most important thing right there in her note. *I'm not missing. You know?*" All I could give her was silence. She stayed with me in it for a long time. Finally she spoke again, her voice softened. "In a lot of ways, your Syd is the type to run away. You know? Her home life was so bad, and her mom was gone. I mean, I know Syd was really good in school. She was trying so hard, sweetie. But I see this all the time. Some things are just too much for a kid. You know what I'm saying?"

The thing was, I didn't. I didn't know what she was

saying. I knew these facts about Syd's life were technically true. But it was impossible for me to conceive of Syd in that way. Syd wasn't a victim. She wasn't a troubled youth. She was a champion. She was the founder and president of the goddamned Life Club. The things Letty was talking about: those were the odds. And Syd had long ago decided to beat them to a pulp.

"She's waiting to hear from Stanford about early admission. Why would she run away? It doesn't make sense."

"It happens. I see it all the time. Plain, old self-sabotage."

"Well, my mom's gone." I sounded petulant, like a child, and I hated myself for it. "I'm not gonna run away."

"Well, you're right," she said. "But Syd doesn't have what you have, Miry."

"Like what? Like because she's poor? Or whatever, because—" I was about to launch into an abbreviated summary of Syd's trenchant ideas about money and power and class, how that can't define a person, but Letty cut me off.

"No, sweetie," she said. "I mean your dad." There was a smile in her voice.

"Oh," I said.

Speaking of. By the end of the day, my father had sent thirty-two texts. Each time my phone vibrated, I broke out in a cold sweat. But it was never Syd. It was always my dad. In history, he wrote to ask if Syd had ever enabled the Find My Phone feature on her phone. *No,* I wrote back. I knew she hadn't.

Do you *have that feature enabled on your phone?* Between the word *phone* and the question mark, he'd inserted an emoji of a crab.

No, I responded.

Would you enable that feature, please? After this one, he sent a lightning bolt. My father was an enthusiastic but perplexing emoji user. It drove me bananas. I never knew what he meant. I decided this little golden bolt was meant to suggest that any second the solution to our Syd problem would present itself in a flash. Out of nowhere. Lightning.

Each of his texts required a response. He'd ask a question about Syd or ask how I was doing. If I couldn't respond right away, he'd text again. *What's up? Everything okay? Hello out there?* As soon as I walked through the door at the end of the day, I saw him relax. I was usually home hours before he was, but today I walked in to find him sitting at the kitchen table, a fresh cup of coffee in front of him.

"Any word?"

"No."

"Okay, here, sit," he said. I sat down and let my backpack clunk to the floor at my feet. My dad had a legal pad in front of him covered in his chicken scratch handwriting. He'd scoured the internet. He'd posted in a few forums for parents of runaways. He'd called the police himself. I expected his diligence would've yielded a long list of things we could do. But all he'd come up with was that I should put up posters around school and on the campus of NMSU, and that I should contact anyone who had a relationship with Syd. The basic idea was to get the word out. Some people, he'd read, felt so guilty about the motives for a loved one's disappearance that they were hesitant to reach out. They were paralyzed by their own shame and fear. This was a big part of the problem. The more time passed, the less likely the runaway would return. This wasn't going to be us, he reassured me.

"Okay." I swallowed. I'd lied all day when people asked me where Syd was. I'd told people she was home sick. The only person I'd told the truth to was Nick, and that was only because of the note. Was I full of shame and fear? Was I a big part of the problem? All day I'd thought of how I'd yelled at Syd the night before. How she'd stared out the window, chastened. How I'd driven off before she'd even made it through the door of the trailer, even after she'd told me she loved me and kissed my forehead. And how I hadn't said it back.

My dad glanced over his notes. He asked again if Syd had been involved with a boy. I didn't know a lot, but I knew Syd didn't get *involved*. Boys were a hobby. Besides, what boy was there? Medium Hottie?

"Nothing happened last night?"

"Well," I said.

"What?" His eyes shot to mine.

"We had a fight." I laid it out there. It was a fact and he needed the facts. "Last night. I screamed at her. I told her she acted like she was the only person on Earth."

"Why?"

"She did something embarrassing. To me." I felt like I was giving confession. "I never screamed at her before, Dad."

"No." He pointed at me for emphasis. *"No."*

"What?"

"This is not your fault."

I almost laughed, thinking of how many times my father said those exact words to me in the weeks and months after my mother left. How many ways he'd attempted to convince me they were true.

For weeks after my mother had gone to the Garden, I held tight to the notion she'd wanted me with her. I believed there was some secret plan in the works that would involve the two of us being reunited. Things weren't finished yet. Any second she'd call to say she was coming home—or coming to get me. She was better. Cured.

But after a month or so, that fantasy began to dissipate. She wasn't coming back. It was just my dad and me, and it was going to be just my dad and me. For good. I was silent, obedient. I didn't cry or mope. Outwardly, I was fine. I was *stoic*, as I overheard my dad tell Benny on the phone. I looked the word up. I agreed. I was totally acting stoic. But inside, I was filled with terrible thoughts— thoughts I couldn't shake. I worried. At night, especially, my worries bred, they'd grown in the dark, fed by the logic of my sadness and shame. I became sure my father hated me and wanted to get rid of me. My father, barely hanging in there himself, tried his best to help me deal, but even that made me feel awful. He asked if I wanted to see a therapist. I said no, but then he took me to see one anyway. When that one failed to make me less stoic, he sent me to another, and then another. I was a burden on everyone. That was how it felt. I was a burden on everyone I'd ever met. Even my dad. Especially my dad. My mom had escaped the vortex that was my neediness—she'd gotten away, lucky her. And my father, he was sad for having been left behind, left responsible. I was so far gone, I started having fears my father was going to put me up for adoption. I got hooked on that thought. In bed at night it would grip me, and any effort to stop it only made it worse. Finally, one morning, after I'd spent the entire night awake—had not slept even for one moment—I found my dad drinking coffee on the patio and I just asked him. Was he going to put me up for adoption? I just needed to know, either way. Either way was fine. It was the not knowing that was killing me.

"What're you talking about, chicken head?" He said this in his earnest way, tossing down his *New Yorker*. I guessed he couldn't quite comprehend the notion I was presenting to him. Maybe he thought I didn't understand the meaning of the phrase *put up for adoption*.

"Are you going to send me away? I just need to know. I won't be mad if you are." Saying the words felt good. They'd been trapped inside my body—inside my brain— and now they were out there, floating around the patio. They were free.

It was strange, the way they landed on my dad's face. I could see him get what I was after. I thought it was promising he looked so surprised by this notion. Maybe he hadn't been considering it at all. Then I worried I'd planted the idea for him. *Now that you mention it . . .*

My father pushed his chair back from the table. He kneeled in front of me and grabbed my shoulders, holding them tightly. He looked into my face, very seriously. I didn't know what was going to happen. He seemed angry, but not really angry, just very serious. "I am never going to leave you." He squeezed my shoulders when he said it.

"Okay." I was a little scared.

"I need you to tell me you understand that I will never leave you, Miranda."

"Okay," I said again. I just wanted this to end. I'd made a mistake.

My father let go of my shoulders. "No, listen. Miry." He took a quick deep breath. His own shoulders fell. He looked a little more relaxed. That helped. "Say it back to me."

"What?"

"Say it: *You will never leave me.*"

It was so difficult to say it. Almost impossible. I had to make the words come up from a secret place, somewhere deep inside my body. When I was little and would go to church with my mom, I was always confused by the idea of having a soul. I thought the soul must be an organ. And even when I understood it wasn't, I still liked to think of it that way. Some little gland, deep inside, where each of us kept the magical thing that made us a person. That was where I had to go to get the words. As they came out of my mouth, I saw them form above my dad's head. "You. Will. Never. Leave. Me."

"Okay," my dad said. He put his arms around me and pulled me into a tight hug. "We're going to be okay," he said into my hair, then he pulled back and looked me in the face. "Oh my god, have I not said that?" I shrugged. "Well, we are. No matter what. We're going to be okay."

"Okay," I said. It was such a relief. It felt like I'd been running for days and days and finally—*finally*—someone had told me it was okay to stop. It was okay. I could stop running.

And that was when I started crying.

I cried for two hours straight, sitting on the couch with my dad. It was like I had the stomach flu and was puking. He just sat there with me and let me do it. Occasionally he'd say something like "That's it. That's okay." And then I'd start bawling again. He got up twice, once to get me a glass of water and once to get me a cold washcloth to put on my forehead.

"I don't know why I got this." He smiled, folding it in thirds and putting it to my forehead. "My mom always used to give us a washcloth when we were sick."

When I finished crying, he looked a little surprised. A little shocked. Like, *Now what?*

He took me for ice cream at Dairy Queen, even though it was 10:30 in the morning. We were the only ones there. I was still in my pajamas. We sat in a booth. We didn't say a word. My father looked happy—or not happy, but okay. And he hadn't looked okay in a long time. I fell asleep in the car on the way home. My father must've carried me into my bedroom and closed the door. When I woke, it was night. My room was dark and cool. Everything felt better. Not good, but better. I could hear out in the hall that my father had turned on the white noise machine he kept in his bedroom. It was the low roll of the ocean, one single wave, duplicated, coming and going again and again and again. I didn't know where my father was. But I knew he was out there. I went back to sleep and didn't wake until morning.

How absurd that ten years later, we found ourselves in the same place. Left behind. Only now it was Syd my father was talking about. "She didn't leave because you yelled at her. You know that, right?"

"I guess so," I said.

I made posters that night. I worried that hanging posters would do nothing but advertise the fact that Syd was gone and start rumors flying. I dreaded people knowing she was gone, in part because it would make the whole thing more real. If no one knew, there was still a chance it wasn't true. Syd would show up tomorrow with the stupid lab notes printed out for Erin Harris. But if hanging posters was the only thing I could do, I had to do it.

I used a photo I'd taken of Syd the week before, after she'd finished tennis and I'd finished my homework in the library, waiting for her. In the photo, she was smiling, her skin radiant and her round cheeks pink after practicing in the cold, her wild hair held back in a ponytail. "Say cheese," I'd said when I'd sprung my phone on her as we'd walked to my car. "Butt cheeeeeeese!" she'd yelled as I'd snapped the picture.

I called Ray before school started and told him about the posters. I don't know why, but it felt like I should get his permission. He was distracted, talking to a beer distributor. He'd heard nothing. He knew nothing. He asked me to keep in touch. Then he hung up before I had a chance to say anything else. I thought of what Letty had said, about Syd's bad home life. *It happens all the time.* I pushed the words out of my head.

I had twelve texts before the first bell rang. I knew they'd come. I knew as soon as people saw the posters, Syd would be the talk of the school. I slipped into the bathroom and sat in a stall and watched the messages roll in. *WTF!?* seemed to be the basic question people had for me. Being on the receiving end of the shock was worse than being the only one who knew Syd was gone. It was as if Syd had been our school's prizewinning animal—our Gracie the pig in human form—and I'd let her escape through a hole in the fence the day before the state fair.

That afternoon, my dad greeted me at the door as he had the day before. He told me everything was going to be okay. He cooked eggplant Parmesan for dinner. The rest of the week, I walked the halls with my head down, trying to be invisible, but found I couldn't make it five steps without someone stopping me to ask if I'd heard anything about Syd, or to ask if the Life Club would still meet this Friday morning. I became Syd's default spokes-person, but I had no answers for anyone. I was one big *I don't know.*

Nick's presence became more confusing than ever. Ever since our time together behind the ditch, he made a point of smiling at me when he walked into French. I could swear in his smile there was actual empathy, and without Syd around to hurl insults at him, I'd too often find myself slipping, obsessing about what his smile could mean, alternately hoping it meant something, anything, and wishing I could will myself not to care.

By Wednesday I'd made one crucial decision about my life in the new normal of Syd's goneness. I was not going to become the kind of person who ate lunch alone every day in her car. Becoming that person would've been easy for me, and I knew I had to fight it from the beginning. So I made my way to the cafeteria and forced my chin up and braced myself for the barrage of questions. But by then, only a few people stopped me to ask about Syd, and most were really sweet about it. Everyone was as stunned as I was that Syd had run away.

For a couple days I ate lunch with Marcy Ellis, a Mormon girl I'd been friends with in elementary school, before Syd came in the third grade and the two of us left poor Marcy behind in the dust. Tall and skinny and friendly to the bone, high school was her natural habitat. It was her Goldilocks planet. She wasn't super-smart, but she was talented in the art of being a person, and so, naturally, Syd despised her. "That poor thing," she said once after Marcy had stopped to talk to me in the hall. "She doesn't even know she's straight-up peaking in high school."

Marcy and her friends carved out the same spot at the same table each day for lunch. Their jokes were shockingly lame, and when they prayed before eating, their prayer was like a giant humble-brag, so low-key and sincere, it drew attention to itself. The whole time I ate with them, all I could think was how I'd describe the experience to Syd. How she'd gobble it up, throwing her head back and cackling. Somehow, eating lunch with Marcy and the Mormons, I felt like an awful person and a total loser at the same time. It stunk. And it made me miss Syd like hell. I'd never wanted her back so much as I did when I was watching those strangers pray over their bags of Doritos.

On Friday I hid from the Mormons and avoided the cafeteria in general. But I didn't return to my car. I decided I'd take baby steps. I escaped to the abandoned patch of concrete in front of the band room with Will Carey, who took secret drags from his vape pen while I ate my sandwich. He was happy to have me join him, and it felt good to get away from everyone for a half hour, to escape into the details of Will's excruciatingly complicated fan fiction. But it became clear before I'd even opened my Sprite that Will had abandoned his obsession with fictional characters and had replaced them with a real live human being.

And who was this human being?

That tall guy with a ponytail in our French class.

Syd would've found it hilarious, the way I nearly choked on my ham and cheese when Will said Nick's name. How had I found the one person on Earth who didn't know about the Nick Allison Event? Or maybe Will did know and just didn't care. Either way, it was agony hearing another person obsess so openly over him. He went on about Nick's hair and the cute way he turned red when called on to speak and how he'd cheerfully receive Madame Spencer's teasing about his sometimes tortured pronunciation. Will even asked if I'd noticed that Nick had dashed into class Monday morning, right before Madame Spencer had arrived, grabbed his stuff, and never come back. He was so enamored of Nick, he didn't notice I hadn't come back either.

Will had things wrong about Nick too, and his sloppiness annoyed me. I had to bite my perfectionist's tongue when he pouted about how Nick was going out with Camila Giménez. Nick wasn't going out with anyone. Will was an amateur. I knew Nick's association with Camila was a professional one: Camila's parents paid Nick to tutor her in math. The two of them met in the library after school on Tuesdays and Thursdays—I waited for Syd every Thursday afternoon in the library just so I could watch them from a distance. Camila had no interest in Nick, or math, and checked her phone every five seconds, often staring off into space while Nick was trying to walk her through something. I'd investigated the relationship thoroughly and had long ago rendered it harmless. I'd even seen Camila hand Nick cash.

Still, I felt awful for Will. He'd found something in the

real world to love. But what he'd found was mine—Nick was my secret obsession—and I wouldn't yield even half an inch of my love to accommodate Will's. After fifteen minutes, I had to fake an excuse and escape, leaving Will in his cloud of vapor and yearning.

By the end of the week, I'd skirted the edges of nearly every social group on campus. Even the ag kids, still grateful about my showcasing their pig, were welcoming. People had started to take pity on me, I guess. The newspaper crew was especially nice. I gave assignments for the week and took on the easiest one myself, a piece about the Feminism Club's enchie supper. I knew I could put it off until an hour before deadline.

I sent Syd hundreds of texts, some of them desperate, some of them not. I tried everything. I asked if she'd heard from Stanford. I tried to be funny and told her she was forcing me into Mormonism. I'd already ordered my magic underwear. As the week went on, her absence grew heavier and heavier. Before I opened my eyes in the morning, the truth would slam down on me and I'd jump out of bed and run to the windowsill for my phone to see if the impossible had happened and Syd had texted.

I thought it might get easier, seeing that she hadn't. But it didn't.

In the absence of being able to actually do anything, I fixated on things Syd had said over the last few weeks, trying to find any reason for why she'd leave. I remembered that, walking to the Life Club meeting the previous Friday, she'd said she wished she'd never formed it. When I joked that she was helping a lot of people extract their heads from their asses, she sighed. "Seriously. All I'm doing is teaching otherwise happy people to be as stressed-out and neurotic as I am. Is that what the world needs?" The way she said it—totally flip, edged with her trademark cynicism—hadn't made me think anything at the time. She was grumpy and tired. She was hangry.

But now?

I turned it over in my mind obsessively. Stressed-out and neurotic? I'd never have described Syd that way. She was a force of nature. A boss bitch. But was that the way she saw herself? Had the pressure she'd been placing on herself the last four years gotten to be too much? It seemed impossible. But everything seemed impossible. Maybe Syd had been sending me hints for years. Maybe she'd been asking for help. And maybe I was simply the world's worst friend, unable or unwilling to allow her to be anything less than the bulletproof superstar I'd come to rely on.

One week without her, and Syd had become a genuine mystery to me. Letty's words—*your Syd is the type to run away*—assaulted my thoughts until they lived there permanently, written across my brain in all caps.

It bothered me to no end that I couldn't recall what I'd said in response that afternoon on the way to Life Club.

I probably just laughed.

I probably just told her to eat a sandwich and chill the hell out.

But now?

Staring at the back of Nick's head in French on Friday, I had an idea. It was the only idea I'd had all week, so it felt like a good one. I decided I'd stop texting Syd for twenty-four hours. I'd stop calling and leaving desperate voice mails. Maybe this would persuade Syd to contact me. Maybe she needed a little radio silence, a signal that I wasn't going to do something insane—like call the police or tell Ray—if she texted to let me know she was still among the living. I'd done everything else I could do. I'd written Patience. I'd put up posters at school and at NMSU. I'd had the world's most awkward conversation with Isaac Chavez in which I determined he was, in fact, Medium Hottie, but that he had no idea why Syd left or where she'd gone. Syd and he flirted. That was all. "Don't even," he said, putting up his hands when he realized what I was after. "No way she ran away 'cause of me."

I'd done everything I could think of, and nothing brought relief. I remained a walking panic attack. When Madame Spencer put her palm on my shoulder after class on Friday morning, I swung around so fast that I nearly clobbered her. I felt terrible, especially because all she'd wanted to say was I should consider seeing the movie at the Fountain for extra credit. Missing a quiz had been a bad idea. She feared my A for the semester was on the line, and tonight was the end of the film's run.

And so, it was kind of perfect. The worst week ever would now conclude with my going alone to the very movie I'd refused to see with Nick.

On the way home, I decided to stop by Ray's to see if he'd heard anything. He'd been so uninterested on the phone Tuesday, it occurred to me he could know something and simply never have thought to share it with me. Also, part of me just wanted to go there, to see the graveyard and the trailer and remember that Syd Miller had existed in real life a week ago.

When I got there, though, Ray's truck was gone and Tonya answered the door dressed in sweatpants and flip-flops. She looked like hell and was self-conscious about it, which brought me a modicum of happiness.

"What is it?" she said, as if I were a stranger, or possibly a home invader.

"Is Ray here?" I asked. "I just stopped by to see if you'd heard anything." I thought of asking if Syd had received any mail, say from Stanford University, but Tonya's face wasn't open to questions.

"No, we haven't. And if you hear from her, you tell her we're cutting off her phone. And we reported the car stolen."

"You reported her car stolen?"

Again, I had that disorienting feeling that Syd's life was a total mystery to me, though it'd been happening alongside my own all day every day for forever. What did I think happened when Syd closed the door to the trailer? Did she just disappear? In the hours we spent apart, did she simply not exist?

"That car's Ray's. It's in his name." She was smug, satisfied.

"That's her car," I said. I could feel the tension in my jaw.

"Well"—Tonya smiled—"tell her she can say that to the cops."

I shook my head. It was all I could do.

"Also, tell her we're moving. And I threw most of her shit away already."

I wanted to pop her in the face. I tried hard to imagine what my dad would do in this situation. He'd be civil and strong. He wouldn't lose his cool.

"Please just tell Ray to let me know if he hears anything," I said. I turned and walked down the stairs and heard the door close before I was halfway to my car.

When I got home, my dad was in the kitchen, starting dinner. I walked in and stood in the doorway and watched him for a second before he turned and looked over his shoulder. "Hey," he said. "Where were you? What's wrong?"

"I stopped at Syd's. Tonya was there."

He wiped his hands on a dish towel. "What happened?"

"What would you do if I disappeared?" I asked. I was standing with my backpack still slung over my shoulder, my keys still in my hand.

"Everything," he said without a beat. "Anything."

"Yeah?" I said.

"Of course. Miranda. Yes. What happened?"

I shook my head. I moved my keys from one hand to the other. I wanted to tell him about how rude Tonya had been, how I felt like I'd been the worst friend ever, how I was becoming more and more sure every day that Syd might be gone for good. But before I could stop it, another question came out of my mouth. "Did you do everything to find Mom?"

He grimaced. I'd caught him off guard. We never talked about my mom. I don't think it was a *decision* on his part. My father was all about talking. He'd sat me down many times over the years to have difficult conversations, including cringe-worthy ones about menstruation and safe sex. And he still talked freely and often about how he missed his own parents, who'd had children late in life and had both died before I could get to know them.

Maybe it was because my mother wasn't a *topic*. She wasn't something we could sit down and discuss over a bowl of ice cream, which is exactly how we'd covered both how I'd prefer to acquire my first bra and the dangers both practical and spiritual of sending nude photos. (He'd read an article in *The New York Times*. He was practically hyperventilating.) But my mother's leaving was bigger than talk. For so long it'd been the defining characteristic of our entire existence. It was our *thing*. My dad tried to make it smaller. Maybe he feared we'd die beneath it, crushed especially by the weight of any lingering hope that she'd return. *Someday.* Benny and Letty believed it would happen. They had faith. But my father couldn't allow that for either of us. We couldn't afford *someday*. So he allowed and then encouraged the details of the everyday to slowly creep over the giant hole where my mother should've been. Our house had changed incrementally. Her stuff disappeared, seemingly piece by piece, a book here, a photo there. Then, when he took up cooking, he'd redone the kitchen. He bought new furniture. A few years ago I'd gone to see Benny and Letty, and he painted the guest room, the room my mother had grown up in. When I returned, I checked. He'd painted over the spot behind the closet door where, as a kid, she'd scrawled *I love Morrissey*.

"Your mom didn't disappear," he said. He slung the dish towel over his shoulder and put his hands on his hips. "Your mom's not missing, Mir. She left."

"Yeah," I said. I didn't even know why I'd brought it up.

"Do you think she got married again?"

He dropped his head and spoke to the floor. "I don't know." The question hurt him and I was sorry.

"Never mind," I said. I relieved us both of the question that logically followed: *Do you think she has more kids?*

"Did Tonya say something about your mom?"

"Oh," I said. "No. She told me they reported Syd's car stolen. They threw away her stuff."

"You're kidding me."

"No," I said.

"God." He shook his head. "I want you to stay away from them."

I took off my backpack and sat at the table. I put my keys down. "The other day Letty said Syd was just the type of person who'd run away. Because of her home life. I thought she was wrong. But maybe she wasn't."

"It hasn't even been a week," my father shot back. "Those people. It's been five days. She could come back."

"And all her stuff will be gone."

He pointed at me. "Don't go back there. I don't want you to go back there."

"I won't," I said.

"I'm making pizza," he said firmly, as if pizza was just punishment for our unjust world.

"From scratch?" I stood and picked up my backpack and tossed it onto the floor in the hallway.

"Of course," he said, offended.

7

I thought of asking my dad if he wanted to come to the movie, but I didn't. He took it as a good sign I was going out. "It'll be good to get out of the house." He'd said similar things in the months after my mom left. He'd wake me on Saturday mornings and announce we were going for a day trip to El Paso or Silver City. He'd tricked me into a disturbing number of hiking situations.

I did the dishes after dinner and went into my room to get dressed. I changed my clothes a dozen times, finally settling on a pair of jeans and an old shirt of my dad's, a vintage T-shirt from R.E.M.'s legendary Green tour. My father had gone to the concert with my mom at the Pan Am Center at NMSU when he was seventeen. It'd changed his life. I knew this because he'd told me about it a zillion times. The shirt was my favorite. It'd faded from black to dark gray and was perfectly soft but not yet threadbare.

I checked myself in the hall mirror. "Laters," I called, looking at my phone one more time to confirm that my Syd plan was still, thus far, a total failure.

"What time?" my dad called back.

"Not late." I opened the front door. But then I thought about *She likes you*. I thought of how I'd asked Nick if the note was awful and he'd said no. Did no mean, no, it wasn't awful if I liked him? Or did it mean, no, the note itself wasn't awful, as in it wasn't riddled with profanities and threats against his life? "I'll text if I'm going to be later, okay?" I called down the hall. "I think some kids from class are going. I dunno. We might go out after." I knew it was stupid, but even making a little space for the possibility made me woozy.

"Okay, but no coffee, Mir." Most parents hoped their teens wouldn't smoke meth or get pregnant. Mine hoped I wouldn't drink coffee after 7:00 P.M. because he knew it kept me up and had more than once left me dangling on the edge of a panic attack.

"All right, warden," I said.

"Warden my ass," he called back. "You're the one who wakes me up complaining of heart palpitations. And you haven't slept all week."

"Okay, whatever, I love you, bye," I said as I closed the door behind me.

"Love you too," I heard him call back from inside the house.

In the car, I wondered if I should text Nick and warn him I'd be at the movie. I decided it was better not to. He might've decided not to go. Anyway, it was best if he thought I'd forgotten he was going to be there. It was best if he thought I wasn't thinking about him at all, even if I was thinking about him all the time, even if I'd applied eyeliner and hoped he'd ask about my T-shirt. I'd already rehearsed what I'd tell him, about how my parents traveled to music festivals all over the country and how they'd been at Lollapalooza—the first one ever, and the second, and the third. About how then my dad went to MIT and my mom stayed here, but for some reason he came home senior year and graduated from NMSU. (Hint: reason was born nine months later. So awkward.) About how he married his high school sweetheart and got a job at NASA and got stuck designing what I called his *thingies*, which were boring and complicated, made almost entirely of math, and had absolutely no practical application in the field of aerospace technology—that is, until they were selected to replace the ineffective thingies on the high-gain antenna on the Kepler space telescope, which launched when I was eight, and discovered Kepler-186f, the first viable Goldilocks planet in a distant galaxy. The discovery was confirmed officially the night of my fifteenth birthday. Someone called to tell my dad and he started crying right there at our table at Cattle Baron while Syd and I and the rest of the restaurant stared. Then he got a big promotion and became head of a team working on thingies for the James Webb Space Telescope. Like every single part of that telescope, the thingies he was making weren't like any other thingies before. They'd never been conceived of. He'd started Skyping with the Goddard Space Flight Center in Maryland. He made better thingies, more efficient thingies, more durable thingies. But he'd stayed here, at the tiny NASA facility in southern New Mexico, two thousand miles from where the Webb was being built. He'd never gotten an award. He'd never sat in at a NASA press conference. He just kept his head down and made his thingies and sometimes, in the evening, he listened to R.E.M. or the Smiths or the Violent Femmes while he cooked the two of us dinner.

Well, okay. Maybe I wouldn't tell Nick all of that if he mentioned my T-shirt.

Maybe I'd just say thanks and nothing else. Why did I feel like I needed to talk to him anyway? I didn't need to tell him anything. I still regretted blurting out my sob story at the ditch. I had to remain vigilant.

I parked at the far end of the lot behind the Fountain, and before I got out, I pulled down the visor's mirror and looked myself in the eyes. "Be strong. Don't be a dumbass. Don't be a fool." I squinted at my reflection, feeling strong, but then it dawned on me: these were words Syd would say. I was Syd-ing myself. The urge to text her was stronger than ever, but I sat there and let it wash over me. "Fuck me," I said loudly to no one. That was when I heard a rapping on my window and turned to find myself staring at Nick's lower body. Of course. Why did this keep happening to me? For eight months I'd successfully avoided any meaningful contact with this person. Now I couldn't seem to stop making contact.

He stooped to peer into the window. "Hey." His voice was distant through the glass though his face was only inches away from mine.

I flipped up the visor and grabbed my purse. I reached for the door handle but realized I was still buckled into my seat. *Come on,* I thought. *Really?* I breathed. I reached over and unbuckled my seat belt and then swung open the door so suddenly, Nick had to jump out of the way.

"You came," he said. Was he happy about this?

"I had to." I felt awful being rude. Then I felt stupid for feeling awful. If Syd were here, she'd have already spit a fireball of insults into Nick's face and dragged me away. I tried to help myself out by willing forth the memory of how

I'd slipped out of my dress on prom night last year, how I'd returned it to the hanger and zipped it up in its garment bag and wondered if I could return it. *Has this been worn?* the salesclerk might ask. And how would I answer?

"Spencer told me this was my only hope for an A," I said, hitching my purse up.

"Have you heard anything from Syd?" he asked.

"No." I hated the sound of my voice. It reverberated in my skull like a bad note.

"Can I walk with you?"

My heart swayed inside my chest, weak. "Whatever," I said as dully as I could. Why did he have to be this way? So gentlemanly? So fucking decent? And why did he have to be wearing his forest-green hoodie, my very favorite of his garments?

We walked in silence, but I noted anyone viewing us from a distance would conclude objectively that we were together, we were a pair, a couple. The thought of it dazzled inside me, as bright as the sky full of stars above us. I hated it.

"So what's this movie about anyway?" I asked.

"Life being crap, I believe," he said. "It's in black and white."

"Oh great," I said.

The movie was about life being crap. Literally nothing happened in it. Nick and I were two of only five audience members, and we were the only two people sitting next to each other in the whole theater. I quickly became so preoccupied sitting next to Nick that I wasn't able to pay much attention to the movie. I gave in and allowed myself to be perverse. There was no harm in it. I could think of anything while I stared at the screen, looking bored. I could think of what it'd be like to reach over and touch Nick's hand, for example. It was sitting right there. What would happen if I did that? What would it cost me in pain and humiliation if he recoiled from my touch? Or, on the other hand, what if instead I slipped my upturned palm beneath his, and I heard his breathing change? What if he opened his fingers and laced them with mine? What if he looked at me? Or what if he was too shy—he was so shy! Baseline weird and embarrassed!—and so just swallowed hard and blinked and looked straight ahead? I liked very much thinking about this while he was so close. It felt good and dangerous and bad and creepy all at once. My brain, full of my thoughts, was just a foot away from his brain, full of his thoughts.

I couldn't do all that weird stuff and also read subtitles. So I let go of my grasp on the plot. I thought of other things too. I thought of Syd and wondered if she'd noticed I'd gone nearly twelve whole hours without texting. I wondered when exactly Ray was going to turn off her phone, cutting off my only possible connection to her. I wondered if she'd heard from Stanford. But my mind kept returning to the person beside me. I was touching his hair. He was putting a tentative hand on my waist and his fingers were slowly moving past the hem of my R.E.M. T-shirt. By the end, I'd lost track of everything. In the last moment of the film, something happened. It must've, because Nick looked at me as if to ask if I could believe what we were seeing on the screen. I shrugged, faking bafflement. And then the movie was over. The lights came up and I was forced back to reality. I scrambled to stand before Nick did. He stood and stretched his arms behind his back and asked very casually if I wanted to go get ice cream across the street at Milagro. I wanted to say no, but I couldn't. It was, after all, the very fantasy I'd concocted in telling my dad I'd text him if I were going to be late.

The streets were empty and quiet. We walked across Main Street and down the sidewalk. "That movie was whack," he said.

"I thought it was a classic example of French existential nihilism," I said.

He turned to me. "Really?"

"No," I said. "I zoned out so much, I lost track of the characters."

"Wait, there were characters?" he asked. We laughed.

Against my better judgment, I found myself on the verge of having a good time. I tried to resist but couldn't. Syd would find me pathetic. She'd question my morality, my self-worth, and probably even my feminism for laughing with a guy who'd gone out of his way to hurt me. *He wasn't just hurtful,* I could hear her now. *He was abusive!* But I couldn't resist. Maybe I was weak. Maybe I was a terrible feminist who hated herself. But while Nick considered his ice cream choice, I made the decision to enjoy the rest of this one evening. Not everything was an emergency. Not everything was an ordeal to be survived. There was such a thing as two people getting ice cream, no strings attached.

I was carrying out this argument in my mind when Nick asked what I wanted.

"Oh, sorry. Chocolate," I said to the woman behind the counter. I dug around in my purse for my wallet, but by the time I had it out, Nick was handing her a twenty. The Syd in my mind went nuts. *Do you see? He's trying to buy you for the price of a fucking ice cream cone!*

"Wait no." I held up a ten-dollar bill like an idiot. The woman behind the counter stopped plunking the keys on the cash register. "I can pay for my own ice cream," I said to her, accusingly. She blinked once and looked at Nick. Nick looked at me. I looked at him then back at her. I didn't know what to do.

"I'll buy your ice cream." He knocked my shoulder lightly with his. My resistance returned. He knocked my shoulder and I was standing again in my dress, peering out the kitchen window to the dark driveway, waiting. Because they'd started to hurt, I'd slipped my shoes off and left them by the door, thinking I'd slip them back on when I saw headlights.

I waited.

I thought of texting, but I'd texted earlier in the afternoon to make sure our plan was tight. Our plan was tight. It was perfect, like something out of a movie. I wasn't even supposed to go to prom with Nick. Syd had arranged for me to go with Quinn Johnson, a friend of Matt Martinez, the guy she was taking. I didn't like Quinn or really even know him. In fact, I couldn't be sure who he was when Syd first suggested it. Syd only knew him because he was on the tennis team with her. I had to look him up. Most of his photos were of him shirtless on the hood of his father's Mercedes. He had so much product in his blond hair, it looked sharp to the touch. Then I remembered. We'd been in American literature together. All I remembered about him was that he used the word *literally* in every sentence. But I agreed, nonetheless. I had no one to blame but myself for Quinn. I'd chickened out asking Nick. I made a plan. I set a deadline. And then, the morning I was supposed to do it after French, I got so

nervous, I ended up rambling about our homework as-
signment instead. Then I scrammed. Nick might've been
weird and embarrassed, but I was a chicken and prom
with Quinn Johnson was *literally* the price I'd have pay
for it.

But that was when the miracle happened. It was Ryan
Gosling Saint Jude, I was sure of it. I'd been reading about
him before bed the night before. Two days before prom
Quinn was diagnosed with mono (along with Marissa
Torres, who happened to be Philip Vigil's girlfriend.
Oops). I heard the news and began scheming, emboldened by the idea that it was destiny. That Friday morning
I told Nick about Quinn, how it stunk, since I'd already
bought a dress and I really kind of *wanted to go*. He did just
what I'd dreamed he'd do: he asked if I maybe wanted to
go with him. He didn't have a date. In fact, he was planning on going camping with Tomás and some other guys.
He'd cancel. "Oh, totally," he'd said. "No problem." And
a sweet smile came so readily to his face, I had to look away
or I'd faint.

Syd was pissed. She said I should have checked first,
since our prom plans had been carefully devised by her
and this would throw everything off. How? I didn't know.
But I was too happy to argue with Syd. I told her we'd have
a great time, and eventually she shut up about it.

I'd texted him earlier that afternoon to say I'd had
Quinn's tickets transferred into my name. If he'd gotten
a tux, we were set. He texted back that he'd rented *the last
tuxedo on Earth*. He'd be at my house at seven o'clock. He
volunteered to be our designated driver. *Not a big drinker.*

I gave him my address.

I thanked Saint Jude.

I praised the God of mono.

I started waiting for the best night of my life to begin. Later, when it became so late that I knew we'd miss dinner with Syd and Matt, I texted Syd we'd meet them at the dance. *He hasn't shown. I'm starting to freak. Should I text him?* I wrote her. *No! Chill!* she'd written back. *Boys are idiots.* I wished she'd offered more advice. I sat down with my father on the sofa, both of us puzzled. We started watching *Dateline.* Some wife had killed her husband by locking him in the freezer at their butcher shop and leaving him in there for days. Or *was* it the wife? That was what *Dateline* was going to find out. My dad was trying so hard not to let me know how bad he felt for me. After a while he went to the kitchen and made popcorn. He set it down between us, but then he started stress-eating it himself.

I didn't cry. Even after I'd gone into my room and unzipped the dress and hung it back on the hanger. I didn't cry because I didn't want to mess up my makeup. Just in case. Pathetic.

At nine thirty my dad started asking what he could do. What could he do? By that time I was wearing pj's and crying freely.

"Do you want me to call his parents?" he asked.

"Oh god, Dad, no." I laughed at him through my tears. When he looked so pathetically happy to see me smile, I fell back to sobbing. I'd texted Syd and she told me she'd be over as soon as she dropped Matt off at the dance. I told her no. I didn't want to ruin her night. She texted, *SHUT UP, I'm on my way.* She walked in at 9:45, looking radiant, her hair down in all its wild, curly glory, a corsage pinned to the amazing red dress she'd found at a consignment shop. Her anger was the only thing that made me feel better that night. She said she texted Nick herself, but he hadn't texted back. I asked what she'd said. "I told him I was going to destroy him." She put her arms around me and let me weep into her hair.

Has this dress been worn? my imaginary salesclerk asked. It was a beautiful dress, deep green, strapless, ankle length with a full, flowy skirt. When I stepped out of the dressing room to show Syd, her eyes bulged. "That dress was made for you," she said. "Your boobies are defying gravity right now." I looked in the mirror and knew it was the one. But instead of Quinn Johnson, I imagined Nick seeing me in it. Maybe he'd be at prom too. Maybe I'd at least lay eyes on him, even if he was with another girl. "Oh my garsh," Syd had said. "Quinn's gonna cream his shorts." She laughed at her own joke and went back to looking at her phone.

Has this dress been worn?

It was too much to forget.

The woman dug the scooper into the untouched surface of the chocolate ice cream. "You know what?" I said, and she looked up. "I don't want ice cream. I'm sorry."

I stared through the glass case at the vats of pastel colored ice cream. I felt disoriented, as if I'd been teleported against my will into this moment. "God, what I am doing?" I said, to myself mostly. I turned to Nick. "I can't." I willed myself to say no more. I turned again to the woman, who now looked happily shocked, as if she couldn't wait to text someone about this weird experience as soon as she could get her hands on her phone. "Sorry," I said again. She fumbled out a "no problem."

"See you in French." I tried not to look at him too long. I turned and made a beeline for the door and walked out into the cold night and down the block and across Main, past the Fountain, and into the now empty parking lot. Not until I got to my car did I turn to make sure Nick hadn't followed me. He hadn't. I was alone, completely and utterly. *The last tuxedo on Earth.*

The only other car in the lot was Nick's, parked a few spots over. Above me, a streetlamp hummed its one dull note of electricity. The night sky bloomed with stars. That streetlamp was the only thing standing between me and the universe. (*Multiverse, Miry,* I could hear my father say in his teasing-not-teasing way, always so eager to expand my horizons, to correct my small-town concept of reality.) I knew I couldn't just stand there looking up, especially now that tears had ruined my eyeliner and were pouring out of my face.

I never returned the dress. It still hung at the back of my closet, zipped up in its gray garment bag. I'd forgotten what it looked like, really, and why I'd loved it so much. Now all I thought of when I thought of that dress was my father shoveling popcorn in his mouth and the butcher shop freezer cordoned off with yellow crime scene tape. Syd showed up before the end of *Dateline.* I never even found out who killed that poor butcher. But I knew who killed the dress, zipped up like a body in a body bag, a reminder of the worst night of my life. It was Nick Allison.

Has this dress been worn? I imagined the salesclerk asking.

And that was why I never returned it.

I couldn't stand the idea of answering.

No, I'd have to say. *Never got the chance.*

8

"Home." I tossed my keys into the bowl. I didn't want to walk down the hall and have to explain my puffy eyes to my dad, though this week had been so monumentally crappy, I had any number of reasons to be crying. He'd never guess it was about a boy. Especially not That Boy. *That Boy* was how my dad referred to Nick when he brought him up. *Did That Boy ever apologize to you? Did That Boy ever explain himself?*

"How was *le cinéma*?" He muted the TV.

"Fine. Weird. Super-French." I tried to sound okay. "Going to bed."

"Okay," he said. "Get some sleep." The sound came back, the familiar roar and squeak of a basketball game, the crowd calling *de-fense*. I'd slipped under his emotional radar. At least I'd done one thing right.

"Night," I said.

"Love you," he called back.

"Love you too."

I closed the door to my room and caught a glimpse of myself in the mirror above my dresser. I was wrecked. My eyeliner was history. I didn't have it in me to walk down the hall and wash my face and brush my teeth. It'd been that kind of night. All I wanted was to be done having it.

I put on my pajamas and climbed into bed. It felt good to be under the covers, to be surrounded by silence. I considered reading about some saints, but I was too exhausted for martyrdom and stigmata and trying to decipher whether or not my mother was crazy from her marginalia. I switched off the light, said a couple Gettysburg Addresses, and was drifting to sleep when I heard my phone ding from inside my purse across the room. It was a miracle! My phone wasn't even in my windowsill. It had received a text from inside my purse on the floor. It was Ryan Gosling Saint Jude at work again! The *IMPOSSIBLE* had happened! My plan had worked! I'd gone fifteen hours without texting and she'd come around! I was a genius who had genius ideas!

But it wasn't her. I deflated.

Instead I'd received a text from *JERK-ASS DIPSHIT*. I'd forgotten Syd had snuck into my contacts last year and substituted this name for Nick's. It made me smile. But then came the deep, piercing sadness: my plan hadn't worked. I wasn't a genius. I missed Syd so bad right then. She wasn't just my best friend; she was *the* best friend. Who else would sneak into my contacts and change the boy who'd hurt me to *JERK-ASS DIPSHIT*?

That was when it dawned on me that Nick was texting. I moved to the window and tapped the screen and squinted as if opening my eyes only slightly would help my heart and head take in his words more cautiously.

Okay, what just happened?

I stared at the words. Did he not know what just happened? Was he a total idiot? I started composing a response—*Are you serious?*—but before I finished, he sent another.

I should have been more clear at the ditch, he wrote. *I wanted to go to the movie with you. Like, together. I'm not good at this stuff.*

It took me about fifteen seconds to read the text sixty million times. There was no way of misunderstanding it, even though I was trying my hardest.

No, I reminded myself. *No.* It helped that the name above the text thread was *JERK-ASS DIPSHIT.* I thought of the dress. I thought of my father trying to get me to forget the disaster and focus on a grizzly murder instead.

No, I wrote back. *I can't.* I pressed send.

Why not? he shot back right away.

I started typing. *Syd was right. I like you.* I typed it. But I knew I could never send that, so I deleted it and wrote, *Do you remember*—but then I couldn't figure out how to finish the sentence. Nick remembered. Of course he did. He'd apologized at the ditch. *For everything.* But it didn't make sense. It didn't add up. You don't stand someone up for prom, never apologize or explain, avoid her for a year, and then, boom, suddenly want to watch French cinema like nothing ever happened. There was only one thing to do and that was to put an end to things. He'd forced me into it.

I don't trust you. I'll never trust you. I typed it fast and then let it sit there until I knew for sure it was the truth. I deleted the second sentence: *I'll never trust you.*

I don't trust you. I tried to find a reason not to send the message, but before I could: *tap.* I'd sent it.

I don't trust you. The words sat there, shining in their bright blue bubble.

I laid my phone down before me in the windowsill. It glowed in the dark, an oracle. This time Nick took a few seconds before he began composing.

Okay, he wrote finally. My heart sank. But then he started composing again. I stood, waiting. The three little dots looked like they were boiling. It took so long for him to send the text that I expected a paragraph, but when it finally arrived, all it said was: *Can we talk?*

Now? I wrote back.

Okay. He'd misunderstood me. I meant *Now?* as in *Are you crazy?*

On the phone? I texted.

No.

I'd have to sneak out. I was surprised I'd even typed this. I didn't know what to do. This was precisely the type of situation Syd was so good at navigating. She wouldn't need to think. She'd simply know the one, correct way to proceed. And that was what she'd do.

I know what Syd meant about telling you the truth, he wrote.

WHAT? I texted. My heart pounded in my ears. *TELL ME.*

I can't do this over text, he wrote.

I took a deep breath and held it. *There's a pecan orchard down the dirt road right next to my house. Meet me there in five. BE QUIET. It's not our orchard.*

Nick wrote back. *On my way.*

For a moment I stood there, dazed. I thought I'd made it to the end of the worst week of my life, but I was wrong. The week wanted to go on. Screw it. I flew into action.

Why had I asked for only five minutes? I checked my face in the mirror. I looked like hell. I figured it'd be dark outside. It wouldn't matter what I looked like. I slipped back into my jeans and put on the R.E.M. T-shirt. I slid on my Vans and rifled through my purse until I found one last piece of spearmint gum at the bottom. I picked off lint and shoved the gum into my mouth.

I tried to decide the best way of getting out of my house with my father awake down the hall. Option one: I could stroll into the living room and tell him I was going out for a walk. Going for a walk at night wasn't unheard of in our household. I knew how to find the craters of the moon using only binoculars. I could grab the pair hanging on the hook by the front door and put them around my neck to look convincing. There was a moon out there. I'd seen it through my tears driving home. *Waxing gibbous,* I'd noted out of habit. He might buy it. He was, after all, the one who'd taught me the phases of the moon and how to find the craters. He'd taught me to look up at the chaos of the night sky and find order in the constellations.

A night walk wasn't unheard of for him, either. The year after my mom left, I'd sometimes wake in the night and find the house empty. I'd wait on the porch and yell at him when he came walking up, earbuds plugged into his old-fashioned Discman. He'd apologize. There was always something happening in the sky and he was always looking for it. But even at nine I knew what he was doing out there was wandering around, lost, wondering if we'd ever see my mom again.

No. It wouldn't work. No way. It was too late now. If I walked into the living room and announced I was going for a walk, he'd say, "Um, no, you're not." Or—more likely—he'd switch off the game and grab his coat, excited to check out Tycho with the binoculars. *Waxing gibbous,* he'd say. *Here we come.*

I had two other options: I could sneak out the front door or I could brave the window. The front door was my preferred method, but only when my father was already asleep. His room was farthest from the front. The door was ancient, squeaky, and the dead bolt was engaged. And he wasn't asleep. So I was left with the worst-case scenario: I'd have to open the old, heavy, wood-paned window in my bedroom and climb out of it without impaling myself on the giant agave cactuses my father had planted beneath it, most likely to discourage me from doing the very thing I was planning on doing right this very second. The window was treacherous. I'd only done it once, with Syd, when Benny and Letty were visiting and my dad was sleeping next door in the guest room. It was easier with Syd. She was dexterous and strong. She'd scrambled out first and then coached me as I tried, eventually yanking my long legs out the window at a diagonal, away from the razor-sharp spines of the agaves.

I went to my closet to get my coat. As I grabbed it, I was aware of the gray garment bag hanging farther back. *Really?* it seemed to ask me. *You're going to climb over a frickin' cactus to meet That Boy?*

I shimmied the window open inch by inch, trying to be quiet and failing. There was no screen, thankfully, only the sky above and the sea of agaves below. I grabbed the chair from my desk and moved it beneath the window, then climbed to the sill and carefully swung one leg through. I remembered Syd telling me the most important thing when sneaking out is to be fast. You can even be loud, as long as you're fast. It's the slow, persistent noises that get attention. I straddled the wide windowsill, staring down into the spiny abyss. *You got this,* I imagined Syd saying. I turned clumsily onto my belly, hitched my other leg over. I tried to stay close to the house as I dropped.

Amazingly, I landed on my feet. I was not impaled. I inched out around the agave and tiptoed into the side yard and hopped the low adobe wall at the edge of the dirt road. I looked toward the street and saw no sign of Nick's car, so I turned and walked along the road toward the orchard, waxing gibbous hanging just above the bare treetops. I felt like I was floating. I looked up and found Orion, then Cassiopeia. They calmed me down. I zipped up my coat. It was cold, but the cold felt good. I felt alive. I reached the orchard. I waited. I swallowed my gum. I pulled my hair back into a ponytail and secured it with the elastic band around my wrist.

I looked again to the sky. It was a perfect night. If it was just a little darker, if I was about twenty miles away from the city lights, I'd be able to see the Milky Way. I tried to eke out a little prayer. *Four score and seven years ago.* But I was too nervous. I peered down the road. I thought of walking back toward the street. Maybe Nick was lost. I took a step and felt something strange and warm on my ankle. In the same moment, a searing pain shot up my leg. I freaked. My first thought was I'd been bitten by a rattlesnake. It was my biggest fear, living in the desert, and I'd seen plenty. But I'd heard nothing. Could you get bit by a rattlesnake and not know it?

I fumbled for my phone and turned on the flashlight and pointed it at my ankle. Two ribbons of blood were flowing across the top of my foot into my shoe. I hitched the leg of my jeans up and shone the flashlight on a three-inch gash across my ankle, oozing blood. *Profuse* was the word that sprang to mind. This was profuse bleeding. Immediately upon seeing it, the pain doubled. I heard Syd saying, *Don't barf, okay?* the way she had when she poked my finger with the pin.

"Oh my god." I sat on the ground. "Oh my god." I was sure I was going to puke or die or both.

"Miranda?" I heard a voice. I couldn't tell if it was Nick or my dad.

"I'm here," I said. I flashed my phone's light in the direction of the voice. I heard footsteps and pointed the flashlight to see Nick standing there, squinting.

"What's wrong?" he said.

"I cut my leg." I didn't mention how close I was to puking, though that felt like a much bigger, more immediate problem.

"How?" He crouched beside me.

Don't barf don't barf don't barf.

"Climbing out of my window."

"Okay." He took my phone and shone the light onto my leg. It was weird how commanding he was. "Here." He sat down and straightened my leg and lifted it onto his lap. He rolled my jeans up carefully until the gash was revealed. It was so bad, it looked fake. "Oh man," he said. "That's gnarly."

"Thanks so much," I said, feeling more pukey than ever.

"Sorry. Don't look," he said. "Just keep your eyes on me." For a moment his eyes met mine and he nodded and I forgot about the pain. I kept my eyes on him. He reached into his back pocket. At first I thought he was going for his phone—to do what? Take a photo for his weird Insta-gram? But when he brought his hand back, he was holding a neatly folded piece of cloth. *A handkerchief?* I thought. *Who carries a handkerchief?* I felt woozy and didn't know if it was Nick's weird-perfectness or me beginning to bleed out. He pressed the cloth firmly to the cut. I braced my-self, thinking that would hurt more, but it didn't. It actu-ally felt better. "I'm going to apply pressure for several minutes," he said, holding my calf with one hand and pressing the cloth firmly to my leg with the other. "What happened? You broke the window?"

I laughed. "No," I said. "There's a cactus outside my window."

"Oh," he said. "Agave?"

"Wow, Sherlock," I said. "So am I going to live?"

"I think so. But you're going to need to clean the wound with hydrogen peroxide and put on a mondo Band-Aid. If you have one of those butterfly-closure things, that'd be perfect. You know those things? You might need two actually. You might actually need stitches if the bleeding doesn't stop."

"You know a lot about wound care. You inflict a lot of wounds?" I was trying not to be distracted by the way he was holding my calf while he applied pressure with the other hand. *Gentle,* I thought. *How can someone so gentle be such a dick?*

He looked at me and smiled. "Well, since you're prob-ably going to die right now, it won't matter if I tell you something, but you have to swear not to tell anyone."

"What?"

He raised the cloth and took a quick peek at the cut. "I'm an Eagle Scout."

I busted out laughing. "Shut up. That's hilarious."

"Yeah." He was embarrassed. I felt like a jerk.

"You're a Boy Scout?"

"No. I mean I was, yes. Now I'm an Eagle Scout."

"You're being serious right now?"

"I think it's pretty obvious I'm serious." His cheeks reddened in the moonlight.

"Oh my god," I said. An awkward silence commenced. "That's—interesting."

"It's pretty dorky, actually. I know. I joined when I was a kid. It's basically the only way I get to do anything outdoors."

How on Earth had I missed this gem? I'd seen every photo of Nick online. He was rarely in the foreground, but I could find him. Anywhere. Tomás's Instagram was my gold mine. *The Allison in his native habitat*, my favorite photo was captioned. In it, Nick sat on a log in early morning light, barely awake, his hands pushed between his legs, staring at a fire. Cumulatively, I probably stared at that photo for at least three hours.

Had those been Boy Scout trips?

"Huh." I tried to fit this information into my brain. What could I find sexy about an adult-size Boy Scout?

"Do you wear that costume?"

"It's a uniform. And no. Only when absolutely required. Like, I've worn it once."

"Wow." I guessed it was going to be like the ponytail. I never thought I'd love an Eagle Scout. Now I had no choice. "Guess you're earning your first-aid badge right now."

He lifted the handkerchief, which, in light of his Eagle Scout revelation, made a little more sense. He revealed the cut. It was weirdly precise and bright red, but where I expected the blood to come gushing out of it again, it stayed. Applying pressure for several minutes had worked.

"I already have my first-aid badge." He smiled. "I have, like, all the badges."

"Right," I said. "Of course." I wanted to ask where he kept them. Were they sewn onto a sash like Luciana's Daisy Scout patches?

He used the handkerchief to wipe the lines of blood on my ankle. He attended to the task with such care and tenderness, I could almost watch him do it without wanting to barf. But I couldn't. I looked up at his face. *His face is right there,* I thought. He looked into my eyes. For one second it felt like we might kiss—we might kiss!—like that might be what was going to happen next. It didn't make sense, but that was how it felt.

But then again he broke the gaze and looked away.

"Do you hate me?" I blurted out.

"No," he answered plainly.

"I think you really hate me."

"That's not the case." He looked back at my leg. "Can I ask you something?"

"What?" My heart quickened.

"Do you have any blood-borne diseases?"

"What?"

"According to the *Boy Scout Handbook* I'm supposed to ask that." He seemed to understand immediately that he'd made a super-lame joke.

"Oh." I fake chuckled. "That's funny." I felt like a fool. A few seconds ago I thought he might kiss me. "So what's the deal? I can't be out here bleeding all night."

Nick looked as if a giant weight had been returned to his shoulders. He moved my leg carefully to the ground and sat beside me on the orchard floor, his arms wrapped around his knees. It'd been a long time since the orchard had been irrigated. The top layers were cracked like the pieces of a giant jigsaw puzzle. He picked up a puzzle piece and it crumbled, turning to dust in his hand. He took the world's deepest breath and exhaled. He looked up into the bare branches of the pecan trees. I couldn't stand it anymore.

"Do you know where Syd is?"

"No," he answered. "No. But I need to tell you something. About last year. About what happened." He looked like he was in actual pain.

"What?" I tried to soften my voice. "Just tell me."

"That night. You know. I didn't come to your house." He stopped, unable or unwilling to continue. I was getting impatient.

"I'm familiar with the events of that evening, yes, Nick."

"Okay. Well. It was Syd." He propelled the words from his mouth with such force, it was almost a shout. "She told me not to come."

"What?" I was baffled.

"She texted. She said you'd changed your mind."

I must've looked like I was watching a TV with no sound, trying to decipher the dialogue by reading lips. When I said nothing, he continued. "She told me not to text you. She said to just leave you alone. So I did. I thought maybe you were sick or something, but she wouldn't tell me. And then, the next day, she started doing all that stuff. Calling. Texting. She did that stuff to my locker.

Everyone was telling me I was a dick. I didn't know what was going on."

I stared at him. Somewhere far away, maybe up there, on the moon maybe, my leg ached.

"That's what she meant. In that note," he said.

"*Tell her the truth.*" I blinked hard and looked up to the stars. "And so?" I braced myself for the truth.

"So I needed to tell you. I should've told you at the ditch. I should've told you last year."

"Wait. No—I mean why?"

"Why what?"

"Why did she do that?"

Nick gave me a puzzled look. "I have no idea."

"Oh." For eight months I'd been trying to come up with a decent explanation for what happened that night. I hadn't been able to do it. Now here it was, and it was more absurd than anything I could've ever imagined. "You were going to come?"

"Yes," he said. "I was getting dressed when she texted."

"Oh." Tears rolled over my lids. I just let them. I remembered that when I asked her what to do that night, Syd told me not to text Nick. *Boys are idiots,* she'd said. And so I didn't. Syd had so much faith in my obedience to her. She'd simply waited for me to ask her what to do.

"I told my parents your appendix ruptured."

I wiped my tears. "Ah. My ordeal."

Nick reached over and put his hand on my knee. It was the first time he'd touched me in a non-first-aid-related way. The first time ever. His hand was warm. "I should've just told you the truth." He gripped my knee. "And I didn't. And I'm sorry."

"Okay." I tried to come to a conclusion about how to

feel. But I couldn't. My natural instinct was to wish I could ask Syd what to do. But Syd was suddenly the very thing I didn't understand. She was the problem. I felt like I'd been busted open, like a window, air passing through me. Unbelievably, I laughed through my tears.

"What?" Nick looked at me like I was crazy.

"Oh. I just thought about how you asked me if I broke my window."

He smiled. It was unbearable. "Oh yeah," he said. "I was confused."

When I heard Syd had disappeared, it was the worst. But at least I knew how to feel. At least I knew I could begin worrying, agonizing, searching, even if it was all in vain. I knew it was right to feel 100 percent terrible, even if it felt 100 percent terrible. But this? This made no sense.

"Can I see her texts?"

"I erased them," Nick said. "I wish I hadn't now. But there was so much dog poop. I finally just erased the thread. After she stopped sending them."

"I knew you were doing that on purpose." I looked at him. There was no doubt he was telling me the truth. "You wanted her to see that you'd seen them."

"It was all I could do. Just letting her know that I knew what she was doing was a lie. It was insane. I thought she was insane."

"I can't believe this."

"I thought you were in on it," he said. "I mean, not at first. At first I was just like: whoa. She asked me to prom and then she stood me up. That really sucks. But then when Syd started all of that stuff, I thought you had to know what was going on. But when I'd see you, I'd realize you didn't know. I wanted to tell you. But, I mean, she's your best friend."

"Yeah," I said.

"French has been hell. I don't know about for you. But for me, it's been hell."

"Yeah," I said, shooting him a glance. "It's sucked." I heard my voice waver and I corrected it. "By the way, Will Carey is super-hardcore crushing on you, in case you hadn't noticed."

"Oh." He smiled. "Yeah, I know. He's a really nice guy. Not my type. But oh man, he's not very good at hiding it."

"Yeah." I wanted to stop myself, but I just let it go. "Have I been any better?" I looked at his chin, unable to look in his eyes. "At hiding it?"

Silence descended from the trees. When I got the courage to look at him, I found his cheeks pink. But he didn't say anything.

"So what are we supposed to do now?" I asked, scrambling away from my weird confession. If he didn't know it before, he knew it now. Syd was right. *She likes you.*

"I don't know." He put his hand to the back of his head and grabbed the scruff of his neck. He was nervous. Had I made him nervous? "I mean." He glanced at me. "I would really like—to kiss you?"

"What?" A wave of anticipation washed over me.

But then Nick froze. "Oh my god, that was so weird. Why did I say that? I'm sorry."

"Oh." I tried not to sound totally deflated. "Yeah." Why hadn't I just leaned over and kissed him? I'd chickened out again.

"But okay, can I just say one thing?" he said. "While

I'm in the middle of saying weird things? Before this is over and I lose my nerve?"

I swallowed hard. "Say it."

He looked me steadily in the eyes. "I want a do-over."

"A do-over?"

"Yes. Where I get to buy you a stupid ice cream, maybe after going to a stupid dinner or something. Or you can buy my ice cream. You know. Because—feminism."

"Okay." I laughed. I nodded. "Feminist do-over. Granted."

He smiled. "Tomorrow?" he asked.

"Tomorrow?"

"Is that crazy soon?" he shot back. "No. Sorry."

"No," I said. "No. Tomorrow's good."

"Cool," he said.

We sat there in the silent orchard. I was becoming acutely aware of my bloody leg and the gross wound that needed tending to. I bent forward and folded my pant leg down. After that, I didn't know what else to do or say. I didn't want it to end.

"So where are you going? To college?"

"Oh." He seemed relieved I'd spoken, but unenthusiastic about the question. "Well. It's kind of complicated."

"You say that a lot."

"You don't know my parents." He shot me a glance. "No. Um. I'm applying to Harvard. And Tufts. My parents—my dad—really wants me to go to Harvard. Obviously. That's where he went and it's, like, this big deal. My brother, Jason, goes to Tufts. So that's why Tufts. But I'm also applying to UNM. But I'm not telling them."

"Why not?"

"I don't know." He poked at the ground. "I'm not what my parents think I am?"

"Oh crap, you're a werewolf," I said. "I knew it."

He laughed. "Yeah, no. My dad wants me to study math, like him. He thinks I have *a gift*." He rolled his eyes. I could see how hard it was for him to talk about the subject. It boggled my mind. My dad had never once suggested what I should study. "Jason applied to Harvard, but he didn't get in. So now it's, like, my turn. On the chopping block." He cleared his throat. "It's, like—the test. You know? Who will make my father proud?"

"Math is really hard," I said. "Not everyone has a gift. I don't. Camila doesn't."

He screwed up his face. "How do you know about Camila?"

I wanted to answer: *because I know everything about you, you idiot. Now kiss me.* Instead I said, "I've seen you guys in the library."

"Thursdays," he shot back. "You're there Thursdays but not Tuesdays." We locked eyes for a long moment. He swallowed. "I see you too."

I could feel my face turn red. "So what is it you want to study? Do you secretly want to be a circus clown?" I asked.

He smiled. "I don't know. There's a forestry program at UNM. I think I want to work for the Forest Service. I've read a lot about it." He gave me a hesitant look, as if what he'd just said was totally shocking. "Literally, I've never told anyone that before."

"Huh," I said. "That's kind of cool."

"I just—I like it here," he said. "I didn't want to move here from Chicago. My mom and I had these big arguments. But then we came here and everything changed. It's hard to explain. But now I don't want to leave. You know?"

"Yeah," I said. "I totally know what you mean. This is—your place." I wanted to say, *This is your Goldilocks planet*, but that would've been way too weird and dorky.

"Exactly," he said. I tried to sit crisscross, but when I pulled my wounded leg in, a shock of pain made me wince. "This is nice, Miranda. I'm so glad we're talking right now," Nick said in his sweet, straightforward way. "But the Eagle Scout in me thinks you need to take care of your leg."

"Yeah." I tried to hide the disappointment in my voice.

When I stood up, my leg ached more than ever. We started walking slowly back down the road. I could see in the distance that the lights in my house were off. My father had gone to bed. I tried not to limp, and felt self-conscious about it, but Nick didn't seem to notice. What he said was still swimming in my head. I don't think I'd ever heard anyone talk about the future like that, so simply and clearly. It felt strangely freeing, to not know, to not have to be sure.

"I sometimes think I'd like to be a nun." I laughed as soon as it came out of my mouth. "I've never told anyone that."

"Really?" he said.

"Yeah." I couldn't stop laughing. "But I mean: it's totally ridiculous. I don't go to church. I don't even know if I believe in God." I thought about telling him about my *zero* God from childhood. He was a math genius. If anyone could understand, it was him. But no. It was too weird and personal and screwed up. If I started there, I could end up telling him the real reason I'd been reciting the Gettysburg Address at the ditch that morning. And there was no one who needed to know that, especially not Nick. "Now that I've said it, it sounds insane."

"Still," he said. "It's cool." I remembered, talking to him like this now, what it was that had drawn me to him freshman year, and what I'd missed so much in our silent standoff the last eight months. Nick was never put off by anything. He never judged anybody. He was open—even his face was open. I could see right into him through his eyes. It's probably exactly what Will was crushing on too. Nick was as close to a character refined by many mutations of fan fiction as Las Cruces High School would ever see. He was reserved and shy, but once you got to his eyes, you were in. In this way, he was the complete opposite of Syd, who trusted her own ideas and opinions to a fault. She was right about nearly everything, and brutally honest, but she wasn't open. I'd never have told Syd what I'd just told Nick. She would've laughed in my face. Then she'd have launched into a tirade on the patriarchal structure of the church. *Dude, you don't want to be a nun. Nuns get screwed. Be a priest. Oh right, YOU CAN'T.* She'd dispose of the whole notion within minutes.

I realized that in some screwed-up way, this was what had made my friendship with Syd so easy: I never really had to be myself. I only ever had to be Syd's friend.

"I don't know," I said. "My dad wants college to be this life-changing thing for me. He's been saving my whole life so I can go to some great school and have this big— Whatever." I shrugged. "I don't even know if I want to go to college." I looked at him. "I've never told anyone that, either."

"I've thought about that too," he said. "Just running away. I could live in a tent. You know, like just walk into the Gila one day and never come out."

"You could be one of those guys who's totally off the grid and eats berries and rattlesnakes and wears nothing but leather underpants."

"Exactly." He smiled.

"You could come into civilization, but only to visit me at my convent."

"Deal," he said. We both laughed.

"Syd was dying to get out of this town. Get into a good school. Get away and be the best. Make a million dollars. She was obsessed. Now she's gone and I realize I never really formed an opinion about it either way. You know?"

"Kinda. I think so."

"I'm just saying: I'm sure it sucks. With your dad. I totally get that. It does sound very complicated. But I also think it's cool you're not just—on autopilot. You know? Just plowing ahead out of fear or whatever."

"Yeah, right," he said. "I'm not scared of leather underpants."

We laughed again. "You're not like anyone I've ever met," I said. His eyes hit the ground. I'd made him self-conscious. "That's a good thing," I said.

"Okay," he said. We stopped walking before we arrived at my house.

"I've got to get back in there," I said, nodding across the road to my window.

"Do you want help?" he asked.

"Not at all," I said. "Actually, will you promise me something?"

"Yes," he said.

"Promise you won't watch me try to get back in my bedroom window. It's not going to be pretty. There's going to be so much ass involved. Like, way too much ass."

"I promise," he said, smiling. "Promise me something?"

"What?"

"You won't become a nun."

I smiled. Then I laughed. "Oh god." I rolled my eyes.

Nick turned so he was standing in front of me. It was clearly going to happen now. We were clearly going to kiss. There was no other way this ended.

But then it didn't happen. Again. The two of us were the worst ever at this. Nick swallowed and put his hands in his pockets. "So I'll text tomorrow." He then extracted a hand, raised a palm, and forced me into the world's most awkward high-five.

"Great," I said. "Good night."

Nick smiled. My heart swelled. My leg ached. "Good night."

He turned and walked away and I stood watching until he got in his car and waved and was gone. I hopped over the wall and looked up at my open window.

When I'd come through that window, my life was an entirely different life.

I walked behind the giant agave and used the little stubby faucet as a foothold, then swung my good leg into my open window. I hung there for a moment, all ass, just as I suspected. I had to will myself to lift my wounded leg. The pain was agony. I sat with both legs inside the window for a moment, recovering. Then I slid down to the chair and stepped to the floor. I closed the window as quietly as I could. Because I'd left it open, my room was freezing.

The first thing I did was take out my phone and stand by the window. I needed to text Syd. I had to do it now. This was the wound I needed to attend to first. I pulled up her text thread, and the column of blue messages sent a flare of anger through my body. I'd been texting all week, begging her to be in touch. She didn't give one crap that her disappearing act had upended my life. I hadn't slept. I'd hardly eaten. She didn't even care enough to let me know she was alive. The cursor pulsed. I thought of the dress in my closet. I thought of Nick having to take off *the last tuxedo on Earth* and hang it back up, having to explain to his parents he wasn't going to prom after all, and then having to make up the stupid story about my appendix. I thought of the months that followed, the sting I'd just this morning experienced as I walked past him in French class.

I thought of Syd, rushing in, wearing her dress, irate. *I told him I'm going to destroy him.* I'd cried into her hair. She'd stayed the night, and in the morning she'd slapped my butt and told me to get out of bed. She was healing the wound she'd inflicted herself. But why had she done it?

YOU'RE DEAD TO ME, I typed into the box.

The cursor pulsed, asking me if I was finished.

I was finished. There was nothing else to say.

I held my thumb above send.

But I couldn't do it. I couldn't bring my thumb down. I thought of Ray. Fucking *Tonya.* I thought of my dad, with his pages of scrawled notes. I sent the cursor back and it ate the message, letter by letter, until the space was blank again.

It was complicated.

I needed sleep. I needed to turn off my phone, let it be dead. I needed to stop waiting for it to ding and change my life. But just as I held down the power button, it dinged.

It was *JERK-ASS DIPSHIT*.

Get in okay?

Yes. I pressed send.

I wish I'd told you the truth earlier.

Let's just forget it.

Also wish I'd kissed you.

My heart flipped. *Me too.*

I'll text tomorrow, he wrote back. *Tomorrow*: the word was flawless, so frickin' profound. It glowed in my dark room, floating in its silver bubble, meaning everything.

Another text. *SNAP. The reason I texted! Kept wanting to tell you. Your shirt is rad. Love R.E.M.* I stared into my phone. It was impossible that only an hour ago I hated this person. Here he was saying exactly everything I'd ever wanted him to say.

Cool, I wrote. I waited. Maybe he'd remember some other compliment he needed to pay me. *Your breath smelled so minty. I'm glad you took off your makeup. Your wound was cute and I liked wiping your blood.*

When nothing else came, I went to his contact information and changed it.

First name: NICK. Last name: ALLISON.

I looked at it a long moment before pressing save.

I'm going to kiss him, I thought.

Tomorrow.

9

My leg still hurt the next day. I peeked under my Band-Aid and nearly puked. I wondered if I should show my dad, but I didn't want him to ask how I'd managed to acquire a wound like this in my sleep. Anyway, the little jolt of pain I felt every time I put my left foot down let me know last night was real. It wasn't a dream.

My father was delighted to see me looking groggy. "You slept!" He was folding a mountain of laundry on the kitchen table and playing the Smiths on the stereo. I checked the clock on the stove and was shocked to see it was nearly 10:30 A.M.

"Oh. Crap." I looked to see that he'd left me a cup of coffee. I shuffled to the fridge and found the milk. "Did you go running already?"

"Yep. I went alone. You needed sleep." He tossed a folded towel onto one of his many piles. "So what's on your agenda for the day?" I remembered right then that Nick said he'd text me tomorrow.

It was tomorrow.

"Oh shit," I said, clunking down my coffee mug and running into my room. I grabbed my phone and turned it on and saw he'd already texted.

It's tomorrow.

That was all he'd written.

I felt floaty.

What is it? Is it Syd?" My father appeared in my doorway, panic on his face, a T-shirt slung over his arm.

"Oh." I looked up. "No."

"What is it? And please don't cuss in the house."

"I have to tell you something crazy, Dad."

"What?"

"I talked to Nick last night, the boy from prom."

"That Boy? What did he have to say for himself?" He crossed his arms.

"He didn't stand me up. Syd told him not to come."

My dad thought for two seconds. He shook his head. "No. He's lying. Miranda. Come on. Syd's gone. He's lying to you. He's a psychopath."

"Okay, that's a smidge dramatic." My dad shrugged in honest disagreement. "He's not lying. Syd left him a note. It said to tell Miranda the truth. That was the truth."

"And why didn't this boy tell you about it until now?"

"Syd did stuff. She made everyone at school think he did it. But it was her. I have no idea why. But I know. For sure."

My dad slung the T-shirt over his shoulder. He was stumped. His eyes searched the floor. "Goddamn it," he said.

"I don't know what to do."

"Well." He exhaled sharply. He was trying to keep his

cool. "Me neither. I'm angry. I'm very disappointed, and I'm angry." It was hard for him to proceed. "But, Mir, we're all Syd has. You know? She has you, Miranda. You're her people. Her mom's a drunk, and her dad—I mean, that guy's a piece of shit. Pardon my French. But we can't shut her out. Even if we want to."

"Well, she's gone, so—"

"Even if she's gone."

"Well, that's very Jesus-y of you."

"Sorry."

"I think I hate her."

"That's fine. But I think that has to be beside the point right now."

"Why?" It felt like he was taking Syd's side over mine.

"Because that's not how we treat people, Mir."

"I know," I said. I was suddenly on the verge of tears and I didn't want to be. I wanted to hate Syd. But I couldn't. I was a failure. My dad put out an arm and I walked zombie-like into a hug. "He's coming here tonight," I said into my father's armpit.

"Who?" My father stood back. "That Boy? Why's he coming here?"

"We're going out," I said to the floor. When I looked up, my father was staring at me. "What?" I said finally. "Come on. Stop."

He blinked hard a few times. Then the dumb smile appeared.

"Nuh-uh," I said. "Don't."

"That was him?" He nodded at my phone.

"Oh my god, I hate you so much." I pushed past him and stomped to the kitchen and picked up my coffee.

He followed close behind. I opened the fridge and stared into it.

"You're going on a date. You've never gone on a date."

"You don't know what I've done."

"You've gone on a date?"

"No. But still, you don't know." I slammed the fridge shut.

"I know Imma meet ya boy tonight." He did a stupid dance move.

"He's not ma boy."

"Well, hell." He snapped at me with the T-shirt. "*Pos, mi'jita* going on a date."

"That's offensive to me." I tried to keep my scowl on. "As a Latina."

"And you're sure he's not a scuz bucket?"

"No. He is not. He's a good guy." I smiled against my will. "Please, seriously, just be cool."

"Mos def, mos def."

"Oh my god, please never speak to me again." I looked down at my phone and tried to stop smiling.

"Text your boy. Tell him to be here at seven. Sharp! Breathalyzers will be administered." He turned back to his laundry, twirling the T-shirt in apparent celebration.

I stared at my phone. "I think eight." When my father said nothing, I said, "Eight's better, right?"

"Oh, now you want my help."

"No." I thought about it for one more second. "I'm saying eight."

"Whatever," he said. "Let go and let God."

———

As the long hours of the day passed, what Syd had done began to really sink in. The tightness returned to my chest. Last night I was ready to never see her again as long as I lived. The injury was clean, painful but straightforward, like the cut on my leg. But now everything was muddled again. There had to be some reason she'd done it.

Was she was secretly in love with Nick? She'd discouraged my crush from the very start. When I started talking about asking Nick to the prom last year, she'd set me up with Quinn within a week. I knew she hated Nick, but I always thought it was because he was her greatest academic competition. The few semesters Syd hadn't ranked first in our class, it was Nick. When he became captain of the Academic Decathlon team last year, she dropped out. It was the only time she'd ever dropped out of anything. Granted, her liking him didn't make sense. Nick was the polar opposite of the boys she usually liked. He was timid, which she took as a weakness. In fact, she'd cataloged in great detail his many unattractive qualities: ponytails were lame; he wore dorky hiking shoes to school; he had no style, which was worse than having bad style; and, as far as she could tell, he also had no personality. Overall, her assessment of Nick was that he was the worst thing you could be in Syd's eyes: boring. It seemed unlikely she was in love with him. But everything seemed unlikely right now. And it made perfect sense to me. I honestly didn't know why everyone wasn't in love with Nick. I'd begun to think Will and I had cracked the code. We were geniuses. And somehow I got to be the person Nick would be picking up in a few hours for a date. I couldn't wait.

But then, fifteen million years later, when it was eight, I found I could've easily waited. The rest of my life, even. I didn't want to come out of my room. Without Syd to tell me how to do it, I found I couldn't dress myself. I'd tried on every article of clothing I owned, but the more I tried on, the less I knew what I should wear, how I should act, if I should continue breathing or just stop while I was ahead and perish quietly on my bedroom floor among the soft rolling hills of a million discarded outfits. The only thing I looked good in was a black sweater Letty had given me for Christmas the year before, but it was too dressy, and besides, when I tried it on, I remembered why I'd never worn it before. It itched like crazy. I settled on jeans, a plain black T-shirt, and a gray hoodie. It was a non-outfit, really. It drew no attention. It had no opinions. It was the best I could do.

My clock flashed 8:00. It was pencils down. I sat down on my bed, totally cashed.

Then it was 8:05. Nick was late.

Then it was 8:06, and I knew he was standing me up again. I was *sure*. The whole thing had been a lie. Nick had been planning revenge for the maxi-pads for eight months. My bloody leg. The handkerchief. The several minutes of applied pressure. Lies, lies, lies, lies, lies.

Then I heard his tires on the gravel. And I wished I had another fifteen million years before I had to walk out of my room and answer the door. My father beat me to the door, which was fine. I was so nervous that even a few extra seconds were precious. I looked at myself one last time in the mirror. My dark hair sat behind my shoulders and my cheekbones glowed.

I stepped out of my room just as my dad turned the

doorknob. He winked at me. "That's not helping," I whispered. He swung the door open and there was Nick, dressed in dark jeans and a button-down shirt.

He was wearing a tie. Why was he wearing a tie? And it took me a nanosecond to process that something else was different. His ponytail was gone. *His ponytail was gone.* His hair was short, the way I'd loved it before, the little puff of obedient curls returned to the top of his head. "You cut your hair," I announced way too loudly, the way a five-year-old might.

"Oh. Yeah." Two seconds in and he wanted to die.

"When?"

"Today." He touched the top of his head self-consciously, as if to make sure it was still there.

"Oh." I wanted to tell him I liked it—because I did; I loved it—but I couldn't even figure out how make my voice a normal volume. There was an agonizing silence made more agonizing by the fact that my father was standing between the two of us.

"Hello," Nick finally said to my dad. I could see the dread on his face as he addressed my father. He'd texted earlier to ask if my father was going to shoot him. I said no. Then he asked a pertinent follow-up: When I'd said my dad was looking for life on other planets, were we talking NASA or a crackpot?

"Oh shit, sorry."

"Miranda!" My dad turned and looked at me as if I were insane.

"Sorry." I took a step toward Nick, giving my dad the evil eye and edging him out of the way. Then, to justify having done this, I gave Nick a weird side-hug. "Dad, this is Nick." I looked down at my outfit as if it was covered in vomit. "We're going to two different places."

"Oh, no. You look great." Nick glanced nervously at my dad. "You look fine." The three of us were standing so outrageously close to each other. How did we get here? I wanted to start over, from the beginning. Like, at birth.

I watched Nick's eyes go from my face to my dad's and back. I couldn't tell if he was nervous or if he was simply plotting my father and me on the skin-tone spectrum and trying to make it work. My dad reached for Nick's hand. "It's nice to meet you. I'm Mir's dad, Peter. Call me Peter if you want. And yes, Nick: I am the whitest man on Earth. And yes, Miranda is my daughter. She takes after her mother." I could feel my entire body blush, even my toenails. I braced for a joke about prom, but miracle of miracles, it didn't come. My dad turned to me. "Home by midnight?"

"Okay," I said. "I'll text if I'm going to be later."

"Okay. But not much later." My father cuffed Nick's shoulder. I felt like we were in a movie. Again my toenails blushed. "Have a good time." Then he did the coolest thing he's ever done. He grabbed his beer from the hall table where he'd put it down to open the door—he must have rushed to get there, not even taking time to set down his Tecate on the coffee table—and walked back down the hall to the living room and disappeared, swallowed up again by a basketball game.

As soon as he was gone, the doorway—or was it the whole universe?—filled with silence.

"Your dad's cool." Nick somehow seemed even more nervous than me.

"Oh, he's not. Believe me." I gestured again to my T-shirt. "I'm changing."

"You don't need to change." Nick tucked invisible hair behind his ear.

"I'm just going to throw on another shirt." I walked to my room as I said it so he couldn't stop me.

Every single shirt I owned was laid out on my bed and floor. I'd tried them all. I grabbed the first thing I saw that wasn't a T-shirt. It was blue and red stripes, silk. It was Syd's shirt, one of her greatest thrift store finds. I couldn't wear it. I had to keep tonight as free of Syd as possible. I tossed it back and hastily grabbed the black sweater Letty had given me. I threw it on in a panic.

Why was I panicking? Hadn't Nick and I had the best, most soul-baring conversation last night? Hadn't he said he wanted to kiss me and hadn't I told him I wanted to be a nun?

I found Nick standing exactly where I'd left him, with the front door still halfway open and cold air pouring into the house. I grabbed my coat and Nick stood watching as I put it on. It seemed to take an hour. "Okay," I said.

"Okay." Nick seemed only then to realize he'd been standing in front of an open door. He stepped aside and let me pass before he closed the door behind us.

He'd washed his car. Even that made me nervous somehow. On the way to the restaurant (La Hacienda, fine Mexican cuisine—thank god I'd changed), we chatted about what we'd done that day (oh, nothing much, except that he'd totally altered his appearance). He asked if I'd heard anything from Syd and I said no and he offered no follow-up question or comment. I couldn't think of a single thing to talk about. I not only felt like Nick was a stranger, but like I was a stranger, paralyzed by my own self-consciousness. The decision to wear the beautiful black sweater was beginning to reveal itself as terrible one. The itchiness was already pure torture. "So," he said after we'd driven at least a mile in silence. "I realized I didn't ask you. Where are you applying?"

"What?" I had no idea what he was talking about or if he was speaking English.

"To college. I didn't ask you. Last night."

College was the last thing I wanted to talk about. "I don't know," I said. "I'm applying to four." I pulled the number directly out of thin air. "But I'll probably go to UNM."

"Really?" he said. He sounded surprised.

"Yeah." I scratched at my neck and vowed to put the sweater in the Goodwill bag the second I got home. "Why?"

"Just seems like you could go anywhere. You're such a good writer."

"How do you know that?" I sounded like I was accusing him of having read my diary. I wished I could change the way the words were coming out of my mouth. I wished I could change everything about the evening so far, including the fact that Nick had cut his hair and washed his car and worn a tie. Why had he cut his hair? It felt meaningful and weird, like he'd done it for me, like he'd known I'd only reluctantly accepted the ponytail into my heart. Did I want him to cut his hair for me?

"I always read your stuff in the paper. I really liked the ones about that pig. That series. I really cared about that pig! I think it was the way you wrote about him." I couldn't believe Nick had read my articles about Gracie the pig.

I didn't think anyone but my dad and the ag kids had read them.

"It was a her," I shot back.

"Oh." I noticed a nick on his neck where he'd cut himself shaving. "Sorry. Girl pig. Right."

"And she got slaughtered after the fair." *Oh god, please make it stop.*

"Oh," he said.

"Her name was Gracie."

"Dang."

"Yeah." *What was wrong with me?* "Those essays were real gripping investigative journalism." I'd begun to sweat under my coat, and the sweat made the itchiness exponentially worse. There was no way I'd make it through the night. Nick laughed nervously without taking his eyes off the road. He looked as miserable as I felt.

Aside from the crushing anxiety, I was beginning to feel like I'd made a terrible mistake. I was ruining the perfect version of Nick I'd created in my mind. I was living in real life now, after living so long in my imagination, where my interactions with Nick consisted almost wholly of slaps on the cheek and passionate kisses and didn't involve him driving like a ninety-year-old and me scolding him for getting a pig's gender wrong.

"I thought they were great." His voice got a tiny bit higher every time he spoke. He shot me a quick, nervous glance. Was he beginning to sweat?

"My dad's basically forcing me to apply to Brown. And Vassar."

"Awesome."

"Not really," I said.

"I bet you get in."

"Why?" I said harshly.

"I don't know. Because you're smart. I don't know." The thought of sitting through a dinner at La Hacienda with Nick and this sweater started to make me feel ill.

But it was too late. He pulled into the parking lot and eased into a spot. When he turned the car off, the engine made a few polite clicking noises that made the vast, terrible silence surrounding us even worse. I couldn't believe this was the way things were working out. I looked over at Nick. He looked despondent.

But then: "I have an idea," he said. I was sure his idea was going to be total surrender, calling it off and taking me home so we could both begin forgetting as soon as possible that this ever happened. And honestly, I'd be thankful. It even occurred to me I could get out of the car right now and call my dad and have him pick me up. It could be over even sooner that way.

"What is it?" I said to his tie.

"Can we do a do-over? Right now?" he asked. "Like a do-over for the do-over? This is going—kinda poorly, I think."

I forced myself to look into his eyes. He smiled and his smile ripped me out of my own mind and into the present moment. He was sitting right there. His hair looked so cute, really, it did.

The relief was instantaneous, like the lights coming on in a dark room.

"Oh my god, yes," I said.

He squinted, thinking. "What's the burrito place inside the Pic Quik?"

"Santa Fe Grill. Yes. Please. Let's do it. Seriously, I've never wanted to spill a burrito all over myself in front of another person as much as I do right now. *Vámanos.*" We laughed. "I don't know what just happened."

"Whatever," he said, turning the car back on. "It's okay if we suck at this." He loosened his tie, then pulled it off over his head and tossed it in the back and unbuttoned the top button of his shirt. I could see he was wearing a light gray T-shirt beneath his button-down. *Bingo.*

"Can I ask you the weirdest favor?"

"Please. And I'll be the judge of this weirdness."

"This sweater is trying to murder me. I'm allergic or something." I pointed to the little triangle of gray cotton peeking out from under his shirt. "Can I wear your T-shirt?"

He smiled. "That's not weird." Then, with no warning, he pulled his shirt out of his jeans, unbuttoned it, and tugged the sleeves off. Then he reached behind his back and peeled the T-shirt off in one motion, revealing his surprisingly muscular chest and arms. He turned the T-shirt right side in and handed it to me. "Here."

Just then an elderly couple strolled past the car. When the woman glanced down and saw Nick shirtless, she grabbed her husband's arm and looked away. We laughed. "You didn't need to do that. Like, right here."

"I'm realizing that." He slid his arms back into his shirt and buttoned it up.

"That's a very muscly situation you have going on there." I made a gesture with my open palm toward his chest and arms.

"I climb. Rock-climbing, you know. I think maybe that's how—or why."

"You don't have to explain," I said. "It's not a bad thing."

I held the still-warm T-shirt in my hands. I resisted the temptation to put it to my nose. My heart quickened, and for the first time tonight it wasn't from pure anxiety.

He pulled out of the parking spot, checking his mirrors intently. Now his ultra-cautious driving seemed adorable rather than bizarre.

"You wanna know the worst part about Gracie the pig?"

"Worse than the part where she got slaughtered?"

"Well, okay, yeah, there's that. But after, the FFA tried to give me some bacon."

"No." His face was familiar again, open and kind. "No! Gracie bacon?"

"Gracie bacon." I felt bad laughing about it. "And I took it."

"No!" He pulled onto the street after looking both ways twice. "You monster."

"Well, it was, like, a thank-you gift. I couldn't say no. I gave it to my dad and he ate it. He was, *Oh yay, free bacon*."

"Your dad ate Gracie?"

"He's a flawed man. I'm telling you."

After that, the night flew by. The second we pulled up to Pic Quik, I dashed to the bathroom and took off the sweater and put on Nick's shirt. It was soft and smelled delicious, but it was also very big on me and he laughed when he saw me walk out in it. We ordered our burritos to go, then went to the plaza in the old part of town, right in front of the church my mother's family had gone to, to eat them. We talked so much, I had to remind myself to stop every once in a while and take a bite of my burrito. I couldn't have told you if the plaza was busy or if we'd been the only ones there. I had no idea. Only once the whole night had I thought of Syd and felt the jolt of sadness and anger go through my body. I asked Nick if he had any idea why Syd had done what she'd done. "I've been thinking about it all day," I said, sipping my Sprite.

"Yeah. I've had, like, eight more months than you to think about it." He shrugged. "I have no idea. Syd was cool to me until she dropped out of Academic Decathlon last year. We were in the semifinals in El Paso, and she, like, froze up. It was crazy. She missed every question. We lost. Everybody's parents were there. I thought maybe she was, like, feeling bad because—you know—her parents weren't there."

"I remember that. I had a cross-country meet. She dropped out after that. After you became captain."

"She dropped out that day. She left right after we were done. She said she wasn't coming to practice. And after that she, like, hated me. Even before prom. I thought maybe she was embarrassed. Because she'd frozen up in front of us. But she was fine with Ian and Bea and everyone else. It was weird."

"Maybe she had a crush on you?"

"No." He didn't even blush. That was how certain he was. "I thought maybe—she had a crush on you."

"Yeah." I laughed. "Like a boy fantasy thing? No. Sorry. That was not the case."

After dinner, we went back to Milagro and had ice cream. I was glad the woman from the night before wasn't working. After that, we took a walk on the river road. The river was dry, only a solitary vein of water running through its very center. On the mesa, one long, squat adobe was out-lined in pale white Christmas lights. Our shoulders knocked every once in a while. At some point earlier, while we were eating our burritos, I stopped wondering when we'd kiss. It was bound to happen—right? I guessed so. Probably? But things became so easy, I forgot to even worry about it. We came to a bend in the road and saw a footpath leading down to the river's edge.

"Look," Nick said. He took my cold hand into his warm one. My chest filled with heat. He pointed his chin to a bench next to the riverbank. We walked down to it, holding hands. But when we sat down on the bench, I felt my phone in my back pocket—I hadn't thought of it all night. I took it out and checked the time.

"Oh my god, it's eleven thirty." My heart sank. Nick was sitting beside me under a waxing gibbous moon, on a bench by the river. And now the night was over. We'd have to walk back to Nick's car and drive home and say good-bye. "We should go, right?" I stood and looked down at Nick, who hadn't moved.

"Yeah," he said. He stood. I had started back up the path to the road when I felt him take my hand from behind. He stopped me. I turned around, and before I knew what was happening, he stepped close and leaned down and put his lips on mine. Just like that. We'd been kissing awhile before he stopped momentarily. "Is that okay? That I did that?" I didn't even answer. I simply returned my lips to his. The butterflies in my stomach turned into an electric energy, a warmth that spread slowly throughout my body. His smell was everywhere. It made me go a little nuts. I had the weird feeling I wanted to see his chest again, and his back, everything.

I wanted to know what he looked like when he was putting on his jeans or reading a book, when he didn't know he was being seen. I wanted to see him sleeping, brushing his teeth, conjugating verbs for French. It wasn't about sex, not really. But I guess it was. I wanted to climb into Nick's smell and stay there awhile. And I also wanted to take his clothes off.

Every time it felt like we were going to stop, we'd start again, and stopping would feel impossible. I tried to convince myself time wasn't passing, but eventually I couldn't fool myself. I could see my father checking the clock and then checking his phone and then huffing out of bed into the living room and turning on ESPN.

"I have to go." I pulled away and my whole body complained. "But I don't want to stop." I looked down when I said it, but it was the absolute truth. It felt good to say it. Standing there at the edge of the river, I felt like I could say anything to Nick, like there was nothing between us. *I want to eat you. I want to climb inside your body and sleep. I want to touch your chest bone with my palm and show you the craters of the moon. I may want to lick your ears. I've never felt this way before.*

Nick was dazed. "Me neither." He brought his hand to his hair and seemed surprised not to find his ponytail.

We walked back to his car, and even though we were late, he drove just as carefully as he had before, never once going over the speed limit. He pulled into my driveway at 12:15. (I'd texted my dad I'd be late and he texted an emoji of a piano keyboard and an avocado. I had no idea what it meant. I texted back a thumbs-up.)

"I'm wearing your shirt," I said.

"Good," he said. "I have a reason to come back." I gave him one more kiss before getting out of his car.

My dad's light was off, so I didn't call down the hall to let him know I was home, though I was sure he was still awake. I got into bed, still feeling buzzy. To calm down, I read about Saint Lucy, patron of the blind, who'd had visions so threatening to the powers that be, the emperor demanded her eyes be gouged out. In many paintings, she's shown holding them up on a golden platter. My mother adored Saint Lucy. *Eyeballs on a platter!* my mother had written in the margin. *LOVE THAT DRAMA QUEEN.*

I slipped the book into the drawer and turned out the light.

I slept in Nick's T-shirt.

10

I never sent Syd a *YOU'RE DEAD TO ME* text. In fact,
I didn't text her again that year. There was never anything I was sure I wanted to say. And she didn't text me
either, of course. I kept waiting for things to become clear,
and they never did. After a month I figured it was safe to
assume Ray had turned off her phone and that the last thin
strand of possible connection I had to her had been cut.

Patience wrote back a week after I'd written her. The
note was short and her handwriting was weird, like a
child's. She'd heard nothing from Syd and told me to leave
it alone. Syd was an adult, she reminded me. She could
make her own decisions.

On the last day before Christmas break, I came to
school to find the custodians had taken down all the posters, including the ones of Syd I'd put up. It was a relief,
actually. It'd been unbearable having Syd's gaze follow me
through the halls all those weeks. That she looked so
happy in the photo only made it worse. Seeing her yell
"butt cheeeeeeese" at me between classes was a misery I
was glad to give up. The posters weren't doing anything

anyway. I had no leads, no ideas, nothing. Each day that passed, Syd became more of a mystery to me, more of a stranger, and I hated it.

She was gone. I thought it might begin to recede, the pain of not knowing where she was or why she'd left, but it didn't. And I missed her. It was that simple. I hated her for what she'd done to Nick and me, and I hated her for leaving. But she was still my best friend. We'd adopted each other. We were bound to each other by blood. I couldn't stop caring about her. I still wondered sometimes about Stanford. Had she heard from them? Maybe she'd gotten in.

I dreamed someday, in a year or two or three, my obsessive Google searches would produce proof that the Plan had worked. She'd get an award. She'd start a club. I convinced myself that someday notice of her success would appear in my search results. The Rhodes Scholarship or the National Merit Scholarship or a Fulbright.

But then again, she'd flunked herself out of school. I felt this irony strongest the afternoon my father came in clutching a letter addressed to *The Parents of Miranda Black*. With Syd gone, all the seniors moved up one place. For the first time ever, I'd been bumped into the top five. I was genuinely surprised. My father entered instantly into a state of ecstasy that bordered on delirium. He took the letter as just one more sign I'd be accepted at one of the fancy schools he'd talked me into applying to.

"And look at ya boy," he said, pointing to the name in the number-one slot. *Nicholas Allison*.

Seeing that name in print was still enough to send the horses in my heart galloping.

At school, people were confused to see us together, and

neither of us was good at fending off questions about what happened. Why the change of heart? I figured people assumed Nick had taken pity on me. My best friend abandoned me and he'd given me another chance. But the thing was: I didn't care. My life was no one's business. My life was mine alone. I'd stopped being Syd's spokesperson. I felt free. I was just me, and for the first time in my life I didn't care what anyone thought.

We spent every day of winter break together. We hiked in the Organ Mountains; we watched the sun go down at White Sands. I took him to my father's lab at NASA and watched with pure wonder as Nick understood every part of the math and engineering gibberish my father used to explain what his thingies did and how they did it. He took me to the climbing wall at NMSU and, though I'd talked crap all the way there about how I was made to climb—"look at these ape arms"—it turned out that I was terrible at it. We ended up splayed out on the mats, laughing.

"Why do I suck at this?" I asked.

"It's hard. You'll get better." He had a streak of chalk on his cheek. When I tried to rub it off, I only added more.

"Show me again," I said.

I loved watching him, the way he carefully assessed the foot- and handholds, putting together the puzzle of his ascension before he'd even left the mat. Then he scrambled up and looked down at me and smiled.

He made it look so easy.

"I don't know," I called up from the mat. "Maybe if you take your shirt off again, it'd be easier for me to learn. I need to see the muscly situation in action."

He shook his head. "You're hopeless," he said. And

then let go one hand and both feet and hung there from the top for a moment before letting himself fall to the mat.

It felt big when we decided to spend part of Christmas day together. Like it meant something, though I couldn't quite say what. Nick had spent plenty of time at my house. He and my dad were like old pals already. Maybe it was going to his house that was the big deal. I think we were both dreading it.

Apparently, it was tradition that Tomás eat dinner with Nick's family, which I found peculiar. I knew Tomás's whole giant family. He was certainly no orphan, and there was no reason he'd have to find another place to eat Christmas dinner. I didn't get it, but in the end I was glad he was there. I felt so out of place in the Allison household, it was a great comfort to look up and see that face I'd known for so long.

Nick had told Jason the whole bizarre story of us, and so when Jason shook my hand in front of their parents, he made a joke about my appendix right off the bat. As soon as we walked into the kitchen, Nick's mom hugged me, just as she had that night at La Posta. His dad only emerged from his office when it was time to eat. When the two of them stood together for a moment while Nick's mom decided who should sit where, I was once again struck by their age difference. Nick's mom, so young and vibrant, made his dad seem even more dour and serious.

The food was all right, but overcooked. It was the kind of meal my father would over-compliment anxiously, in order to conceal his true opinions. Nick's mom had seated his dad at the head of the table, and he loomed there over the meal in his cool aloofness. I couldn't stop thinking about how he was a math genius. Every time he looked in my direction, I felt caught, as if his penetrating blue eyes could look inside me and see my underwhelming math score on the SAT. I remembered the thing Nick said about how there were only seven people in the world who could understand his math. I wished at least one of them was there, to make conversation.

Tomás, thank god, could talk about anything, and did. He talked about school and college and went on for many minutes about the groin injury he'd gotten playing baseball last season, encouraged by Nick's mom's *oohs* and *ahhs* of sympathetic reaction to each gory detail. Before anyone knew it, he'd used the word *testicle*. It was heinous. But the weirdest thing was, no one giggled or smiled or even acknowledged it. No one's face changed at all. Maybe it was because we all knew that as long as Tomás was talking, even if it was about his groin, none of the rest of us would have to. By the end of the meal, I was a nervous wreck. I could see why Nick had made the toothache sound that day on the ditch. Everything felt so heavy. So *ugh*.

Nick's dad retreated to his office after dinner, and his mom and Jason went back to working on a massive jigsaw puzzle in the family room. Tomás and Nick and I loaded the dishwasher. And that was it. Nick's mom hugged me again and sent me home with a tin of slightly burned cookies for my dad, who I guess she assumed had spent the day alone.

Later, when Tomás and I were left outside for a moment while Nick got his coat and my gift from his bedroom, I asked Tomás what the deal was. Why did he eat Christmas dinner with Nick's family?

"Dude. Come on," he said in a low voice, looking up from his phone where he was checking sports scores. "I do it for Nick. That's some intensely somber shit in there, if you hadn't noticed. I've gotta go eat a whole other meal with my family now." He looked up. "Don't tell him I told you that."

"That's crazy," I said, though he was absolutely correct. My jaw was sore from clenching.

"Whatever. Sorry if I'm not into silence. Dude, I just talked about my balls for like ten minutes."

"That was hilarious," I said. He shrugged and went back to his phone. I turned to make sure the coast was clear. "Hey T," I said in a hushed tone, "are you a Boy Scout?"

He looked up and stared, then shook his head. "Shut up. No."

"Nick is one," I whispered.

"So what?"

"You don't think that's weird?"

"Mir, if you think that's the weirdest thing about Nick, you need to look harder." He went back to scrolling through his sports scores. "I think it's weird that Nick's mom was so interested in my balls. That's weird," he said and laughed at his own joke.

"Your family's so quiet," I said to Nick as I drove us to my house, where my father was hosting his annual NASA Orphans Christmas.

"*Quiet* is one way to describe them," he answered. He seemed tired, distracted. I worried he wasn't in the mood for my father's party.

When we arrived at my house, there were so many cars in front, I had to park down the street. It was a perfect evening, crisp but not cold, the sky a deep, glorious blue. It was Christmas-day quiet. The world was still. "Be warned," I told Nick as I trolled for a parking spot. "This is my father's favorite thing ever."

It was always a little weird having a hoard of strangers crowd my house on Christmas, but I'd come to love my dad's tradition of inviting over all the people at his NASA facility, many of them soldiers from the adjoining missile base, who didn't have anywhere else to go on Christmas. Without us, my dad told me, they'd eat mac and cheese and watch *Star Trek* by themselves all day.

I suspected that he did it as much for us as for them, though. There was also a possible version of Christmas where my father and I spent the day moping, thinking but not talking about my mother.

There was a version where *we* were the orphans.

"Did your parents get divorced?" Nick asked me out of nowhere as I was struggling to parallel-park a full block away from my house. "Before your mom left?"

"No," I answered. "My dad divorced her. Like, a year after. It was awful."

"Like you wished he hadn't?"

"Oh. No. I don't know. I guess I just wished she'd come home. I dunno. I was only eight."

"Yeah," he said. He was sitting with my gift in his lap. I could tell it was a book. I was glad he hadn't noticed I was doing a supremely terrible job at parallel parking. "Do you think your parents were in love? Or whatever."

"I have no idea," I said, pulling out again and straightening my tires for the millionth time. "My dad was. I think. It's weird—we never talk about it—but I'm pretty sure. I mean—you're a math genius: pregnancy lasts nine months, my parents got married in February, and I was born in July. My dad had to leave MIT and go to NMSU. His parents were super-mad. My mom didn't even finish college. I think her family—Catholics don't love the abortions, you know." I shot him a look. He was listening to me very carefully, as if I were going to reveal the answer to some big question he was pondering. "I've thought about it a lot. It's a little awkward to bring up, you know: *Hey, did you kinda want to erase me from the face of the Earth when I was a zygote?* But my guess is: sure, they were in love, but they were young and very different. It was a disaster waiting to happen. I was just the accident that set it in motion."

"You weren't an accident."

"You know what I mean. I don't think my dad thinks about it that way anymore."

I was finally tucked into the spot and was so relieved to turn off the car. "What sucks, though, is that even after they got married—after they did everything they wanted them to do—my mother's family sort of shunned us. I don't know why. I'm sure it was screwed up. Stuff I don't know about. Then she left. And it was like they blamed my dad for that, too. My uncle Benny and aunt Letty—they're in town and they might come over tonight—they're the only ones we keep in touch with, really. Everyone else was sort of like, *Smell ya later.*"

Nick was looking out the windshield, up at the sky. He didn't seem to want to go anywhere. "I think my parents are going to get a divorce," he said plainly.

"What?" I shot back. "Really?"

"I don't know. My dad's applying for jobs all over the country. But this time my mom hasn't said anything. In fact, she made a big deal about how she just signed a lease on a new office with another psychologist and she's going to take on more patients. It's this weird show. But I don't know what it means."

"You can't ask? Your mom?"

"It's not really the kind of thing we do. You know? Like, talk like that."

"What does Jason think?"

"Same thing. That it's weird."

I put a hand on his knee. "That really sucks."

"I don't know," he said, cocking his head a little. "Does it suck?" He looked shocked to hear himself say it. "My mom is, like, normal—normal age, normal mom. You know? My dad's old. There's nothing about that situation that's going to change. Sometimes I just think my parents—my mom—would be better—apart. Is that the worst thing to say about your own parents?"

"No," I said. "Not really."

"My dad is—" He shook his head and put both hands through his hair.

I didn't know what to say. So I didn't say anything.

"Anyway." He shook it off. "Sorry." He held up my gift. "It's a book. Open it."

It was a book called *The Beauty Beneath Numbers*.

"It's a math book." I couldn't help but start laughing.

"No. It's about theoretical math—for laypeople. You seemed interested. Is it a terrible gift? My mom thought it was a bad gift."

"It's perfect," I said. And it was. "I'm as lay a person as you will ever find."

I reached into my purse and took out his gift. He opened it and looked up at me, confused.

"It's a necklace." He was trying so hard to be polite, to make it sound like a necklace was exactly what he'd always wanted.

"No, it's a saint." I turned over the little dime-sized silver medallion, and there he was, Saint George, rearing up on his horse, the dragon slayed at his feet.

"Oh." He was still perplexed. "Cool."

"Saint George is the patron saint of Boy Scouts—and Eagle Scouts."

"Ah." He rolled his eyes and gave me one of his adorable, shy smiles. "I love it."

"You don't have to wear it."

"I love it." He took it out of the box and slung it over his head.

"Here." I leaned over and slipped it inside his T-shirt. "You don't have to wear it on the outside. It's not a necklace."

He leaned in and kissed me. "I love it," he said again.

The orphans were eating dessert when we came in. I recognized a few faces from Christmases past, but most of the orphans were new, as usual. I found my father in the living room, glowing with happiness and maybe a little too much wine. He whooped when he saw us. "There's my girl!"

The house smelled like piñon from the fire, and little white Christmas lights hung from the vigas. Every seat in the house was taken. Nick and I took our pecan pie and sat in the corner of the living room, near the kiva stove, on the tile floor. It was warm by the fire and the house was alive with people.

While we ate our pie, I watched my dad make his rounds, filling wineglasses and taking dessert plates. As he did every Christmas Eve, last night he'd dismantled the small Christmas tree we put up each year. He needed more space in the living room. For people. He was just so damn happy. After a while he made his way over to us and plopped down onto the floor and produced from his pocket a small poorly wrapped gift, which he handed to Nick. Nick stared at it for a moment, then looked at me.

"What's that?" I asked. I had no idea my dad had gotten Nick a gift.

"Open it," my dad said to Nick. He smiled and shoved me. "None of your business."

I glared at my dad and watched Nick unwrap his present. It was a Swiss Army knife. With Nick's name etched into it.

"Whoa." Nick lit up at the sight of it. "Thank you so much, Mr. Black."

"It's just Peter, Nick. You just call me Peter. Now, this bad boy here has thirty-three features. But look, I have to show you this. My favorite." My dad took the knife and extracted from one side a ridiculously tiny serrated blade. He held it up triumphantly. "It's a little saw!"

"That is so cool." When my dad handed the knife back, Nick went about pulling out every single tool, and, like two children, he and my father named each one and its multitude of potential uses.

"When would you ever need a little tiny saw?" I peered over to look at it.

"When I need to cut down a little tiny tree." Nick made a sawing motion with the blade. My dad laughed and slapped Nick on the back, then looked at me apologetically.

"Saint George slayed a dragon." I leaned back again. "I'm not sweating it."

"Oh, she gave you the necklace?" my dad asked brightly.

Nick turned to me, eyes wide. I shook my head and palmed my face and tried to look totally affronted, though in the end I couldn't help cracking up.

"He gave me a damn math book," I said.

"Good man!" my dad said, squeezing Nick's shoulder and hopping up. "Merry Christmas, my love." He kissed the top of my head and then stood up again to attend to the crowd.

"I do love it." Nick brought his hand up to his chest and felt for the little medal disk under his shirt. He looked at me, sincere. "I love it." I leaned in and gave him a stealthy kiss. He went back to fiddling with the knife, completely absorbed.

I leaned back against the wall and watched him for a long time, understanding, probably for the first time, what was happening between us—or maybe what had already happened while I wasn't looking.

I wasn't crushing on Nick anymore. Not at all.

I was falling in love with him.

I never would've guessed the two states would feel so different. Crushing was so easy. It was a mild form of torture, an ache that never went away. But falling in love was big and sharp and unpredictable. It didn't ache; it *hurt*. Because it was real, and it was actually happening. The feeling was so sharp, it felt like it could kill me, like it could slice right through to my very center and I could die from whatever I found there, from whatever my love for Nick revealed.

Just then, Nick looked up and brandished the knife with every single one of its thirty-three ridiculous tools pulled out. "Excuse me." He cocked his head. "Do you by chance have any fish that need to be scaled or wires that need to be stripped?" The goofy look on his face was everything. It was him, Nick, unadulterated, and he was giving it to me, all of it, all of him, and it was better than any book or necklace in the world.

Later, after most of the orphans had gone and it was only the small group of close friends that came every year, my dad brought out Trivial Pursuit and we gathered around the dining table, dividing up into two teams.

"This is a very serious tradition in our house," my dad said to Nick. He was definitely tipsy. If my dad had been drunk, it wouldn't have been funny—I'd never once seen my dad drunk—but because he was just a little buzzed it was kind of hilarious.

Just as we were setting up the board, we heard a knock at the door and Letty came in, followed by Benny, who was holding my cousin Luciana, awake but zonked. *Christmas-ed out*, my dad called it.

"Uh-oh," Benny said in his big voice as soon as he laid eyes on my father. "Pedro's been drinking." He put Luciana down. She just stood there, dazed.

"Touché, Benicio." My dad ambled over and scooped up Luciana and she gave him a kiss. He gave Letty a hug, then Benny. My father and Benny were both tall. But where my father was thin, Benny was a giant. He wasn't fat, just huge, alarmingly so, and his hugeness was made even more dramatic by the relative size of Letty. Next to him, she looked miniature. "Where are the boys?" my dad asked, peering out the door before closing it against the cold. Letty shot a look at Benny and Benny looked at my dad. "They're staying down in Deming. With their grandparents," he said.

Letty turned to me sympathetically. She'd always hated the way my mother's family had treated my dad and me. Those were, after all, my grandparents, too. When my dad turned to me, I could see his lip stiffen. I shrugged at all three of their concerned faces. I wasn't hurt. The truth was, I didn't know my grandparents well enough to be hurt by them.

I grabbed Nick and dragged him over to meet Letty and Benny. He was super-polite and adorable, especially considering Letty was being particularly hard-nosed and meticulous in her appraisal. "Miranda speaks highly of you," she said in her best unimpressed-social-worker voice.

"Um." Nick looked at me, completely tongue-tied. Letty frowned, skeptical.

"Come on. Give him a break," I said.

Benny grabbed Nick's hand and what started as a handshake quickly became a bear hug. Luciana raised her arms to me in a silent demand, and I picked her up and she put her head on my shoulder.

"You ready to lose, my brother?" my dad asked Benny.

"I was born ready to lose," Benny answered, slapping him on the back.

We walked to the dining table and joined the others.

I sat down with Luciana still wrapped around me. She fell asleep almost immediately.

"Hey, wait, where's your friend?" My dad's lab-mate, Jerry, turned to me. He was famously over-competitive. I could see a vein already forming in his forehead. He was upset not to find Syd among us. "She was our secret weapon last year."

My dad gave me a quick look. "She couldn't make it this year," I said. "But this guy's pretty smart." I pushed Nick over to the other team.

Jerry sized Nick up. "You're going to have to prove that, son," he said, only half joking. He grabbed Nick by the shoulder and pushed him down into a chair. Jerry had met his wife, Bonnie, at Orphan Christmas a few years ago. They weren't orphans anymore, technically, but they still came every year. It was tradition. Bonnie rose from her seat next to Jerry and came to our side of the table. "Too much testosterone," she announced as she sat down next to me.

Before we began, I carried Luciana into my room and put her in my bed and closed the door. I returned to my seat beside my father, and as we played, he slung his arm around my shoulders. He teased me about my answers to sports questions ("Derek Jeter didn't play football! God, I've raised an idiot!"), and the two of us screamed out the answer to one question at the same time. (The Sea of Tranquility was, of course, where Apollo 11 touched down in 1969.)

I kept looking over to catch Nick watching us, and when I did, he'd smile and look away. I wondered if he was thinking what I was thinking while he fiddled with his knife, but I thought it was more likely he was thinking about his own dad. Somehow I couldn't imagine his dad putting his arm around him.

Nick's team landed on sports and leisure.

My dad drew the card from the deck dramatically. Silence fell upon the room. "How many squares are on a chessboard?" He squinted at the other team.

Jerry's forehead vein bulged and Bonnie shook her head in amusement beside me. Letty tapped me on the shoulder. She knew the answer. I was glad she wasn't on the other team.

"Anyone?" Jerry said, looking at his teammates, beginning to panic. "Guesses?"

Nick raised his hand sheepishly. "I know."

"Say it, boy!" Jerry roared. "Say it!"

"Sixty-four," Nick said quietly.

"We're gonna lose." My father shoved the card back into the box and the other team roared in celebration. Benny nearly picked Nick up out of his seat.

"Nerd!" I yelled at Nick through the commotion.

He gave me a sheepish smile. Then he reached under his collar and pulled out Saint George and let him dangle there, over his T-shirt. "We slay." He sat back and cocked his head. "All day."

He wasn't very good at gloating, but he was giving it everything he had.

And while I sat there looking across the table at Nick, I felt it again, the razor-sharp edge of that huge, scary feeling, the real pain of real love.

Is this actually happening? I asked myself.

This is actually happening.

II

11

In April I marked the four-month anniversary of Syd's disappearance by driving on I-10 until I came to the place where I could see the graveyard from the highway. It was still there. I didn't know if Ray and Tonya had moved away and left the graveyard for the next tenant to deal with, or if they just hadn't left town yet. Tonya could've been using the mere idea of moving as an excuse to throw away Syd's stuff.

I pulled off the highway and sat in my car looking down at the graveyard. I could still make out the divot in the earth my butt had made in front of Manny and the one Syd's had made in front of Isadora. If I wasn't so scared of Tonya and her gun, I'd have pulled over and put on my hazards and climbed down the perilous embankment and sat there and wept.

I didn't know why I thought it was a good idea to drive by. It wasn't. I hadn't seen the graveyard in four months, and though I still thought about Syd all the time, the definition of our relationship—the specific texture of it, the deep familiarity—had begun to fade. Looking out my car window and seeing the graveyard down there made everything fresh again, the sadness and the anger and the giant stomach cramp of not knowing where she was and if she was okay. And it made me miss her more than ever. I noticed, sitting there with my hazards on as the traffic whizzed by, that when I thought of Syd now, I felt a pure kind of grief. It was uncomplicated, uncorrupted. And, for whatever reason, whenever that grief for Syd surfaced, it always brought up with it the ancient grief for my mother.

What I'd learned from the two of them was that grief wasn't about someone being gone. It wasn't final like that. In fact, it was the exact opposite. It was about wanting them so bad and knowing that your want had no end—there was no one there to receive it, to stop it. It just kept going and going, seeking endlessly.

I would've characterized the four months after Syd left as the worst time of my life, if it didn't happen to also be the best time in my life. Everything was as perfect as it was terrible. If someone had told me that night at Ten Thousand Poles that in four months Syd would be gone and Nick Allison would be my boyfriend, I'd have laughed. It was ludicrous. Absurd. But then it happened. It actually happened. And now the idea of being separated from Nick began to hurt as much as the reality of being separated from Syd already did. College loomed, a distant galaxy we were hurling toward at light speed.

After hours of negotiations with my dad and a few thousand pros-and-cons lists, I decided I'd apply to Brown, Vassar, Reed, and Smith. If I didn't get into any of these schools, we'd revisit state colleges and other options, in-

cluding my taking a gap year and applying again the following fall. The process was exhausting. I let my dad's
enthusiasm carry me to the finish line. But then, after
the applications were sent and the pressure was off, I
actually began to hope I might get into one of those
schools. I'd find myself walking across the dusty campus
of LCHS and realize that in my imagination, I was walking along a path on some beautiful leafy campus, and, as
my father said to my million eye rolls, "achieving my potential for self-actualization."

But then, one night after an epic make-out session
with Nick, I came home and scrambled together my application to UNM. I found a scholarship to apply for from
the National Association of Hispanic Journalists. It required an essay and two years' experience working on a
school paper. It was perfect. When I asked my dad the
next morning to cover the application fee, he sighed. "Just
to see," I said. "What if I don't get into any of your fancy
schools?"

"They're not my schools," he said.

"It's just a safety," I said. "I'm not actually going to
go there."

But, in my mind, I was totally going to go there. Nick
would stand up to his dad and go to UNM and study forestry, and I'd go too. We'd be together. It was that simple.
And it remained that simple right up until the impossible
happened and I got into Brown. It'd been my pie-in-the-
sky-no-way-in-hell-am-I-ever-getting-into-that-school
school. I'd even argued for skipping the application. It was
the Ivy League, for god's sake. There was no way.

I was floored. I kept rereading the email, sure there
was a catch.

My father died when I called him at work to tell him. He *died*. After screaming "Shut up!" for a full three minutes, he started going through the halls, yanking people aside to share the news.

"Please stop it," I said.

"Hell no!" he whooped.

That night, we went out to eat. We never went out to eat. "I'm so happy, I can't even cook," he said, driving us to Chope's in La Mesa, down the old highway, through miles of pecan orchards, with the windows rolled down and Le Tigre's "Deceptacon" on full blast and the trees on either side of us making a bright green canopy over the road.

"I wish I could tell Syd!" I hollered over the music.

"God, I wish I could tell your mom!" he hollered back.

He never talked about my mom like that anymore, like a person who was alive, who could receive news or who'd care about it if she did. He'd slipped. That was how I knew he'd lost his mind with joy.

A few days later I came home to find a letter in the mail. I'd won the journalism scholarship at UNM. It wasn't a huge amount of money, but there was only one scholarship and I'd won it. They'd based their decision on an essay I'd written about growing up with a single, white dad; all the ways the world misinterpreted us; and what he taught me about who I was, and who I could be. My father was proud I'd won the scholarship, and he teared up when he read the essay, but there was no doubt he wanted me to choose Brown over UNM. Brown was where I'd have the great, mind-opening college experience he'd been wishing for me, the one he'd been saving for since I was a newborn. And I'd liked it too when I looked at the campus on the website, with its towering trees and grassy hills and carefully curated students sitting in a circle on a vast lawn, talking about big ideas. I liked the idea of going there more when it was a total impossibility. But to actually leave New Mexico and my dad and Nick and the bone-deep familiarity of Las Cruces, which, I'd never hated like Syd had? It sounded awful. After I got the email, I had to google to refresh my memory: I didn't even know what city Brown was in. So yes, I liked the idea of going there. I just didn't like the idea of actually having to *go* there.

The day after I got my letter about the scholarship, Nick showed up after school clutching a letter from UNM. He'd been offered a four-year Presidential Scholarship, as well as a special math fellowship, and, through a partnership with the Scouts, a summer internship with the US Forest Service. If he accepted the internship, he'd leave in early July and spend a month on a trail-building project in a remote part of the Jemez Mountains.

"What the hell?" I teased him. "All I got was a crappy scholarship. What, you also get, like, a personal assistant? Will the president of the university give you wake-up calls every morning?"

The Eagle Scout was over the moon. But when I asked him if he'd told his parents, he screwed up his face. "Why do you ask me these things, woman?" He collapsed onto the couch and I plopped down beside him and swung my legs onto his lap. He ran his finger over the scar on my ankle from the night in the orchard, which now felt like it happened a million years ago.

"So no?"

"No," he said, his chin up. He was giving me a look

that told me there was more to the conundrum. "There's something else."

"What?" I asked.

"I got into Harvard." I could hear in his voice that he didn't quite believe it.

"What?!" I jumped up. I threw my arms in the air. "Oh my god! Nick!"

"Yeah," he said. "Crazy, right? With a fellowship."

"That's so awesome!"

He nodded gravely.

"Oh no, I know," I said, sitting back down beside him on my knees and placing a hand on his shoulder. "It's so sad. You got into Harvard. You poor, cisgender white male."

He knocked me with his shoulder. "It's, just, you know."

"Complicated," I said.

He tried to smile. "Well, it is."

"What did you tell them?"

"I told them about Harvard. I didn't tell them about UNM. Or the Jemez."

"Were they stoked? I bet they were so stoked."

"They're not going to be stoked when I tell them I'm not going."

"What are you talking about? You're not even going to consider Harvard? That's ridiculous. I'm sorry, but that's just stupid."

He looked hurt. "I made my decision a long time ago."

"Well, okay, that's great. But—come on. You made that decision before you got into Harvard. I mean, I'm no expert, Nicholas, but I think you'll probably still be eligible for a job in the Forest Service with a degree from

Harvard." I shoved him, trying to soften his somber mood, but it didn't work.

His eyes searched the floor. "You're considering UNM over an Ivy League school," he said.

"Yes, I am. I'm considering it. I'm not just—you know—making my decision based on some weird fear of becoming my father." It came out sounding much more pointed than I'd intended. Nick looked like I'd slapped him. "I'm sorry. That's not what I meant."

"What did you mean?" His calmness was unnerving.

"I don't know," I said. "I'm sorry for saying that. Really." And it was true. I didn't know what I meant. Wasn't the two of us going to UNM together what I wanted? We'd just be together. Everything was working out to be as simple as I'd dreamed. Why was I arguing against it?

He drew a long breath and stared at the floor. "I didn't think I was going to get in, so I didn't think I'd even have to deal with this."

Something about the way he said it, the tremor of fear—or defeat—in his voice, stoked my anger. "I don't get you sometimes, Nick." I tried to soften my voice. "You like math. You like to work hard. Your brain is—not a normal brain."

He looked up at me sullenly, then back at his feet.

"Your dad didn't invent math. He didn't make Harvard."

He just sat there. "You don't understand."

"Okay. Sure. Maybe I don't. But I know you. And I know you're not going to be a very good underachiever. So if you want to go to UNM because your whole being tells you it's the right thing, then yes. Go there. Live your bliss. But if that's the case, then why can't you tell your parents?"

He looked at me, wounded. "I don't know," he said.

I put a hand on his knee. "You know it's a big deal. Right? You worked really hard. And you do have a gift. Some would even say it's a privilege."

"I get it. This is a white male privilege problem. I'll own that. But it doesn't make it any less difficult. Okay?"

"Okay," I said. "Yes. I totally get that." I cuffed my palm around the warm back of his neck. Even though we'd been together almost four months, I still had moments like this, when I couldn't believe I was touching the neck I used to stare at. Moments like this, it'd be so easy to say the words I'd wanted to say to him for weeks, maybe months: *I love you.* But as soon as it occurred to me, I'd chicken out. There was no going back after those words had been spoken. Even a rookie like me knew that.

"You could always just lie to them about where you end up," I said.

Finally he smiled. "That'd be awesome."

"Dear Mom and Dad. I love college. Harvard is a good college. I'm definitely studying math at Harvard, for sure. It's really great and I'm not in New Mexico."

He laughed reluctantly. He shook his head and shoved me so hard, I fell over onto the couch.

"For what it's worth, I'm totally impressed," I said. "Really. This is a big freaking deal. We both got into freaking Ivy League schools. We need to celebrate."

"Oh really?" He gave me a sideways look and squinted. "I know of an upcoming celebration we could attend together."

I knew that look. "No," I said.

"You don't even know what I'm going to say."

"No!" I scrambled to my feet, but he grabbed me around the waist and pulled me back down. I turned and grabbed his cheeks in my palms. "You don't have to do this, Allison."

"I do, though." I squirmed out of his grasp and took off running. He followed me into the kitchen and we squared off on either side of the island. His face got serious. He picked up the first thing in front of him, which happened to be my father's overcomplicated salt grinder, and held it out to me in a vague formal gesture. "Miranda." He lowered his chin. "Will you go to prom with me?"

I snatched the grinder from him. "No."

His face fell. "Why not?"

"Why do you keep asking? You suck." I finally achieved some success at keeping a straight face. "Seriously," I said.

He looked at me, trying to gauge my level of seriousness. He must've figured it was high enough. He looked honestly disappointed. "Fine."

"I don't understand why you want to go to prom so bad."

"Are you kidding? Look at us. I just gave you that— What is that? Salt? You're my lady friend."

"Aw," I said. "I'm your lady friend, huh?" Again, here was another chance. *Hey, dude. I totally love you.* Just casual. But no. No matter how I planned to say it, the words caught in my throat.

"Yes." He looked a little pained. "You are." I wondered if he wanted to say it as much as I did. We were terrible at this. We were both rookies. "Going to prom would be like perfect revenge."

"Revenge against whom?" I asked. I was curious to see if he'd say Syd's name. The last time I remembered hearing him say it was on our first date. Now it was like she didn't exist. Like she'd never existed.

"Against"—he searched for the words—"the haters," he finally said, satisfied.

"The haters," I repeated. We both cracked up.

"But seriously." He held out his hand out to me. "I want another do-over."

I placed the grinder in his palm. "Oh my god, how many do-overs do we need?"

Nick had asked me a dozen times to go to prom, but my feelings wouldn't budge. Once, he asked if I still had my dress from last year. Wouldn't it be cool to finally wear it? If my mind wasn't made up before, this question sealed the deal. I couldn't even imagine taking the dress out of the garment bag and putting it on. The idea made me actually queasy. The dress not only served as a reminder of the worst night of my life, but it'd also become the very symbol of Syd's betrayal. *Your boobies are defying gravity right now.* I hated thinking of it. And I hated the dress. It was cursed. The only good thing about prom was that it was this Saturday. A few more days, and Nick would have to stop asking me.

I heard the sound of my father's tires on the gravel outside. "Hey, don't tell your dad about Harvard, okay?" Nick looked sheepish.

"What? Ugh. Whatever." It bothered me that Nick saw my dad in any way like his, as someone who was there to approve or disapprove of his decisions.

"Hello, teens!" my father hollered as he came in, dumping an armload of mail onto the table in the hall. He took off his NASA ID badge and tossed it into the bowl, along with his keys. "Miranda. Here." He walked into the kitchen and handed me an envelope addressed to him from Allstate insurance.

"What's this?" I said.

"What does it look like?" he asked.

"You want me to pay my car insurance?"

"Oh," my dad said. "Yes, I'd actually love that, but seeing as you have no reliable source of income—it's not a bill. It's the card. For your glove box."

"Oh." I tossed the envelope onto the table and plopped down in a kitchen chair.

"Miranda," my father said impatiently. "Do it now. Before you forget."

"Jeez." I stood and snatched the envelope up again.

"I should go home," Nick said.

"See?" I glared at my dad. "You made Nick want to leave our house and never return," I said. "Autocrat."

"Hey, now," my dad said, unbuttoning his shirtsleeves and rolling them up. "Don't call me an autocorrect."

Nick laughed at my dad's cornball joke. I glared at him, too. "Oh god, you two are *hilarious*," I said.

"Lemme get my stuff." Nick jogged into the living room. I opened the envelope and pulled out two insurance cards. The fact that the new cards' expiration dates extended past graduation, summer, and deep into what would be my first semester at college, wherever I ended up, gave me a pang of anxiety. "All right." Nick came in with his backpack on and stood next to me at the counter. My father's back to us, he picked up the salt grinder again and handed it to me. I rolled my eyes and put it down. Then, suddenly, while my dad was washing his hands,

Nick placed a palm on my butt and squeezed. "Nice to see you, Mr. Black," he said in his Eagle Scoutiest voice while looking at me steamily. I felt a jolt, like a crack of lightning up through my body from between my legs. It was so totally unlike him. Nick was always the one to back away when it felt like a make-out session could—or should—turn into sex. I widened my eyes and smiled and was immediately sad when he let go and his hand went back to his side.

"Check you later." My dad turned around. "Sure you don't want to stay? I'm making chicken orzo soup."

"Oh, thanks," Nick said. "I gotta get home."

"Want me to put yours in your car, Dad?" I asked, holding up the second insurance card. "You can command me to do so if it makes you feel more comfortable."

"Thank you, Miry," he said. "Bye, Nick."

"Bye, Mr. Black," Nick said.

"Stop calling me Mr. Black, Nick. It's so weird."

"Sorry," Nick said. "Peter." It sounded like a word in a foreign language. All three of us laughed.

"So much better," I said, grabbing my keys and my dad's. Nick opened the front door, and the two of us stepped outside. It felt good to step into the golden light of a gorgeous spring afternoon. I felt light, hopeful even. It had been such a long time since I'd felt that way. Maybe it was the ultra-green leaves on the giant pecan tree in our yard or the bright purple fruit coming out on the cactuses. Maybe it was the memory of Nick's hand on my butt. I had the urge to kiss him right then, and I pulled him to the other side of the patio, into the driveway, away from view of the kitchen window, and then I grabbed him by the back of the neck and pulled him down toward me. His lips were soft and warm. "Ummm," he said from beneath the kiss.

It was absolutely absurd we hadn't had sex.

"Hey," I said. "My dad has his guy thing tonight. You should come over later."

"Okay." He was dazed from the kiss.

"You get me? Like, come back. When my dad is gone tonight."

I saw Nick come to understand what I was saying. He swallowed. "Really?"

The Eagle Scout looked a little panicked.

"Yes. Or I don't know," I said, feeling totally self-conscious. "No?"

"Yes." He nodded. "Yes."

"Okay." I kissed him one more time, a long sweet one.

"I'll text you," he said as he pulled away.

"I'll text you too," I answered. We both blushed and laughed and then I watched him walk to his car, get in, back out of the driveway, and pull onto the road.

I turned and opened the front door and went back inside.

As soon as I walked in, though, I remembered I'd gone out there for a reason. "Oh crap," I said to no one, holding up the insurance cards. "Duh."

"What?" my dad called from the kitchen.

"Nothing," I called back, opening the door again.

I went to my dad's truck first and riffled through his overstuffed glove box until I found his old insurance card along with two others from years past. I placed the new card on top of the mountain of crap. It took three whacks to get his glove box closed again.

I walked to my car, opened the passenger-side door,

and sat down. It was weird sitting in the passenger seat. Syd's seat. It'd always be Syd's seat. There was still an apricot stain on the upholstery where she'd dropped an open lipstick. I swung my legs in and pulled down the visor. I looked at myself in the mirror. I thought about what would happen later, when Nick came back. I thought of his hand on my butt and how he'd called me his lady friend. I'd come close to saying *I love you* earlier. Tonight I'd do it. No matter what. I wouldn't chicken out. I could see it in my own eyes. I smiled and flipped up the visor and opened my glove box, but when I went to put the insurance card in there, I saw something I couldn't quite place. Was it an object I'd seen in a dream once? Or a flat-out hallucination? It took my brain a while to catch up to my eyes. But when it did, there was no mistaking. Lying facedown in its hot-pink-and-gold leopard-print case was Syd's phone.

"What?" I heard myself ask the emptiness of the car. Immediately I felt a shock of pure joy seeing it there. I couldn't help it. It was her phone! It was as close to being her as any object could be. But my joy was eclipsed very quickly by anger. All those desperate texts and voice mails I'd sent had been going to a phone three feet from where I was driving around, oblivious. Syd had gone off into the world with no way to communicate, no way to be reached. And she hadn't known I'd been trying so hard to reach her. And she hadn't known when I'd stopped trying.

She was more gone then than I'd ever imagined she could be.

I had to force my hand to reach out and pick the thing up. Part of me wanted to slam the glove box shut and walk away, to leave it blissfully undisturbed as it had been for all these months. But then, when I did pick it up, I couldn't help bringing it to my nose and taking a whiff to see if it still smelled like Syd. It didn't, of course. It didn't smell like anything. But when I turned it over, I saw that stuck on its face were four hot dog–shaped sticky notes covered in her tiny, precise handwriting. I read them quickly, hoping beyond hope that they would tell me where she was and how to contact her.

Mir, the first hot dog read:

I hope you find this far in the future. If you have, I'm sure you know everything about prom. If not, ask Nick. If he hasn't told you the truth yet, he's a coward and he deserved everything I did to him. If he has, I hope you two are sucking face on the regular. I know you like him and he'll always be your Medium Hottie. I could see tonight he has a boner for you too. So if you two aren't in love now, I hate you both.

I unstuck the second hot dog.

I can't trust myself with my phone right now, so I'm leaving it with you. Guess I'm kind of a coward myself. I know I'll see you again someday. Please don't worry about me. I'll be FINE. BUT I NEED YOU NOT TO LOOK FOR ME. I don't want to be found right now. I hope you understand that. Someday you'll understand. I hope.

I unstuck the third.

I can't believe what I did in the restaurant tonight. I totally deserved the new asshole you ripped me. BUT LISTEN: I know you, Miranda Black, and I know you'll think I'm leaving because of what you said in the car. What I'm doing has nothing to do with that. Please believe me. I'm not leaving because you yelled at me. You're the best thing in my life. I love you. S

The fourth sticky read:

POSTSCRIPT. OKAY. BIG FINISH. DRUMROLL, BITCHES. . . . Look under the map of New Mexico. (Why the hell do you have a paper map of NM in your glove box, Mir? It's so you. I love you so much.)

I lifted the map. Beneath it was a large, creamy white envelope. I grabbed it and turned it over and heard my gasp resonate inside my brain. It was addressed to Sydney Miller and the return address was Stanford University, Palo Alto, California.

For two seconds I entertained the idea that I could simply destroy it. I'd never have to know. But I already knew. They don't send rejections on stationary that fancy. It took it out and read it.

Dear Sydney,

The admissions committee joins me in the most rewarding part of my job: presenting you with an offer of early admission to Stanford University. We've reviewed your financial aid application and are pleased to inform you that, should you accept our invitation, you'll be eligible for full tuition remission as well as other scholarship funds. In short, we understand your financial needs and offer our fullest support should you join the Stanford family.

Keep in mind your admission offer is contingent upon continued academic success as you complete high school. We ask that you don't change your course of study without first contacting the admissions office.

Oops, Syd had written. She drew an arrow to the second paragraph.

I read the letter from beginning to end, then read it through one more time. Then again. It was quite simply the most remarkable thing I'd ever seen, even if it meant nothing now.

Syd's Plan had worked.

I sat there, dazed. I took up the phone again and pressed the button, but it was dead. If I wanted to turn it on, I'd have to take it inside and charge it. I was immobilized by indecision. I read through each hot dog again. For all her drama and drumrolls, Syd hadn't once said she was sorry for what she'd done last year. She hadn't apologized. Maybe it was that I'd had four months away from her. Her selfishness stood out to me. It was a scent I'd become so accustomed to, I was nose blind. Getting a whiff of it now, I smelled it loud and clear. The thing about Nick being a coward if he hadn't told me about her betrayal! It made me irate. Nick didn't deserve anything she'd done to him, and neither had I. And she'd left me her phone because she couldn't trust herself with it. Which is another way of saying: *Here. Take this. It's your shit storm now.*

I looked at the driver's seat of my car. Ten minutes and I could be handing this phone to Ray, if he still lived in Las Cruces. It was his property after all. Or better yet, I could simply walk around the side of the house to the shed in the backyard, close the door, and destroy it quietly with a hammer. It could be over in three minutes. Probably. Depending on how long it took me to find a hammer.

I could be done with it before I even turned it on.

Three minutes, I thought.

I wished so badly I were the kind of person who'd do it. Syd was that kind of person. Obviously. She could slice people out of her life with no regrets. She'd done it to Patience. Now she'd done it to me.

But I wasn't that kind of person. I needed about zero minutes to figure that out. I checked the glove box to see if there was anything else. When I was sure there wasn't, I put the insurance card inside and closed it. I folded the letter and returned it to the envelope and stuck the four hot dogs in there too. I slipped her phone, and then the envelope, into my pocket. I stared up into the green brilliance of the pecan tree and said one long, slow Gettysburg Address.

It brought me no comfort.

12

"What were you doing out there?" my dad asked when I walked into the kitchen. He brought down a large knife, cleaving into a raw chicken breast. He turned around and detected my weirdness immediately. "What's wrong?"

I tried to act like a person. "Nothing. I was just trying to close your glove box. I had to rearrange crap in there just so it'd shut."

He stared at my face for three seconds. "Nothing in there is crap." My rudeness had covered my tracks. I was relieved. He brought the knife down again. "You didn't take anything out, did you?"

"No." I tried to sound bored. "But you have a menu in there from Coop's."

"I like Coop's." He held up his hands like a surgeon and rubbed his nose with his wrist. The raw chicken, laid out on the cutting board like a sacrifice, was sickening. I averted my eyes.

"Coop's closed when I was in middle school." I walked to my bedroom as casually as I could. "You need an intervention," I called from my doorway.

"Dinner in about thirty," he called after me. "And remember I'm going out."

"'Kay." I closed my door. I yanked the phone and letter out of my pocket. I found my charger and plugged Syd's phone into it. I sat on the edge of my bed and stared at it. I pressed the power button. Nothing. The phone was broken. Or it had been disabled. Was that possible? Was that a thing? I reached into my bag on the floor, grabbed my own phone, and ran to the windowsill, tossing Syd's phone onto my bed but watching it as if it were a bomb. I was in the middle of Googling *Can an iPhone be disabled?* on my phone when I looked over and saw the little swirling circle appear on the screen of Syd's. I left my phone in the windowsill and grabbed hers. I sat down on my bed. *Four score and seven years ago.* I continued through four complete under-my-breath recitations of the Gettysburg Address, the circle swirling and swirling like a single planet forming itself in the dark little universe of the screen.

And then: *Hello.*

Syd's entire world. I was holding it in the palm of my hand. I swiped the phone on and entered her passcode—my birthday, 0723—and there was her menu screen.

The phone was no longer receiving service, of course. Still, Syd had 447 new text messages and 33 voice mails. The last had been received at the end of December. Ray really had turned off the service, and not even a month after she'd disappeared. It was infuriating. His own daughter. I remembered my father saying he'd do everything if I disappeared. Anything. Letty was right, after all. Syd's life was just the kind of life a person would run away from. That she hadn't done it earlier was a miracle.

I wanted to read every text and listen to every voice

mail, but it felt wrong. I remembered trying to snatch Syd's phone from her in the graveyard to see what she'd changed my name to in her contacts. She'd held on with a death grip. Phones were private. And I knew there was no middle ground. If I started, I'd have to read every single text, look at every photo, listen to every voice mail. I'd devour it. Syd knew that. Right? Why else would she have left it? Why wouldn't she have changed the passcode?

The phone was the only clue I had. It was the only thing I'd discovered in four months. It was my job to devour it.

I started with text messages, but because of Syd's method of renaming her contacts, I couldn't identify a majority of the dozens of people who'd texted her. At first I couldn't even find myself. I had to look through the threads until I found the last text I'd sent her. I wasn't Goody Two-Shoes anymore. She'd changed my name after all. Now, I was The Good One. I didn't know what it meant, but seeing it brought tears to my eyes. I scrolled up and up through the texts I'd sent her. I begged her to call me. I begged her to come home. *Please,* my last text read, *just text and tell me you're alive and I'll never text again. I swear.* I couldn't stand it. I went back to the list of threads. Her guidance counselor, Ms. Yslas, had sent a few stern texts. Both Isaac (Medium Hottie) and Joe (Big Boy) had written. Erin Harris (Academic Terrorist) had sent a flurry of texts the morning after Syd had disappeared, scolding her about the lab notes. Only one thread, far down, among the stupid names—T. rex, Math Ass, Clown Town—stood out. The name was too simple, too serious: HIM. In all caps. *HIM?* I tapped it. There was only one message in the thread. It'd come at 10:40

the night she disappeared, less than an hour after I'd left her house.

No. This has gone too far, Sydney. You need help. I'm blocking your number.

Syd must've deleted all the texts that had come before it in the thread. HIM had answered no to something. This one was the last text in a conversation.

I remembered her saying the thing that night about college boys acting like it was charity to touch her boobs. Was HIM a college guy? She'd been checking her phone so obsessively that night. I thought she was toggling between checking College Confidential message boards and texting Isaac. But now I knew she'd been doing neither of those things.

The strangest thing, though, was that he'd called her Sydney. No one called Syd by her full name. She hated it and made a point of telling teachers before they took roll on the first day of class that she went by *Syd*. Had Syd gone by Sydney in her classes at NMSU? Why? To seem older?

My own phone dinged from its perch in my windowsill. It felt like a signal from a distant galaxy. I dashed to receive it.

It was Nick.

When should I come over?

He yanked me back into my life. I'd been hunched over Syd's phone, reading her messages. I felt dirty. I'd soiled the entire evening. Nick coming over suddenly felt wrong. Gross. Weird.

Why did I have to find Syd's phone today of all days? Before I answered Nick, I powered the thing down right then and there and shoved it in my nightstand with the charging cord still attached. I wasn't going to let Syd ruin tonight. *Eight o'clock on the dot,* I wrote. I tried to rally back my belief that tonight was going to be the best night of my life. I tried to will it with all my might to feel good again.

He wrote back right away. *On the dot!* I smiled and then—wait. *Wait.* Syd flattened the tires at Nick's house that night. Why had she done that? Could HIM be Nick? My whole body felt hot, like some cumbersome garment I needed to get off me. The room felt small. I grabbed Syd's phone from the nightstand, powered it back on, and waited. In the time it took the phone to power on, I'd convinced myself HIM was Nick. My life was a sham and no one I'd ever loved could ever be trusted. I was glad I'd chickened out all those million of times and hadn't said *I love you* to Nick. At least I still had those words safe inside me. I hadn't given him everything. I plowed through Syd's passcode, went to the messages, and tapped HIM's number. Then I tapped Nick's number on my phone.

They didn't match.

They didn't match!

Of course they didn't match. What the hell was I thinking? I felt even more miserable. I hated that I'd even checked the numbers. Maybe it was me who couldn't be trusted.

"Mir," my dad called from the kitchen. I shot to my feet.

"Yeah?" I called back, trying to sound like I was doing something normal.

"Set the table?"

"Yep." I shoved Syd's phone back in the drawer. I took a deep breath. I reread Nick's text. *On the dot!* I wanted the words to feel perfect, but they didn't. An hour ago everything felt okay. Now everything was wrong. I emerged from my room, looking as bored as I could, and set the table. But when I sat down across from my dad, my mind took off again. I thought about what I'd hoped would happen later with Nick. I thought about Syd's phone, how it took me a second to recognize what it was. I thought about HIM and Syd's hot dog notes and the letter from Stanford. Was she still going to be able to go? Was it still possible? Was her *oops* a reversible *oops*? And where the hell had she gone? And why? All this new crap and I still had no idea.

"You all right?" my dad asked.

"Oh. Yeah. Just thinking about the college thing." I told myself it wasn't a lie, since I was thinking about Stanford, and so was, technically, thinking of a college.

"Getting to be decision time."

"Yeah. What about that scholarship at UNM? I mean, Brown is amazing, but getting a scholarship is, like, they really want me there, you know? And it'd be less expensive."

My dad was silent for a moment. "And Nick's going to UNM?"

"Jesus!" I sounded way more ferocious than I meant. It was the nerves.

My dad looked shocked. "Jesus yourself," he said.

"Sorry," I said. "But I'm not just going to follow Nick. Give me a little credit."

"I know," he said. "Of course. I know that. I just want what's best for you."

"And what's best for you," I said to my soup.

"No."

"Then why'd you say that? What's so bad about staying in New Mexico? You graduated from NMSU." To punctuate this already shitty dig at my dad, I considered getting up and carrying my bowl of soup to the sink. That would be one of the greatest slights I could make. My father taught himself to cook. He cooked for me. His cooking was his love. We both understood this. Before chicken orzo soup, it was all peanut butter and jelly sandwiches, granola bars, and applesauce.

"Hey," he said sharply. "I studied for three years at MIT. And yes, I did graduate from NMSU." He looked at me squarely. "But those three years were some of the most important years of my life."

"Well, this is *my* life," I returned, too harshly.

"I know." He gave me a little grimacing smile.

"I know too. That's what I'm saying."

He took a deep, grudging breath. "What I mean is: you're right. I'm sorry. I shouldn't have asked about Nick. The decision is yours—entirely yours, as in my opinion counts for very little. But I can still have an interest in this matter. Okay?"

Of course he had to go and apologize. I wanted to keep fighting. Now he'd taken the option off the table and I was forced to succumb to his reasonableness. "I'm sorry too," I said. All the hot air escaped my head. I ate some soup. It was delicious, annoyingly so.

After dinner, I did the dishes and my dad headed back to his room to get ready for his night out. I heard his electric razor, then his electric toothbrush. I guessed these Tuesday nights with his NASA buddies were as much of

an effort as he was ever going to make at meeting someone. That he shaved and brushed his teeth gave me hope
and made me feel sad at the same time.

In ten years my dad had dated three women and I'd
only met one, a tall, nervous dentist named Ruth. She
had red hair and a long, thin face. *Aw, that's sweet,* Syd
had written when I texted a photo. *Pete's dating horses
now.* They broke up after six months. But for a long time
after, I stalked Ruth online. I don't know why. Within a
year she met and married a man who had a penchant for
pastel-colored polos and whose name also happened to
be Peter. A year later Ruth and her Peter had a set of twins,
a boy and a girl. Emma and Charlie. I checked on those
babies for months. I guess I cared about them because
I knew, in an alternate universe, my dad could've been
Ruth's Peter and Emma and Charlie could've been my red-
headed siblings and the five of us could've made the most
wonderfully weird, ethnically confusing family of five.

My dad walked into the kitchen at 7:45 while I was wiping down the counters. "Tucked or untucked?" he asked.

"Untucked."

"You didn't even look."

"Is it a T-shirt?"

"Yes."

"Then the answer is always untucked," I said. "Go
get 'em."

"I don't know about that," he said, grabbing his keys.
"Don't drool."

"Don't drool. Got it. Don't you stay up too late."

"Got it," I said.

As soon as he was gone, the house became intolerably quiet. I felt like I could hear the thick, adobe bricks of our house eroding. I couldn't stop looking at the clock. I finished cleaning the kitchen. When everything was neat, I rubbed smudges out of the toaster with my sleeve. I swept the floor. I even went down the hall and peered into the dryer to see if there was laundry to fold. There wasn't. I nearly dropped my phone when Nick texted at 7:55. *On my way.*

I sprinted to my room and took Syd's phone out of my bedside table and put it in my backpack along with the Stanford letter. I made my bed. I put my dirty laundry in my hamper. When everything looked okay, I walked back into the living room and sat down on the couch and put my hands in my lap. After a few seconds, I jumped up and sprinted back to my room and grabbed my backpack and tossed it to the very back of my closet and closed the door. I went back to the living room and sat down again. My stomach was in knots. I knew I was supposed to be feeling anticipation, but this felt different. This felt like dread, pure and simple. When I heard Nick's car pull into the driveway, I popped up. He had his hand on the doorknob when I yanked it open. I startled him.

"Whoa." He stumbled into the doorway. "Hey." He stepped inside and closed the door.

"You're here," I said.

He put his car keys on the table and opened his arms and I walked over and buried my face in his chest. "I'm on the dot," he said. His face was beaming. I pulled away and looked into his eyes for a long time, but I couldn't find anything to say. "Are you okay?" he asked.

"Yeppers," I said. It was the first time the word *yeppers* had ever come out of my mouth. I wanted to push it back in. My body didn't belong to me. I took his hand and led him the few steps down the hall into my bedroom. I closed the door and locked it. Then I checked to make sure it was locked. I put on music. First it was too loud, so I turned it down. I closed the blinds and pulled the curtains shut, and then, when it became comically dark, I clicked on the lamp beside my bed. I just tried to soldier on. I'd *written a check*, as my father would say. Now *my ass would have to cash it*. I went here and there, mechanical and silent. Nick stood in the doorway. I couldn't bear to look at him.

"Are you sure you're okay?" he asked.

"I am. Are you?"

I walked over and peeled off his hoodie, pulling it awkwardly down his arms and dropping it to the floor. Nick watched me. His face was close to mine. I could hear his breathing. We stood looking at each other for another long moment.

"I'm going to take off my clothes," I said with embarrassing straightforwardness, as if I were announcing I was going to start puking.

His eyelids fluttered. "Okay. Are you sure?" I felt my cheeks burn. "It's okay if you don't want to do this. It won't change anything."

"No. I'm good." I was trying my hardest to make it true.

"So that's a clear yes?" he asked. He hadn't laid a hand on me.

"Well, yes. Unless it's a no. For you."

Nick tilted his head and looked confused. "It can be. Yes. A no for me. Yes. It feels like a no for you. Honestly. Even though you're saying it's a yes. I'm just—seriously— I'm just on the level of straight-up consent 101. Your yes doesn't sound like a yes."

I couldn't believe we were having this conversation. Syd was ruining everything once again.

I looked into his face for a few thousand years, not knowing what to say. I tried once again to rally. I imagined how Syd's phone would shatter so satisfyingly under a hammer.

"I'm just nervous," I said.

"Yeah, okay." He smiled an actual smile and everything felt better. "Me too."

"Did you earn a Boy Scout badge in consent 101?"

"Shut up, please," he said.

"Enthusiastic yes," I said, giving him a Scout's salute. Then I kissed him.

"Here." I led him to my bed. We sat down. I thought of Syd's stupid phone at the back of my closet. Why hadn't I taken it out of the room? I leaned in and gave Nick another prolonged kiss. He responded, pulling me closer. It was all systems go. I could feel it. Nick put his hand on my waist, and his fingers moved down.

"Can we stop?" I asked suddenly. His fingertips had traveled no more than a millimeter under the waistband of my panties.

He pulled away, looking guilty. He looked like he wanted to throw his hands in the air. "Of course. I'm sorry. This is what I didn't want to do—I didn't want to pressure you. We don't have to do this." He swallowed.

He looked a little relieved, too, but also a little frustrated. "That's what I was saying."

"I know." I put my face down into my palms. "I'm sorry. I want to jump your bones, Nick. So bad. But I just can't. Tonight." I considered telling him a lie—I'd started my period at dinner? But I didn't need to do that. Nick didn't need a lie. I sat there for a moment. My body was so confused. It wanted to keep going, but my mind wouldn't let it. "All I need is, like, twenty-four hours." I shot Nick a glance. "Twelve, even."

Nick put his hand on mine and knocked my shoulder with his and pointed at the alarm clock on my dresser. "Twelve hours from now we'll be in French. So, that'll be super-convenient."

I laughed. It felt so good. I leaned into him. "Do you hate me?"

"Why do you ask that when you know the exact opposite is true?"

"Yeah?" *And what was the exact opposite of hate?* I swallowed hard. This was it. It was going to happen. Right now. It had to. What Nick just said was an invitation. "You know . . ." I began. But the fear scaled my spine again and stopped me.

"I do not. Know." He bit his lips together. He was just as bad at this as I was.

I clasped my hands together and clenched my jaw and tried, but it wouldn't come. I looked at him. He looked at me. Finally I just spat out the first thing I could think of. "Do you know what a Goldilocks planet is?"

Oh my god. What was I doing? And why did I have to go outside our solar system to do it?

But then Nick's eyes lit up. He sat with his back a little straighter and searched the ceiling with his eyes. "Okay, wait." He closed his eyes. "Okay." He quietly cleared his throat. "A so-called Goldilocks planet is a planet that orbits within the circumstellar habitable zone of a star and has a planetary surface that, given sufficient atmospheric pressure, could contain liquid water and thus could support biological life. This habitable zone is commonly known as the Goldilocks Zone, an analogy taken from the fairy tale about a girl who chooses among three bowls of porridge, rejecting the one that is too hot and the one that is too cold, and finally choosing the one that is, quote, just right. Unquote."

He opened his eyes. He beamed, triumphant.

I stared into his face, dumbfounded. "What the hell was that?"

"Academic Decathlon." He grinned. "I can do lots. The fundamentals of microeconomic development in Latin America. Titles of paintings by Frida Kahlo. Songs by American folk music icon and Nobel Prize–winner Bob Dylan."

"That is totally insane."

He shrugged. "I'm very smart. Number one in my class, if you remember."

"Okay, whatever." It was back to the task at hand. My heart started racing again. I could hear my breath get shaky and hoped he couldn't. "I've just been wanting to say—to you. That I've thought about it and—I think— it's like you and me. It's like, I think this is my Goldilocks planet. I think— You're in my habitable zone." I looked at the floor. That had gone even more miserably than I could've ever expected. Not only had I not said the words I'd meant to say—*I love you*, three simple words—now I'd added the fuel of the world's stupidest metaphor. The Dumpster fire blazed brightly. If anything, now that it'd come out of my mouth, it sounded like I was telling him I was pregnant. I shrunk with embarrassment. When I ventured to look up at him, I expected total bewilderment on his face.

Instead he was smiling widely. "Seriously?" He looked down at me.

"Seriously," I whispered. Two more seconds and I'd be in tears.

He looked at the ceiling again, the way he had before, as if he were trying once again to recall the correct answer. "Okay. Yeah." He nodded. "I love you too, Miranda."

"Oh." He said it. My heart burst in my chest. "Really?"

"Is that what you were saying? With your space metaphor?"

"Yes," I said. "But I didn't say it."

"Well, one of us had to." He put his hands in his lap.

"We're bad at this." I reached over and took his hand and squeezed it, hard. "So: I love you." I nodded once, for emphasis.

"So: I love you too." He leaned in and kissed me. We looked at each other for a long moment, as if trying to detect a change.

"Okay." I felt supercharged suddenly. Unstoppable. I swung around so I was suddenly straddling him. "Twenty-four hours." I pushed him down onto my bed. "Things are gonna get real up in here, sucker."

"You are so weird," he said, looking up at me dreamily.

"So are you," I answered.

That night, I couldn't sleep. I read (quite appropriately) about my favorite of the virgin martyrs, Saint Cecilia, who, determined to remain chaste for the love of God, told her husband she was betrothed to an angel. I read Saint Patrick, famous for having driven the snakes out of Ireland, though that wasn't an actual confirmed miracle. *Evidence shows postglacial Ireland never had snakes,* my mother had written at the bottom of the page. *Sorry, Patrick.* I read Saint Peter and Saint Ignatius and the harrowing story of Saint Joan of Arc, with whom my mother had clearly been obsessed. *"I was in my thirteenth year when I heard a voice from God to help me govern my conduct. And the first time I was very much afraid."* Oh, Joan. Oh, JOAN. My mother was a sucker for the voices. She wrote so much about these tortured saints, I'd long ago begun to believe she'd heard voices herself. Maybe she was crazy, as many people in town obviously believed. Maybe it was her voices that told her to leave.

I switched off the lights and tried to sleep. But I couldn't.

My dad came in at 11:15, put his keys in the bowl quietly, kicked off his shoes, and walked to his bedroom. I heard the water go on and I heard him brush his teeth. I heard him pee loudly and then flush. Then it was ultra-quiet. After a few minutes he blew his nose so loudly, I was startled. If I'd been asleep, it would've woken me up. I smiled and rolled my eyes in the dark. I lay there and wondered if he'd ever have anyone living in this tiny old house with him after I moved out, someone to smile when he blew his nose like an elephant in the night. Was he going to live alone in the childhood home of the woman who'd left him? Was he going to die here, a lonely old man, in the room where my mother had slept as a newborn?

Eventually, my thoughts wandered back to Syd. Her stupid phone was burning a hole in my closet. Who was I fooling? I threw back the covers and tiptoed to retrieve it and then climbed back in bed.

I read everything. I read the texts Ray had sent, all business.

That car is in my name and you need to return it.

You have a stack of mail here.

The last read: *Shutting off this phone.*

It was as heartbreaking as it was infuriating and made me feel like I'd been a terrible friend to Syd. Why hadn't I forced her to live with us? Why hadn't I ever even asked her?

I read Big Boy's texts and Math Ass's texts.

I read her texts with Erin Harris. Syd would've loved them so much, the way they built to an end-of-times fever pitch. *THANKS SO MUCH FOR RUINING MY LIFE!* Then, the next day, after I'd put the posters up and everyone knew Syd was gone, she sent one more. *Yikes, hope ur okay. Now that ur missing, I got an extension on the lab. XO.*

I read every thread. I looked at every photo. I listened to all her voice mails. I devoured everything on the phone, just like I knew I would. If she hadn't deleted all her social media apps and her Gmail, I'd have scoured those as well.

I guess I hoped the phone might help me figure out

where she was and what she was doing and why. But in the end, I'd learned absolutely nothing. The biggest unknown quantity was the single message from HIM. I kept going back to it. What had *gone too far*? I got out of bed and grabbed my own phone off my windowsill and entered HIM's number into new a text message to see if one of my contacts would come up. But no. *Nada*. Whoever HIM was, he wasn't in my phone.

I glanced at the clock. It was after midnight.

Who cares? I thought. *Who is this?* I typed into the text box on my phone. But then I realized if I received a text from a strange number asking *Who is this?* the last thing I'd do is answer. I deleted that.

Do you know anything about Syd Miller? I typed.

I let it sit. I acknowledged it felt wrong to send it. But then I pressed send. *Delivered*. As soon as the word appeared under the text bubble, I regretted it. What was I doing? I felt gross again. Dirty. I deleted the thread from my phone and tried to pretend it never happened. I stashed Syd's phone in my bedside table and turned my own phone off and threw it in the drawer too.

As I lay in the dark, I made myself three promises.

First: if I received an answer from HIM on my phone, I'd simply delete it. Unless HIM wrote back with a physical address and a video of Syd holding up that day's newspaper and asking me to come get her at that address, I'd pay it no attention. I wasn't Encyclopedia Brown, hot on the trail. I was Miranda Black, who needed to come to terms with the fact that her best friend was gone. She was gone, of her own volition and without a desire to be found. Her note said: *I'm not missing*. Her other note said: *I NEED YOU NOT TO LOOK FOR ME*. She'd removed herself from her own life, and so she'd been removed from mine, too. This was the truth. *I'm not missing.* I needed to start reciting it to myself like the Gettysburg Address. I needed to stitch it into my consciousness. Yes, it sucked. But the truth often sucked. And I'd survived worse.

Second: first thing in the morning, I'd take Syd's phone out of my room, preferably out of the house, maybe to the shed, and I'd leave it there until the reason I had to retrieve it was because Syd was standing in front of my face, in the flesh, asking for it. *I'm not missing* was never going to sink in if I spent my days poring over Syd's life. That was sick. She'd burdened me with the responsibility of her phone because she couldn't be trusted with it. But I couldn't be trusted with it either. So I'd get it out of my house. If the shed wasn't enough, I'd destroy it. With a hammer. Or a brick.

Third and most important: barring natural disaster, zombie apocalypse, death, or dismemberment, I was having goddamn sex tomorrow for the first goddamn time in my goddamn life with the goddamn boy I loved and it was going to be goddamn great because we were goddamn in love.

Full stop.

Amen.

Good night.

13

As she did at the beginning of each class, Madame Spencer was standing at the whiteboard, dry-erase marker flying, drilling us on the verb conjugations we'd likely see on the AP exam. I was concentrating hard—the irregular verbs always tripped me up—when Nick turned around in his desk and looked at me. He still sat a row over and three desks up. Will wouldn't budge. He was not going to allow me even that simple gesture of concession. I allowed my eyes to move for one second from the whiteboard to Nick's face.

What? I mouthed to him.

He shot his eyes up and to the left then turned to face forward again before Madame Spencer noticed.

I followed to where his eyes had gone and found the clock above the window. It was 8:25. Twelve hours later. I stifled a laugh and Will snapped around and glared as if I were being totally disruptive and compromising his entire educational career. "Sorry," I whispered, and he turned back around. Still, I couldn't stop smiling.

I'd woken up feeling resolved. Making those three

promises last night had given me strength that carried me forward all day long. After my dad left for work, I put Syd's phone in a shoe box along with the Stanford letter, and I walked out to the dusty shed, ceremoniously pushed open the heavy, stuck wooden door, and hid the box beneath a tall pile of painting tarps my dad had neatly stacked on a shelf. I hated the shed. It was full of spiderwebs and the lurking possibility of scorpions and worse. Somehow this seemed like insurance enough that I could leave the box out there. I could leave it alone.

Throughout the day, the sound of my phone dinging with a new text caused me a small panic attack. It was like the first days after Syd disappeared all over again. But once I'd made it to the end of the school day without hearing back from HIM, I knew I was in the clear. If HIM was going to text back, he'd have done it by now.

After school, I walked Nick to his car. I had to stay on in the newspaper office because we were putting out a double issue on prom that had to be at the printer by six o'clock. Our journalism teacher, Ms. Boone, was having a meltdown about the deadline and so it was all hands on deck.

And Nick had been tutoring a middle schooler for the last few weeks and they were having a cram session before the kid's big math test. "What are you doing after?" I asked.

"Nothing," Nick said, suppressing a grin. "Nada."

"Come over," I said. "For real."

"Okay." He attempted to nod casually. "I'm sorry, I mean yeppers."

It turned out Ms. Boone's freak-out was a false alarm and the newspaper was actually much closer to being finished than we'd thought. Anyway, most of what was left to do was up to the photographers. Copyediting the stories on prom preparations—all those dresses and limos and dinner reservations—had started to make me anxious. I kept having flashbacks. I scrammed as soon as I could.

I thought I might have time to make things perfect before Nick came over. Light a candle? Is that something sex people did? I hauled ass home. But when I turned into my driveway, I was surprised to find Nick's car parked in the space where I usually parked mine. I got closer and could see he was sitting in the driver's seat, doing his homework. He looked up when he heard my car. I gave him a bewildered look. He put his notebook down and picked up a small bouquet of flowers—lilies and poppies and some strange blossoms I couldn't identify.

"Oh my god," I said, and rolled my eyes. We got out of our cars. He handed me the flowers.

"Thanks." I put them to my nose. "What happened to the cram sesh?"

"He has strep throat." He smiled.

"Oh, that's so freaking awesome." I grabbed his hand and we dashed into the house and I tossed the flowers onto the table in the hall as we fumbled into my bedroom. I locked the door. We looked at each other. Neither of us had to ask or say anything. But then, because he was Nick, he did anyway. "This is a yes?" he said as we started peeling off our clothes.

"Oh my god." I looked up into his face. "Yes!" I pulled off my T-shirt. When I reached behind my back to unhook my bra, Nick's face lit up, as if he were having a really great idea. My bra hit the floor. He sighed heavily. He took off his T-shirt. Again, his muscles surprised me.

His shoulders were even more perfect naked, dusted with light freckles. He looked at me so sweetly, so thoughtfully, my body ached. I must've looked flushed or funny, because he leaned down and kissed me.

"I'm nervous," I said. "Are you nervous?"

"Yes." His breath was shaky.

"Do you want to stop?" I asked.

He shook his head. "Do you?" he asked.

"Absolutely not." I swiped off my jeans and tossed them. Then my panties. "Shit's getting real," I said. He laughed. I fumbled with the buttons on his jeans and when I couldn't undo them, he took over. He stepped out of his jeans and stood in his boxers and socks. He slid off his boxers. We stood there a long minute, neither of us daring to look down.

"Okay, I can't just be standing here in my socks," he said. He flicked them off in two quick motions.

I led him to my bed and pulled him down. He was so warm. We kissed for an eternity, each kiss pulling us closer together. He moved down, kissing my neck and chest and my breasts. Rockets blasted off in my brain, ricocheting inside my skull. "I have a condom," he said blurrily. "It's in my wallet. But it's banana flavored. I'm sorry. I didn't realize that until just now when I was in the car. It was from the health fair."

"It's fine," I said, breathless. "Any flavor will do. I don't think you're supposed to eat it anyway."

We laughed again. He leaned over and grabbed his jeans on the floor and then his wallet. I liked watching him move without his shirt on, his back muscles, his arms, his shoulders. He tore open the condom, but then he didn't seem very good at putting it on, sitting at the edge of the bed, bent over for a moment while I lay back and waited. I was about to ask if he needed help when he appeared again above me, eager and beautiful. We kissed a long, serious kiss then locked eyes as his hand moved down. I felt fumbling, fumbling—and then an extraordinary rippling sensation, like a giant stone had fallen from out of the sky into the center of a small, placid lake. It was enormous and tiny at once. I looked up at Nick and wondered if I looked as surprised and happy as he did. We moved together. After a while he buried his face against my shoulder. "Oh," I heard him whisper. And then he pressed his face into my pillow and let out a low moan. It was such a personal sound, pure, like a secret, something intimate and vulnerable and made entirely of him.

"Oh my gosh," I said as Nick rolled away and made some gestures I took to mean he was removing the condom and disposing of it. He lay back and I curled into him and felt his chest rise and fall with a deep breath. I looked up at him and he looked shyly down at me.

"I'll do better next time." He was still breathless. He didn't look scared anymore, but he was self-conscious. "Sorry."

"What?" I poked him hard in the ribs and rolled over onto my elbows. "What are you talking about? That was amazing. I want to do that all the time. Why haven't we been doing this the whole time? I should've jumped your bones when you took off your shirt that night in the parking lot of La Hacienda. Seriously. I wanted to." I kissed his neck. "Let's drop out of school and just do this. For careers."

Nick laughed. "I think it was more amazing for me than for you. I can work on that. Next time."

Next time. It was bliss. There'd be a next time, and a next time after that. Lying there with Nick, the *next time* of everything was infinite, wide-open, a universe we'd never have to worry about reaching the edge of. It was so simple: we'd just be together. College and life and everything headed our way was nothing. We'd walked through this door together. Where I thought we'd find ourselves on the other side of something, we'd instead found ourselves on this side of a million more *next times*.

"If you'd like"—he folded his arm and propped up his head—"I could try something."

"Something?" I said.

"I've done some research."

"Research! I love you, nerd." I kissed his shoulder. "Are you going to tell me everything you know about Nobel Prize–winning songwriter Bob Dylan now?"

"No." He held up a finger as if to say hear me out. "Just." He indicated I should lie down. Then he kissed his way all the way down my chest and belly until he was between my legs. I couldn't quite believe it.

Basically, it was the most amazing thing I'd ever experienced in all my days on planet Earth.

Every now and then, I lost my concentration. I thought of Syd. I thought of HIM and the phone and my stupid midnight text. But if I closed my eyes, I'd be back in my body again, at its very center, and my brain would be dipped again in honey. It was profoundly strange having an orgasm with someone else in the room. But the fireworks in my skull kept me from feeling too self-conscious.

"Holy crap," I said as Nick returned to his place beside me. "Hi, Bob Dylan." Nick laughed. He was relaxed and happy. We lay quietly for a long time. I wished we could stay like that forever. We weren't even holding on to each other, just touching down the lengths of our bodies. Together. "I don't think that's supposed to happen, like the first time." I turned my head to face him. "I feel like there's a chance I might be an inspiration."

"Yeah?" He was sort of dazed and dreamy.

"Like to all mankind. Or womankind, I should say. Superhero status." Nick busted out in a giant laugh. "And you, sir." I shoved him a little. "I'm sorry. Where did you say you conducted this research?"

"The internet," he answered plainly. We laughed. "Not what you think. There are some very good resources for interested young men." I gave him side eye. "And a little of what you think." We laughed again, and I scooted over and put my head on his chest. I was just drifting into the woozy space before sleep when his voice pulled me out of it.

"Hey," he said softly. "Can I ask you something?"

"What?"

"Will you go to prom with me?" He'd said it so tenderly, it took me a moment to understand what he was asking. I was about to launch into my usual denial, but when I looked at him, there was no joking in his face. "Really. Just please."

"Fine." I couldn't believe I'd said it.

"Really?" He was clearly surprised too. "Prom's in two days."

"I know. We need tickets."

"I'll get tickets."

"You need a tuxedo."

"I'll get a tuxedo."

"And," I said, "I have to check with Quinn Johnson. He has dibs."

"Quinn Johnson is *literally* going to have to fight me."

Right then we heard tires on gravel. We'd lost track of time entirely. "Oh god, it's him," I said. Nick scrambled up and put on his boxers and started turning his jeans right side in. I pulled on my pants, tossed my underwear into my closet, and threw on my T-shirt. I straightened the bed while Nick hopped frantically into his jeans. I grabbed his shirt and tossed it to him. We were a well-oiled machine of pure panic. I opened the door to my room and turned on the ceiling fan to circulate the air, but because it hadn't been used in months, dust rained down on us. It looked like a snowstorm in my room. I turned it off. I grabbed my laptop and flipped it open, and within twenty seconds Nick and I were sitting on the floor with our backs against the bed, barefoot, but otherwise looking like respectable citizens, watching the first video I clicked on. It was a Chihuahua doing—oh, whatever.

"Hello, teens!" my dad called out.

"Hello, old person!" I called back. I looked at Nick. He was watching the Chihuahua so gravely, it looked like he was watching a horror movie. I elbowed his ribs.

"You shouldn't have," my dad said from the hallway. I heard his keys crash into the bowl. Nick and I looked at each other in terror.

He walked into the doorway, carrying the flowers, waving like Miss America.

"Oh. Ha." I was suddenly sure my room smelled like a banana sex palace.

I'd totally forgotten about the flowers. I couldn't account for them. I looked at Nick for help.

"I got those for Miranda," He blurted out. "For finishing the prom issue of the paper."

"It was a double issue," I said. I went back to watching the Chihuahua. I concentrated hard. What was he doing? Oh, he was walking on his back legs. And he was dressed in a little suit and tie. "This Chihuahua is ridiculous. You have to see this, Dad." I snapped my laptop closed. Nick was forced to look up.

"Cool." My dad nodded. I had no idea how to act around him.

"Nick was just getting ready to leave," I said.

My dad looked at Nick, his bare feet. "Getting ready to leave?"

"Yeah. I have to go. It's hot dog night." Nick looked my dad in the face, never wavering. It was a disaster. He must've realized what he said didn't add up, so he added, "I love hot dogs." *Oh my god,* I thought. Of all the foods on all the nights, why did it have to be hot dogs?

"Oh. Okay." My dad looked at me. "Miranda?" I looked at him standing there with the flowers, eyeing me suspiciously. Or was he?

"What?" I sat up straight and tried to look like *no big deal*.

"The flowers," he said. "You need to put them in water."

"Oh." I jumped up and snatched the flowers and ran to the kitchen, elated to have somewhere else to be and something to do.

"You bring in the mail?" he called to me from the hall.

"No, sorry. I forgot." I heard my dad open the front door. I found the one and only vase we owned in the back of the cabinet. I filled it halfway with water. Nick appeared in the kitchen, still looking horrified, and sidled up to where I was busily snipping the ends off the flowers and plunking them into the vase. He put his mouth to my ear and spoke as if we were secret agents on a mission. "The condom wrapper is on the floor on the other side of the bed." The front door opened and closed and my father strode into the kitchen with an armful of mail.

"Okay, bye," I said to Nick a bit too forcefully.

He was happy to leave, though his shoes were still untied. "Bye, Mr. Black."

"Peter," my dad said.

Nick smiled, grabbed for the doorknob. "Bye, Peter. Peter. Sorry. Bye." He closed the door behind himself. I was on my own.

I looked up to see my father standing on the other side of the island, and returned to arranging the flowers as if my life depended on it. I wished there were more of them. I'd plunked them all. Now I was just moving them around. He folded his arms. I glanced into his face, then down again. I spotted a tiny packet of flower food taped to the plastic wrap. I yanked it off and read the instructions. My father stood watching me. I wanted to climb into the garbage disposal.

"Miranda. My dear." I couldn't look up at him. There was a possibility he was smiling. Or maybe he was frowning. I didn't want to know.

"Uh-huh?" I read the instructions on the packet as if they were *War and Peace*, though there was only one step: *Empty packet into water containing flowers.*

"Miranda." I looked up hesitantly. He wasn't smiling or frowning, just looking at me. I was relieved.

"What?" I said. I went back to the packet, looking for the notch to tear it open.

"You know I trust you." I could feel I'd commenced to turning all possible shades of pink and red, but I made myself look him in the face.

"Uh-huh." It was the best I could do. I thought I was doing pretty well, all things considered, but just then my nervous fingers got the better of me and I tore open the flower food with such force that it exploded, sending a cloud of powder everywhere. "Oops."

I never stopped looking my dad in the face. He half-smiled. He was being as kind and as cool as he could be. I was grateful. My dad. He really was a good guy. He deserved to be in love, the way I was in love with Nick. He was young enough. He could start over, get married again. We could be a family. An actual family. My father in love! It was the best idea I'd ever had. We had to make it happen.

"I want you to make good choices, Miranda."

"I'm making good choices," I said. "I mean, not flower-food-wise. But in life."

"We're talking about the same choices?"

"Yes," I said. "I'm making good choices." I swallowed hard and forced myself to say it. "Nick and I are making good choices."

"All right." My dad's face changed. It was as if someone had been bending his finger back to the breaking point and had suddenly released it. For a moment he appeared as if he were going to laugh, but then I realized he was actually heading in the opposite direction. "Damn it," he said. His eyes welled up. He was still wearing his tie and NASA ID.

"Are you okay?" I asked.

"Yep." He pulled himself together before he'd produced any actual tears. I was grateful for that, too. "I'm just gonna miss you. When the hell did you grow up?"

"I'm not going anywhere," I said. "But yeah, I'm gonna miss you too." I felt a sharp bite of sadness. In an alternate universe, I could tell my father everything: the rippling, honey-coated feeling, the way Nick had said, *Okay, yeah, I love you too, Miranda*, after my stupid planet metaphor. The way Nick's shoulders made me want to cry and my secret desire to follow him to UNM or anywhere else on the planet. "I hope . . ." I dusted flower food off my wrists. "I want you to be happy, Dad. I don't want you to be lonely. You should meet someone. You could have a whole other life after I move out."

He laughed. "Don't worry about me," he said. "I'm going to live it up in this joint. I'm going to have ragers as soon as you're out of here. The women are going to come from all over. Deming, Hatch, *Tucumcari*."

"I'm serious," I said. "I want you to make good choices too."

"I'll try." He nodded. "But for a while I'll live on beer. And flower food."

"These poor flowers. I spilled their food." I dusted the powder off the counter into my palm and turned and poured it into the sink. "They're nice, aren't they?"

"Yeah," he said.

"I love Nick, Dad." The words flew out of my mouth. I couldn't have stopped them if I tried.

"I know."

"But it's so huge."

"I know."

"And it hurts. Why does it hurt?"

"I don't know." He frowned in sympathy and shook his head. "I don't know why."

I wanted so badly to ask him if he'd felt this way about my mom. If my mom had made him feel this big, pure pain of love.

"I've been thinking about Mom," I said. His face seemed open to further discussion, so I continued. "Do you remember how she prayed?"

"Oh yeah." He brought his fingertips to his temples and closed his eyes.

"Yes!" It made something inside me jump to see him make that familiar gesture. "I used to pray. All the time. Or I mean, I don't know, it's not like I was praying to God. Like Mom was. I don't know. She taught me how. But when I tried, I only ever saw the Milky Way. Remember that time out behind Uncle Benny's? Oh god, it sounds so stupid now."

"I remember that. You asked how far away it was."

"When she left, I couldn't do it anymore. Not even the Milky Way."

"I never knew that," he said.

"Yeah." I wasn't as embarrassed as I thought I'd be telling my dad this weird detail about my life. I decided to spare him the part about the Gettysburg Address.

"Huh." He did something that wasn't a smile or a frown.

"Don't make fun of me."

"I would never," he said. "That's great. You talk to the Milky Way. I mean, that's basically what I do for a living. Both waiting for the same thing, I guess."

"I don't anymore, though."

"Right." He gave me a sad little smile.

"For a while I wanted to be a nun."

His sad smile turned immediately into a melodramatic look of alarm.

"No," I said. "Because nuns pray. I wanted that. But it got all screwed up, like maybe it was just Mom I missed, not the Milky Way. Or God or whatever. You know?"

"Yeah." He nodded. "But for the record, being a nun would be going too far."

I let a long moment pass, both of us looking at the flowers. UNM is so close."

"It is close," he said.

"It's close to you."

"Yep."

"I'm so sick of not knowing what to do," I said. "Syd always knew what to do. She made it seem like things were supposed to be one way only."

"Well, you're not Syd. He grabbed his ID badge and took it off over his head and held it in his hand. He loosened his tie. "You'll figure it out. I've been thinking about this a lot. So many things in life are like this. Like a test. Not just when you're young, either. Your whole life. You come to a point and people are telling you what they think you should do and you just have to listen to yourself. That's what it's all about. Who the hell am I to tell you Brown is what you want?"

"Was it like that for you when Mom got pregnant?"

My father's eyes bulged. "Jesus." He looked around as if trying to find backup, someone to help him. "I guess this is the conversation we're having right now?"

"I'm not an idiot. And you had to leave school."

He rubbed his chin. "I did. Yeah." He stood thinking a moment. "And damn, yes. There were people, my folks, my father, especially, telling me—telling your mom and me—we shouldn't do it. We couldn't." He looked at me, assessing whether or not he should go on.

"But you did."

"Yep." He swallowed. "And sure, part of me thought they were right. I was mad. You know. I had to change my life." He paused a moment. "And so, you know, if you're asking me if that was the single most insane, ill-informed decision I've ever made, I'd probably, honestly, have to say hell yes. But was it also the single best thing that ever happened to me—the best thing that will ever happen? Well, hell yes on that one too." The kitchen was quiet. I tried to absorb the magnitude of what he'd said.

"If I go to UNM, I could come down on weekends," I said.

"Do you want that?"

"Well. What are you going to do?"

"I'll be fine. I might not even stay here."

"What?"

"I could go to the Jet Propulsion Lab. I could go to Goddard in Maryland."

"Really?"

"I mean, you know. Yes. My thingies are kind of a big deal."

"Seriously?" I'd always felt sort of sorry for my dad and his thingies. I assumed his contribution to aerospace engineering was so measly, the people at NASA were happy to let him languish in the desert, unknown, small potatoes.

"I stayed here because, you know—you were in school. We were here."

"You're telling me right now you're moving to Maryland?"

"No. I mean, I could end up in Maryland. I don't know. All I'm saying is, you don't need to worry about me."

"Maryland? Is that close to Providence, where Brown is?"

"Miranda."

"Really? *Maryland?* Okay. I see how it is."

"Oh god. Listen to me. This telescope has been in development since before you were born. It's basically the most sophisticated piece of technology the world has ever seen to date." He lowered his head. "I assure you, Miranda. The James Webb Space Telescope is not a ruse the National Aeronautics and Space Administration has cooked up so I can follow you to college." He slapped the counter. "Please. Get over yourself."

We both laughed. "Dang," I said. "Would you sell the house?"

"Never. We'll never sell it. You never need to worry about that."

"Oh my god. Will you get to do the press conferences?"

"No. That's—no. That's not even on the table at all."

"Roll in, grab the mic, be like: *Um, who ordered the Goldilocks planet?*"

He smiled. "That's just how I've always imagined it."

"How big a deal are your thingies?"

"I don't know." He shrugged. "Google it."

14

That night I googled my dad. It was weird. I didn't know what to call his thingies, so I just put in *Peter Black engineer NASA Webb Space Telescope*. The articles that came up were mostly too technical for me to understand and only mentioned my dad briefly, or mentioned his in a long list of names. But buried beneath those, I found a short profile on the NASA website, complete with a photo of him standing between a small model of the Kepler and another of the Webb. In a sidebar Q&A, when asked his proudest achievement, he said it was raising his daughter. *She's my life's greatest blessing.* That was a direct quote: *my life's greatest blessing.* I stared at the photo for a long time. I'd never once in my entire life heard my father describe a single thing as a blessing. It was sweet, but so strange. I could never mention it. I was sure it'd embarrass both of us. If he'd said, *She's my highest priority,* I'd mention it. If he'd said, *She's got a pretty good head on her shoulders and I'm proud of a number of her decisions,* sure. But not this. *She's my life's greatest blessing.* I must've read the sentence a million times before I closed my laptop and put on my pajamas.

In bed, I read about Saint John the Apostle. My mom didn't have much to say about him (*Assumed author of Book of Revelation*), but at the end of the day, he was probably my favorite saint. John was the only one of Jesus's apostles who lived to be an old man, the only one who'd been spared a gruesome martyr's death. As an old man he'd be asked to give mass and all he would say at the altar was, "Little children, love one another." That was it. The whole mass.

I was trying to concentrate on John, but my mind kept returning to the afternoon, to Nick's shoulders, his moan. The way he'd asked me to prom so sweetly—"Really. Just please"—and I caved. When my phone dinged in my windowsill, I figured it must be him. He was having the same trouble sleeping. But when I scurried to the windowsill and grabbed my phone, it wasn't Nick. It was HIM. After everything that had happened today, I'd nearly allowed myself to forget I'd ever even texted HIM. Finding Syd's phone—having the wound of her absence ripped open again—and then texting a stranger from mine: hadn't that happened in a different lifetime? Wasn't I on the other side of the door? Finished. Complete. Wasn't I was going to be like Saint John the Apostle, the one allowed to bypass the horrible pain and suffering and grow old in peace?

Who is this? That was all. I stared at my phone and remembered my promise: if HIM texted me back, I'd delete the text thread. No matter what, I'd be done with it.

But now, here was HIM. And here was me, finding it impossible to let it be.

Who are you? I texted, before I could talk myself out of it.

How did you get this number? he shot back.

I considered telling him the truth. I was Syd's best

friend. I found his number in the phone she'd left me the night she disappeared—the phone that contained a stern text from him. But I knew that wasn't a good idea. *I'm Syd's cousin. She put this number in my contacts. Sorry!* I pressed send.

Have you heard from her? he answered right away. He began composing another message, but then stopped. I sensed desperation.

No, I answered. *Have you?*

It took him a while to answer. *No.*

I paused and thought of all the training Ms. Boone had given us in how to sniff out a story, or how to get to the real story hiding beneath the surface of another. He'd waited a full twenty-four hours to return my text—but he'd returned it. He could've ignored it, but he didn't. Or he couldn't. Maybe he'd made himself a vow and broken it too, unable to contain his curiosity. Maybe he was guilty of something and was worried I was on to him. Maybe he wasn't. Still, I knew I'd have to be delicate with my next communication. I didn't want to scare him away. He'd told Syd in that last text he was blocking her number. I didn't want him to do the same to me. I wanted him to talk. This was something Ms. Boone preached to the newspaper staff: be open and wait. Everyone talks. Eventually.

I waited two minutes. I timed it. I wanted to see if he'd say more. But he didn't. So I texted, *Hey, would you mind letting me know if you hear anything? Just want to know she's okay, you know?* I added an emoji of a hand giving the peace sign, for effect.

I hoped I hadn't gone too far in my casualness. I feared I wouldn't get a text back. But then: *ding. I will. You do the same? Please use this number to reach me.*

I remembered the thing Syd had texted me on prom night: *Boys are idiots.* Aside from the fact that she'd been lying to me at the time—and I was lying right now—the hypothesis felt so true, at least for this particular boy. He thought I was just a slightly concerned, kind of dopey cousin of Syd's.

Sure thing! I pressed send. I waited, but he didn't write back. I put the phone in the windowsill and crawled into bed and returned to Saint John. After a moment I found myself staring off, thinking of the shed, resisting the temptation to sneak out of bed right now and retrieve Syd's phone from the kingdom of spiders and scorpions. I'd already broken one of my promises. I looked down at the illustration of Saint John as an old man. Beneath it, my mother had written: *Actually, not all other disciples died as martyrs. Judas fell on his sword. Died by suicide.*

I closed the book and turned off my light.

The spiders won.

But it turned out my resistance to Syd's phone would survive only until the morning. After my father left for work, I walked around the side of the house, past my enemy agaves, across the dusty backyard, and pushed into the shed. I slid my hands beneath the tarps and grabbed the box and took out the phone and letter and shoved them into my backpack. When I got in the car, I took out the phone and laid it on my passenger seat. It was still turned off. I threw my car into reverse and made it all the way to the paved road before I regained my senses.

I was not going to fall on my sword. Not that Judas was a great example. But still.

I drove forward, put the car in park, took the phone and letter around the house, back to the shed, returned them to the shoe box, and shoved the shoe box back under the tarps. As I batted at spiderwebs both visible and invisible, I considered the possibility I was developing a full-blown OCD-style ritualized relationship to the damn shed, but I encouraged myself to ignore that fear and just feel proud for having returned the phone to its rightful place: out of my life. Away. Saint John.

I tried all day at school to forget it, and to forget HIM. I filled every minute of the day with activity. I dropped into the newspaper office before school and, with the issue at the printers and nothing to do, I cleaned up the desks and wiped the whiteboard clean, then ultra-clean. At lunch I went from table to table, like Syd would have, checking in with people. Marcy and the Mormons were especially happy to hear me blather on and on. I even stopped Quinn Johnson to congratulate him on being nominated for prom king. He looked down at me with his watery eyes and said thanks, but I got the honest sense he didn't know who the hell I was. I tried everything. But there was no use. Something about HIM's last text kept bugging me, like a splinter in my skin; the more I worried it, the deeper it got. While I was telling Heather Thomas about how a picture of her in her prom dress would be the front cover of the newspaper, my mind was busy turning over this one question.

Why had he said, *Please use this number to reach me*?

Wouldn't *this number* imply there was another number I was not to use?

All day I tried to convince myself I was just being obsessive. But by the time Nick asked me after school if

I wanted to go do homework at Milagro—or just go make out in his car—my mind was made up. I gave a lame excuse and exceeded the speed limit all the way home. As soon as I pulled into the driveway, I once again walked around the house, across the yard, pushed into the shed, slipped my hands under the tarps, and grabbed the box. My mouth was watering in anticipation. I felt every spider staring at me, every scorpion.

The moment I took out the phone and turned it on, I felt I understood how it must've felt for Patience to take her first drink of wine after all those weeks in rehab. It was an absolute relief. Suddenly I had no other responsibilities. All I needed was Syd's phone.

I tapped the text from HIM. I tapped his contact page. I scrolled down. And there it was, shining like a little nugget of gold: *home phone*. Beside it, another number.

I didn't think twice. In fact, I hardly thought once. I took out my phone and dialed the number. The phone rang once. Twice. Three times. It was ringing so slowly. The shed was dark and hot and silent. With each ring, I became more aware of what I was doing and lost a little more of my nerve. I was about to hang up when the ringing stopped.

A decade passed.

"Miranda?" It was a familiar voice.

"Nick?" I grabbed the old wooden shelf in front of me, sure if I didn't that I'd faint and fall and break my head open on the stack of cinder blocks in the corner.

I thought immediately of Judas falling on his sword.

"Oh," I scrambled. "Hi."

"Hey. Why are you calling my landline?"

Just then someone picked up another line.

"Hello?" It was Nick's mom. I clenched my teeth and tried to die.

"Mom, sorry, hang up. It's Miranda."

"Oh, hi, Miranda!" Her voice was as bright as the shed was dark.

"Hi, Dr. Allison." I tried to make it sound like I wasn't having a nervous breakdown among spiders.

"I hear you two are going to the prom. It's so fabulous. You and your appendix get a do-over." Even though my head was on fire and I was about to vomit from nerves, I thought it was cute that, like her son, she, too, had called it a do-over.

"Mom," Nick said.

"Okay. Sorry. But I do hope you stop by before the dance. I want pictures. Jason never went to prom. Miranda, sweetie, you're our family's only hope."

I laughed and said, "Okay," at the exact same moment Nick said, "Hang up!"

"Hanging up now." She hung up.

"So what's up?" Nick said. I had absolutely no way of answering. I'd almost forgotten I was having a nervous breakdown.

"So this is your landline?" I tried to sound bored.

"Yep," he said. "This is it. Pretty cool, huh?"

"We haven't had a landline since I was, like, ten."

After a short pause—too short, I thought—Nick said, "Miranda, did you just call to make fun of my family for having a landline?"

"No, sorry. Okay. Sorry. I'll text you later."

"Wait, what?"

Ah, Nick. *Wait, what?* A better question had never been asked.

"Oh, no," I said. "I just called—I must've written your number down. I just found it here. In an old notebook. I thought it was your phone number. I just called. To make sure. I guess I could've just looked it up." Of course, it hadn't occurred to me until I said it that it was true. I could've looked up the number and avoided this hideous web of lies I'd begun spinning.

"Oh. Okay." That was all he said. "I got a tux."

"You did?"

"It's the same exact one I got last year. There's a hole in the pocket. Same hole."

"That's crazy. Can we hang up? Phone calls make me nervous."

There was a long, painful pause. Then Nick said, "You're such a weirdo."

"Okay, fine, nerd. Bye." I hung up.

It was such a pure relief to be off the phone. It took a long, cool moment for my brain to start working again. It was like the circle on Syd's phone when I'd first turned it on, swirling and swirling.

It didn't make sense. Nick's number and HIM's number didn't match. I checked. They didn't match! Syd hated Nick and Nick hated Syd. Nick wasn't HIM. There was simply no way Nick was HIM.

But then again Syd let the air out of Nick's tires the night she left town. That had always bugged me.

Why had she done that?

Wait. My mind snagged on something. The world stood still. *Wait.*

Syd hadn't let the air out of Nick's tires that night. Not Nick's tires.

It was so overwhelming, I had to sit down. I looked around the dark shed and found the stack of cinder blocks was the only thing available, so I perched on them until it came to me. That night at La Posta. In the middle of Syd's bizarre performance at the Allisons' table, she'd stuck her hand out, first to Nick's mom, and then to his dad. His mom looked confused. But his dad—hadn't his dad looked absolutely horrified? Caught off guard? I remember he'd stood up halfway and stayed that way the whole time. He was bright red. She shook his hand so long, it became utterly unbearable, as she gushed about how she'd seen him lecture on computable model theory and how she'd loved it. It'd blown her mind, she'd said. She said she introduced herself to him after class. *Sydney Miller,* she'd said coolly. *You probably don't remember me.* And Nick's dad had stumbled on that. At first, he said he was sorry, it was a long time ago. But then a moment later he said of course he remembered her. Now that I thought about it, though, I don't remember her telling me she introduced herself to Nick Allison's dad after his mind-blowing lecture on computable model theory. She'd told me about the lecture, yes. I remembered very well. I'd pounced on the opportunity to ask questions about Nick's dad. Was he tall? Was he short? Fat? Funny? Hot? She'd seemed totally uninterested, as if she couldn't remember a thing, though it'd just happened.

A couple months later she dropped out of Academic Decathlon. She choked in the semifinals. *Everyone's parents were there,* Nick had said. Syd quit that day. She walked out and never returned. And then she started treating Nick like he had the plague. A month later she set me up with Quinn for prom. When Quinn couldn't make it and Nick stepped in, she was mad. And when Nick didn't show that night, she said she'd texted him, but he hadn't returned her text. But of course, that was a lie.

Everyone's parents were there.

I grabbed Syd's phone and went to the HIM text.

I grabbed my phone and Googled: *Allison Math Department NMSU.* Two taps and there he was: Dr. Samuel Allison, Ph.D., smiling smugly.

Things were falling into place. I tried to stop them. I waited for something to stand out, to make me say to myself: *Stop. See. You're being insane, Encyclopedia Brown.* But I couldn't find a damn thing.

That night at La Posta, I thought Syd was hell-bent on humiliating Nick when really her humiliation was aimed at someone else. *Wanna get tacos at La Posta?* she'd suggested out of nowhere at the party, right after she'd received that last, annoying text.

I looked again at the photo of Dr. Allison, his sleepy eyes and windblown hair.

Half of my mind knew it was ludicrous. I was looking at an old-ass math professor, for crying out loud. The other half knew it was true.

Either way, I had to find out.

I clicked OFFICE HOURS. Tuesdays and Thursdays, 2:30–4:30. Today was Thursday. It was three thirty. If I left my house right now, I could catch him. *Catch him.* It was a terrible notion. There was nothing I wanted to do less than to catch Dr. Samuel Allison doing anything. I still remembered the dread I'd felt at the dinner table on

Christmas, the fear he might at any moment toss me an impossible word problem to solve.

Still, I had to do it. If it was nothing, it was nothing. I'd make something up. *I was just on campus and thought I'd stop by.*

If it was something, though, it was everything. I understood this somewhere deep in my body.

I drove crazy. My father would've killed me. I cruised through a light that had just turned red and thanked god there was never any traffic in Las Cruces. I drove under the highway and past the high school. The parking lot was still half full. There were students hanging out, sitting on the hoods of cars. I longed to be one of them, just a normal teen doing normal teen things. I pressed the accelerator. I passed strip malls and Laundromats and the Baskin-Robbins.

My heart jumped when I heard my phone ding inside my purse. I dug around and grabbed it. It was Nick. He wanted to know what kind of flower I wanted in my corsage. *You're getting one, my lady friend. Even if you don't want one.* I tossed the phone down and winced in shame. Suddenly I screamed at the top of my lungs to relieve the tension. That helped a little. Then I glued my eyes back to the road and drove faster.

The only place by campus I knew I could park was the west end, which was devoted to the corrals and stables and barns of the agricultural school. It smelled bad and was far away, but I knew I could park there without a permit, and I wasn't going to waste time looking for a spot on campus. I pulled off the road and parked haphazardly beside the arena where the rodeo team was out practicing in the cool afternoon sunlight. I jumped out of my car and started huffing it. As I passed the arena, someone blew a whistle and a girl on a fast horse took off, running the barrels at lightning speed. It looked dangerous. I was glad she was wearing a helmet. The horse kicked up a wall of dust as they made their way across the dirt. A bunch of cowboys were hanging over the fence, watching the girl, whooping encouragements at her and the horse. They never even noticed me go by.

The closer I got, the more I felt the fear trying to enter my body. But I wouldn't allow it. I couldn't. Once I got onto campus, I simply stopped thinking. I let the breeze push me past the engineering complex, the administrative buildings, the student union, until I was walking up to the squat, ugly math building. I didn't stop outside. I knew stopping would mean thinking, and thinking wasn't an option, so I flung the glass door open, glanced at the directory on the wall, then made my way down one corridor and into the next. The building was cold and musty. It smelled like math. My sneakers squeaked on the linoleum and I made them stop. I watched the office numbers go up: 116, 118, 120. Dr. Allison was 122. His door was wide open. The hall was ultra-silent, abandoned, lousy with fluorescent light. I could hear my pulse thumping in my neck. I stopped just before I got to his door. I wanted to take the last two steps, but my body wouldn't let me. It demanded I leave the premises immediately. *Just run, dingus,* I could hear Syd saying. *Go!*

But I thought of how she'd called me The Good One. It was time now to be The Good One.

I took the two steps.

He was sitting behind a gigantic desk, reading something, his mouth turned downward in concentration. His desk was a mess. Crammed bookshelves lined the walls. I stood there for a moment, frozen. He looked up without moving his head when he finally sensed me standing there.

"Oh." He was perplexed. "Miranda." I understood immediately I'd made a mistake. I tried to recall the excuse. *I was just on campus.*

But I didn't say anything. I couldn't.

"I'm sorry," he said, looking behind me into the hall. "Is Nick here?"

"No," I said, my voice was shallow, a puddle. "I'm here alone."

"Oh," he said. He blinked.

I tried again to begin the excuse. *I was just on campus.* But instead what came out of my mouth was: "Did you know that I'm Syd's cousin?" I kept my eyes on his.

He blinked again. He turned his head slightly as if trying to hear me better. He gave a smile of confusion. "I'm sorry. Come again?"

He was innocent. It was time for the goddamn excuse. Why couldn't I make it come out of my mouth? My heart was flying and my legs were shaking. But then I noticed his phone sitting beside a stack of folders on his desk. I looked at it for a long time. I looked back at him. And then, as he watched me, dumbfounded, I took my phone out of my pocket. I went to the text thread.

ARE YOU A LIAR? I looked into his confused face and pressed send.

It was an immaculate kind of silence that followed.

Everything was suddenly clear. I was standing in front of my boyfriend's father, acting like a lunatic. I cleared my throat and tried once again. I smiled stupidly. Finally it came. "I was just on campus—"

And that was when it happened.

His text alert was set to an unfortunately humorous duck's quack. He pursed his lips and allowed his eyes to look at it. He looked back at me.

"Would you check that?" I had no idea why, but I maintained total coolness.

He reluctantly tapped his phone. He read the words I'd sent.

"Okay—"

But before he could finish, I'd already typed another message.

LIAR.

Send.

Quack.

"Okay, listen—"

LIAR.

Send.

Quack.

He put up a palm meekly, as if to call a truce. But I couldn't help myself. Fueled by a white-hot rage, I typed it once again. Then I stared him in the face as I pressed send.

Quack.

"I can't discuss this—" he began, all seriousness.

"Oh, no." I couldn't believe how sturdy my voice was. It clearly surprised him as well. "You don't need to talk. I'll talk." He closed his mouth. He entwined his fingers and placed his hands on his desk and stared at them. He looked like a penitent child.

I stepped forward until I was standing at the edge of his desk. It occurred to me I hadn't thought of what I'd say. But that wasn't going to stop me. I took my time. "There is probably only one person in the world I love as much as I love Syd Miller." I swallowed. I was silent. I knew my silence would force him to look up at me. And it worked. He raised his sleepy eyes and squinted at me. "And we both know who that person is."

He heaved a heavy sigh. "What would you like me to do, Miranda?" He sounded impatient and it infuriated me. "I've lost my job. What else can I do?"

"Tell me where she is."

"I don't know that."

"Are you lying?"

"No."

There was no way to tell if he was lying or not. I stepped forward. "I'm going to find her," I said. "Someday. And when I do, if I find out you knew where she was—right now—and didn't tell me, I will destroy you." I was as stunned as he was I'd uttered those words. I saw his jaw twitch and I was happy. If I'd caused him even one moment of suffering, this was all worth it. I understood then what my father had said that afternoon when I asked him what he'd do if I disappeared. *Everything,* he'd said. *Anything.*

I knew now I'd do anything for Syd.

"May I ask what you plan to do with this—information?" Dr. Allison said.

"Anything I want to do," I snapped back.

I took one more look around his office and saw on a high bookshelf behind him a framed photo of Jason and Nick as kids, wearing their Boy Scout uniforms. Nick was probably seven or eight. His curly hair sat wild on top of his head and he held his hands obediently in front of himself. For once, I thought, he'd known what to do with his hands. His smile. It was so pure, so innocent.

I was going to turn then and leave. I should have. But I was emboldened by the photo. I thought of Nick and my dad sitting on the floor on Christmas night, looking over that stupid knife. "One more thing." I looked down on him. "I have a little advice for you. If you ever meet my father—if you're ever even in the same room as my father. *Run.*"

I turned and strode out the door and never looked back. The sound of my footsteps down the hall was unbearable. All the way to the big double doors, I braced myself as if I were walking away from a bomb whose fuse I'd just ignited. I pushed through into the bright afternoon sunlight, then turned and looked over my shoulder. I was sure he'd be there, but he wasn't.

I jogged the whole way back to my car. It became clear what I'd just done. The righteous indignation I'd conjured up in Dr. Allison's office—that great euphoria of justice—began to leave me as quickly as it'd come. Minutes ago I was speaking truth to power. I was settling scores. But as I swung open the door to my car, reality crashed down upon me. I'd just chewed out my boyfriend's father—threatened him, even. And still I was no closer to finding Syd, even if now I could guess at why she'd left. I closed the door and looked out at the arena. The corrals were empty now, entirely so. The horses were gone, put up in their trailers and driven away. I missed the cowboys who'd stood watching their teammate practice, woohooing her speed and her grace.

The car was stifling hot. I was sweating. I tried to slow down my mind. I tried to breathe. I tried to pray. As usual, nothing came. This time, it was more painful than ever. All I wanted was one measly prayer. What had I done to deserve this gigantic nothing? Why had my mother taken this one comfort from me? All I'd ever done was love her. All I'd ever done was worship her as if she were a god. Maybe she was a god! Maybe that was the whole problem. My mother was my god, and when she left, she took everything. She took the whole galaxy with her, the whole universe. She wasn't taking calls. She wasn't coming home. She wasn't even going to send me a stupid birthday card. Even Patience had done that a couple of times over the years.

I punched the steering wheel with the side of my fist. It hurt, but I did it again. Then again. Each time it hurt more. And each time I did it again. I remembered what my dad had said about things being a test. *You come to a point,* he'd said. I was at that point. I knew I'd arrived there. And it filled me sadness to think there might never come a time when I'd pass this test, when I'd acquire whatever skill or talent or magic it would take to forgive my mother for leaving us. To let her go. To forgive Ray and Patience and a world that seemed so dead set against goodness and rightness.

What would you like me to do, Miranda? I felt like I couldn't breathe, or like I didn't want to breathe. I didn't want the responsibility of breath. The world sucked and Syd was gone and Nick was finding holes in the pockets of his tuxedo, oblivious to the fact that everything in his life was about to explode because his dad had had an affair with his girlfriend's best friend, a fact my own brain was still fighting against with all its might, trying to bar the mental images that were trying to get in. Was it possible Syd had kissed that man? Had seen him naked? Had let him touch her? I closed my eyes tightly and demanded my brain stop right there. I couldn't allow it to go any further.

I turned on the car and rolled down the windows. The breeze came rushing in. It smelled heavily of cow shit, but it didn't matter. It was better. It wasn't good. It was nowhere near good. But it was better.

My phone dinged. I reached into my pocket and retrieved it.

It was my dad.

Thinking about LASAGNA. Would you stop for mozzarella, maybe get an onion?

After that, three emojis. One of a shooting star. One of a cow. One of a snowman.

I dropped the phone in my lap and put my hands over my face and sobbed, the sudden rush of tears dripping onto my palms.

How many times would my father save my life without even knowing it?

I took a long, slow breath. I stopped crying. I picked up my phone.

Will mozz it, dude. Sounds super, I wrote back.

I added an emoji of a fish.

I added, *Love ya.*

And then I drove to the grocery store.

15

I couldn't face Nick. I simply couldn't do it. I couldn't tell him the truth and I couldn't keep it a secret. It was an impossible situation. He texted while I was checking out at the grocery store and asked if I wanted to FaceTime French homework. I made a lame excuse. It was excruciating.

Gettin' stoked about da prom, he wrote later that night. I didn't even write back. I kept seeing that photo of him in his Boy Scout uniform, standing next to Jason, that familiar wide smile beaming its innocent light out to the world, his hands clasped in front of him. I couldn't stand it.

I avoided meaningful contact with him all the next morning, too. I was always rushing off to some imagined elsewhere I had to be. The newspaper was in shambles. I had to talk to a teacher. By lunch he was suspicious. "Is something wrong?" he asked while we were walking to the cafeteria together.

"No," I said.

"I think I know what it is."

"What?" I looked into his face. Was it possible he knew?

"You don't want to go to prom."

"Oh. No, that's not it."

"We don't have to go. Really. I pressured you. You don't want to go. What kind of a jerk makes a girl go to prom when she doesn't want to go?"

Prom! It was so insignificant. It was almost funny in its smallness. Charming.

"No," I said. "I want to." I took his hand and gave it a squeeze. "I'm actually getting quite stoked about da prom myself."

But after that, it only got harder to be around him. In each class period I convinced myself I had to tell him. And then each time I saw him, I didn't. I couldn't. After the last class of the day, I went into the bathroom and washed my hands in hot water, trying to scrub away the guilt. I looked myself in the mirror for a long time. I couldn't go on like this. I just had to tell him. I coached myself the whole way to Nick's locker. I told myself I needed to be strong. Solid. I was doing the right thing. Honesty was the right thing.

But when I arrived, I found him standing in the abandoned hallway, staring at his phone. His locker was wide open. His backpack was slung open on the floor beside him. I knew right away the other shoe had dropped. He already knew. His world had exploded while I was busy Lady Macbething it in the bathroom.

"Hey," I said.

He looked up. He blinked. He shoved his phone in his pocket and wiped his palms on his T-shirt.

"Nick?" I said.

"Okay," he said, disoriented.

"What's wrong?" I was the worst actress ever.

He was pale. "Can we go somewhere? Can we go to the ditch?" He didn't wait for me to answer. He slammed his locker and picked up his backpack and started walking. I followed. We didn't speak the whole way. He was furious. Was he furious? I was sure he was going to break up with me. In five more minutes I'd have lost him.

He stopped when we got to the footbridge and let me go over first, then followed behind. There was no real reason to hide at the ditch after class. You didn't need to be invisible then. But when he sat down and leaned his back against the dirt, I sat down beside him. Everything was different since the last time we'd been to the ditch. The fields were thick with green chile, lush and fragrant. Nick brought his palms to his face. He exhaled loudly. "Fuck," I heard him say. I realized it was the first time I'd heard him cuss.

I put a hand on his shoulder.

"My dad lost his job," he said to the ground.

"What?"

"My mom just called. He got fired two weeks ago. He didn't even tell her until today." Nick looked at me, hard. "She called. She told me over the phone." He shook his head.

"What happened?" I asked.

He looked out to the field of chile. Then he looked back at me. "He had—a relationship." He ran both hands through his hair and seemed to force the words out of his mouth. "He had sex with a student. It's happened before. My mom sends him for all this therapy. She's a doctor, you know; she thinks she can fix him. But he can't be fixed. I mean, oh my god. She was his student when they met. It started with her."

"She was?"

"Yes. Of course she was. He's just . . ." He looked up to the sky. He started crying. I waited with dread for him to get to the part about Syd. "It happened at Berkeley. Another undergrad. I remember hearing my parents fight about it. We moved. And then it happened in Chicago. Twice. He's, like, a sex addict. The second time was almost a lawsuit. He was asked to resign. We came here because some friend got him a job. And now it happened here. No charges. But the woman—the girl"—he pursed his lips together and looked at me—"she was really young."

I tried to read his face. Was he trying to tell me something? "Who was the girl?" I had to force myself not to look away.

He swiped away tears. "I don't know. They do. She reported him. There was an investigation. That's why he lost his job."

"Oh." I felt bad, but I was relieved. "God, this sucks. I'm so sorry."

He took a deep breath and exhaled. "At least it's almost over for me. At least I'm almost gone."

All of a sudden, Nick's white boy Harvard problem became very real to me. It was, after all, so fucking complicated. Who'd want to follow that legacy? Who wouldn't want to escape, even if it meant walking into the woods and living with bears?

"Everyone's going to know." He shot me a look. "I don't want anyone to know. I didn't even want to tell you." He put his head down between his legs. I thought he might puke. I remembered what he'd told me that night in the orchard when he was attending to my wound. He told me to keep my eyes on him.

"Look at me, Nick." He looked at me. "It's going be okay."

"No, it's not." He looked away. "I don't want this to be happening."

"Well, it's happening."

He gave me a wounded look. "Thanks."

"No. I didn't mean that. I just mean: this is your life. Maybe this is a sign. That you need to stand up to your parents."

"Are you really saying this right now?"

"Well, I am. Yes. When are you going to tell them about UNM? When are you going to tell them about the Jemez? If that's what you want, why can't you tell them?"

"What does that have to do with anything?"

It felt terrible, like I was kicking Nick when he was already down. But the more he retreated, the more frustrated I became. "I just think you're stronger than you're acting right now."

"Why are you so concerned? It's not your life."

"Why are you so scared?"

"I can't believe you're saying this right now." He put his head between his legs again. It was like he was trying to hide.

"I mean, dude! You have to know about your father's pervert sex life but you can't tell him where you want to go to college? That is fucking ludicrous! It's so stupid!" The long moment of silence that followed only underscored the fact that I'd been shouting. A breeze moved through the fields, wagging the chile peppers on their stems. Nick kept his head down. I felt like an asshole.

"God, I'm sorry." I laid a hand on Nick's shoulder. "I'm sorry. I need to shut up."

"You're right, though." He lifted his head. Then he leaned back against the slope of the ditch and closed his eyes.

"Just tell them. About UNM," I said. "Not because they need to know, but because—you know. It's true. Just tell them you're thinking about it. This is about you, Nick. Not your dad. Just let it be about you for once."

"Yeah." He pressed his palms to his eyes and then looked at me. He smiled meekly. I considered it a triumph.

But did I deserve a triumph? I'd been so busy life coaching, I'd almost forgotten I was the one with the truth that needed telling.

When I looked at him, though, all I could see was that Boy Scout in the photo, with his wild hair and a smile beaming a million megawatts of innocent light out to the world. All I could see was Nick's goodness.

Why did he need to know? Why did Nick need to know it was Syd? Couldn't we just go on with our lives? Couldn't I tell him in a year or two or fifty?

"You're right," he said again plainly. He stood up. "Okay."

"Wait. What?" I said, looking up at him.

"I'm just going to do it." He looked more scared than I did. "You're right."

I wished he'd stop saying I was right. "You don't have your car," I bumbled. "I drove. You want me to drop you off? Or wait in the car?" *Stop making suggestions,* I thought.

"Yeah. Okay," he said. He put on his backpack. I took out my keys. And then we walked silently up the ditch and across the bridge, into the math wing and through the empty halls of the school to the parking lot.

The car ride felt exceptionally short. We passed the bowling alley, the mall, and a thousand strip malls, including the one that housed Desperados and the nail place next door to it. Nick was silent the entire ride. I kept whispering to my brain that there was nothing to be scared of. I wasn't even going inside.

I pulled into the driveway. Nick stared at the garage door as if in a trance.

"I want to come in," I heard myself say.

"Really?" Nick said. *Really?* I thought.

"Yeah. Really. I can help. I want to be there. You know?" I nodded.

"Are you sure?"

"Yes."

And the next thing I knew, I was opening the car door and stepping out. When we got to the front door, I gave him a look of solidarity. He tapped on it and then turned the knob and we walked in. "Hello?"

As soon as we stepped inside, I heard his parents in another room. It was only a second, but I could tell they were arguing.

"Hey," Nick called out. "I'm home."

"In here, Nicky." I blushed a little on Nick's behalf. Under normal circumstances, this was something I could tease him about.

"Miranda's here," Nick said, just as his mom walked into the living room. She lit up with surprise when she saw me standing next to Nick.

"Miranda!" She made a beeline for me and gave me a hug. It made me want to weep. I felt so bad for her all of a sudden. I remembered Nick saying he thought his parents might get a divorce. When he said it, I felt sad. But now I understood. A divorce was just what this woman needed.

"Hi," I said. She smelled good, like lilacs. "You smell good," I blurted out. I was immediately embarrassed.

"Oh, thank you. That's so nice." She leaned forward and touched Nick's arm lightly. They passed a look back and forth to each other. I'd been watching the doorway, knowing any moment Dr. Allison was bound to enter the room. Hadn't he heard us come in? Hadn't he heard me say hi and tell his wife she smelled good? At this point, the fact that he'd not entered the room was uncomfortable. We'd heard his voice when we'd come in. We knew he was there.

"Sam," Nick's mom called. "Nick and Miranda are here."

I felt my stomach seize. His shoes were so heavy on the wooden floor. It took him forever to arrive. I squeezed Nick's hand and he squeezed mine. And then: nothing. Dr. Allison entered the room, aloof as he'd been before, when he was just Nick's weird, snobby dad. "Hello, you two. Nice to see you, Miranda."

"Hi." I must've smiled. I must've smiled the way people who are at the deepest point of being pranked on TV sometimes smile, in total bafflement and with an edge of anger, hostility, and simmering violence. There was something so infuriating about Dr. Allison's performance, something so pathetic, I understood quite suddenly that

I had power over him in this moment. I held this man's life in my clammy hands and he knew it.

"Nice to see you," I said. I refused to take my eyes off him. Was he nervous? I hoped so.

"Can I get you guys anything?" Nick's mom asked.

"No, thanks," I answered before Nick could. I could tell my talking was making Nick nervous. I couldn't tell if it was making him angry. I didn't want to make him angry. No matter how much I hated Dr. Allison, I had to remember the boy I loved was standing beside me doing one of the hardest things he'd ever done.

"You guys excited about the prom?" Nick's mom was trying so hard to keep things from going off the rails. It made me feel tremendous empathy for her.

"Totally," I said.

"Miranda knows what happened," Nick blurted out. "I told her."

I looked up at him and could see how much it cost him to say it. I nodded as if to reassure him, to transmit that I believed in him. When I realized he wasn't going to say anything else, I turned to his father. But I found I had nothing more to say to him. I'd said it all the day before. So I turned to his mom. "Your son is—incredible, as you know." I could feel my voice quaver, but I didn't stop. I didn't even hesitate. "If I were you, I'd do whatever I could to keep him in my life."

I looked at Dr. Allison. His face had changed. He glanced at Nick and then his eyes darted around the room before settling back on me. He looked angry, but I knew deep down he was full of shame. He was rotten with it. At least that was what I told myself. I looked up at Nick.

His face was inscrutable. I felt him release his fingers, disengaging them from my own sweaty palms. My heart fell. "I'm sorry," I whispered to him.

"Here," he said, taking me by the shoulder and walking me back to the front door. "Wait for me in the car, okay?"

"Okay," I said. "I'm sorry."

"Just wait in the car."

"Okay." It felt so weird leaving without saying good-bye to Nick's parents. It was a courtesy my father would have insisted on. But I stumbled out into the bright sunshine and did what Nick asked me to do. I got in the car.

I waited. I put on my seat belt.

I took out my phone and checked the time. A minute passed. Then three. Five. Ten. I rolled down the window because it was hot, but also because I wanted to see if I could hear anything coming from inside the house. I couldn't. I stared out at the lawn, neat and tidy and green. My father would've hated it. *Lawns don't live in the desert.*

I kept thinking of what I'd said, alternately wishing I'd said more and wishing I'd said nothing at all. I thought of Syd and felt a great swell of sadness. I'd have given anything to have her there with me right then. Not because she'd know what to do—I didn't think of Syd that way anymore, as the one who always knew what to do. I just wanted to see her. I missed her.

I was lost in thoughts of Syd when the door flew open and Nick emerged with a backpack slung over his shoulder, the big kind you'd take on a backpacking trip. My eyes must've widened when I saw it, because Nick gave me a sad little smile and raised his eyebrows. He walked around the car, popped the trunk, plunked the backpack inside, then came around the other side and got in.

"What happened?" I asked as I turned on the car.

"I left," he said matter-of-factly.

I eased out of the driveway and onto the street. I looked back at the front door, sure one of his parents would appear at any moment to call out to him. To stop him. But no one came.

"What are you talking about?"

"I told them everything," he said. "I told them about UNM and the Forest Service and that I didn't want to study math and that I wasn't going to Harvard. My dad just sat there. My mom. Oh my god, she's so desperate."

"It's okay, Nick," I said. "It's going to be okay."

He nodded.

"I'm going to text my dad and tell him you're going to stay with us."

"No," he said. "I can stay with Tomás."

"Stay with us," I said. "For tonight, at least."

"Okay," he said. "Thanks." He looked at me. "Thank you for what you said." He ran a hand through his hair. "God, that was so bizarre." He let out a short, stifled laugh. Then he went silent.

"Tell me what happened!"

"Oh." He snapped out of it. "Yeah. So. You left. And I was standing there with my parents. I told them about the Jemez and UNM and I was just thinking, *This is it*. Like: this is it. You know? And my dad did this thing—he's always done it—like, to try to get me on his side, you know, like it's always us against the world. Like we've been wronged and misunderstood and we need to stick together. He said: *Your girlfriend is very opinionated*. And I just, like—laughed in his face. It was so awesome. I wish Jason could've been there. I told them everything. I knew what he'd say. He basically said exactly what I thought he'd say. He told me I was throwing away my gifts. I was making a mistake. Blah, blah, blah. And I listened. Then I just looked him right in the face and I said, 'You're such a hypocrite.'"

"No, you didn't," I said.

"I did," he said. "I did!" He didn't sound happy about it, or sad, just amazed and maybe a little relieved. "I went to my room and packed my bag. I said good-bye to my mom. I told her I'd call later. I couldn't even look at my dad."

I was stunned. "This isn't what I thought would happen."

"I know," he said. "But there wasn't another way. I've been thinking about this for a long time. Before you— before we even moved here."

"Yeah?" I thought again of what my dad had said. Life is a test. *There comes a point.*

"Yeah." Nick laughed again. "Oh my god. I packed the stupidest stuff. I think I packed two pairs of swim trunks. I wasn't even thinking. I grabbed anything. I think I have my Scout's uniform."

"What?"

"I keep it in my camping pack. I realized while I was packing that I hadn't taken it out. So it's in there."

"That's actually kind of funny," I said.

"What did I just do?" Nick said.

"It's gonna be all right," I said, channeling my dad. But not even I believed what I was saying.

16

Nick really had packed the stupidest things. He'd grabbed every pair of underwear he owned, but had no socks. He had a winter scarf and what turned out to be not two but three pairs of swim trunks. But he'd only packed one pair of jeans. Most disappointing to him, he'd left the tuxedo he'd rented for prom hanging in his closet.

"Maybe it's a sign," I said, sitting on my bed, feeling a little discombobulated surrounded by Nick's stuff.

"It's not a sign." Nick was still high on adrenaline. He kept stopping in the middle of sentences to put his hands on his head and laugh maniacally. I imagined it wouldn't last long.

I excused myself to the bathroom and sat on the side of the tub and texted my dad. I told him Nick had a huge fight with his parents and needed a place to stay for the night. *I told him he could stay here. I thought that's what you'd have done.*

My dad wrote back right away. *Sit tight.* I wished he'd followed his text with some baffling emoji, a flamenco dancer or an octopus. It would've helped.

Nick was all over the place. Over the next hour, his mood went from giddy to despairing to furious and had settled on silently stunned. He couldn't believe what he'd done. He checked his phone a few times and seemed more relieved than sad his parents still hadn't contacted him.

When I heard my dad pull up outside, Nick and I were sitting side by side on the couch in the living room, silent, each of us lost in our own galaxy of problems. I didn't know how long it'd been since either of us had spoken. "Oh, I texted my dad," I said absently. "He knows."

"Everything?"

"No. Just that you had a fight with your parents and are spending the night. He said it's fine for you to stay here."

"Oh," Nick said.

"I mean, of course it's fine." I touched Nick's knee. "He was glad."

"Okay," Nick answered from a million miles away.

Thank god for my dad. Predicaments, crises, problems, snags both minor and major: these were so his jam. In the movie where everyone's gathered around some radar screen at NASA, watching the blip representing the imminent end of humanity at the hands of an alien army, he's the guy who leans in very calmly and says something like: *It's now or never, Mr. President.* When I saw the bag of groceries in his hand, I almost burst into tears. My dad was good in a crisis. But he was golden when things could be made even a little bit better by cooking something.

"Jeez," he said when he saw the two of us sitting there. "Nick, I'm really sorry about all this. But listen, I need you to tell your folks you're staying with Miranda and me for the night. You can give them my number if you need to. You can tell them you're sleeping in the guest room. Which you are, by the way. But I need you to tell them you're here."

"Okay." Nick picked up his phone. I was surprised he hadn't resisted, even a little. But then again it was *now or never, Mr. President* time. "Okay," Nick said again after he'd sent the text. He put his phone back on the table.

"Can you help with dinner?" my dad asked. Nick and I looked up, unsure which of us he was addressing. "Nick," he said. "Miranda, can you go down and get the mail?"

"Yes." I was relieved to have one simple action I could complete. And I was glad he'd asked Nick to help with dinner.

It was a beautiful evening, the light like a thick gold net. The sky was losing its blue, and a burst of clouds hung over the mesa, turning pink. As I made my way to the mailbox at the end of the driveway, I thought of Syd. I couldn't help but feel she was more gone to me now than ever. I'd followed clues. I'd come to the end. All I'd found was that Syd was as much a mystery to me now as she ever had been. I knew, too, that for all her coolness and experience and bravado, there was no way she was prepared for whatever had gone down between her and Dr. Allison. Maybe she wasn't as prepared for anything as she pretended to be. It was only after she was gone that I realized how worthy of escape Syd's life had been. Before they'd come here, Ray had dragged her and Patience all over the desert southwest. He'd been a rodeo clown; he'd gone to jail. Then they came here and Patience gave up. She left Syd with Ray like an abandoned pet. Syd made her plan. She lived by it. But maybe she just couldn't wait.

Maybe she had to escape, even before her escape.

For the first time, I considered the very real possibility that I might never see her again. Ever. In a month, high school would be over. I'd go away to college. Even my dad was thinking of moving. Why would Syd ever come back here?

And if I did find her on the internet like I dreamed I would in a year or two, living a new life with new friends, would I even have the courage to contact her? Would our friendship just die? Or had it already? It still felt like a small death. I knew if I never saw Syd again, I'd lose part of myself, too. Part of me would die without her.

I walked back into the house, carrying an armload of magazines and junk mail. In the kitchen I found Nick hunched over a cutting board, awkwardly peeling an onion while my father whacked away, tenderizing some unidentifiable piece of meat. I stood in the doorway and watched the two of them. Nick didn't look up from his onion.

"Hey," my dad said cheerfully while continuing to abuse the meat. He nodded to me without Nick seeing, as if to reassure me everything was going to be okay. I was unconvinced.

"I'm tired," I said, inexplicably. I wasn't tired. If anything, I felt like putting on my shoes and going for a long run, sweating in the dry evening air and watching the sun go down, thinking of exactly nothing but forcing my body to move forward.

"Go lie down." My dad looked up momentarily. "Dinner in about an hour."

"You sure?" I said.

"The men can handle it," my dad said, giving Nick a look.

Nick's attitude had lightened considerably in my father's presence. He smiled at me and returned to wrestling the onion out of its skin. I'd never loved helping my dad in the kitchen, but I'd been forced into it over the years and I knew a few things. For instance, I knew how to peel an onion. Whatever Nick was doing was not working. I watched him another few seconds, until I felt like screaming about his technique, then turned and walked into my room and closed the door. I pulled the curtains closed. I slipped off my shoes and got under the covers with all my clothes on. I stared at the ceiling and felt the weight of everything settle upon me. My whole room smelled like Nick.

I must've fallen asleep, because I woke up disoriented. It was dark and I was sweating. I sat up and reached over and opened the drawer in my bedside table and paused for a moment, not knowing whether to pull out *Lives of the Saints* or Syd's phone, which I'd stashed in there after taking it out of the shoe box. But before I could choose, I heard voices rise in the kitchen. I felt a tremendous grief for Nick, and a tremendous gratitude for my dad. But then I heard music. Loud music. My father was suddenly shouting over R.E.M.'s "It's the End of the World as We Know It (And I Feel Fine)." I flung the covers off and pushed the drawer closed. I opened my door and heard Nick. At first I thought he was crying. Maybe he'd broken down again. But when I walked into the room, he wasn't crying. He was laughing.

"That's what I mean!" my dad shouted. "It's a perfect

song!" I knew this was my dad's favorite song. He'd played it for me a million times, explaining it was the most important song of his generation, the song that spoke most clearly to him. I'd never understood what was so great about it. It was just a stream of nonsense words over annoying music.

"It's so loud," I said. I sounded grumpy and was self-conscious about it. I hadn't checked to see what I looked like in the mirror before stepping out of my room. Now I smoothed my palm against the back of my head. I wondered how long Nick would be staying with us. Would I have to start worrying about how I looked, getting showered and dressed before I saw him in the morning? Would we be giving each other kisses while we brushed our teeth? It started to feel suffocating, and he'd only been here a few hours. The music wasn't helping. Neither were their chipper, buddy-buddy moods. Why the hell were they so chipper? It was the end as the world as I knew it. And they felt fine.

They hadn't heard me and didn't even seem to notice me standing there. They were huddled over my dad's laptop on the counter, presumably Googling inane facts about bad music.

"Hey." I spoke much louder than I had a moment before. The two of them turned to face me. My dad was holding a beer and so was Nick. When I gave him a look of shock, he turned the bottle to show me his was root beer. I felt embarrassed for him.

"It's loud," I said. I noticed the table was set. They'd even put down a tablecloth.

"Sorry, Miry." My dad walked over and turned down

the stereo a negligible amount. "I was just schooling Nick about the greatest song of the 1990s."

"Oh," I said. *This again?* I thought. "What time is it?"

"Eight oh five," my dad said, looking at his watch. "Nick thinks 'Smells Like Teen Spirit' is better than this?"

The song was boring a hole into my brain. I looked at Nick. He had a smile on his face. For some reason, it pissed me off. Wasn't he supposed to be sad? Wasn't he supposed to be freaking out? Why didn't I get to feel super-great and drink root beer? Why did I have to carry this weight on my chest? These two seemed to be celebrating.

My father detected my annoyance. "You okay?"

"Yeah." I tried to feel okay. I offered a tiny smile. "Dude, everyone knows 'Smells Like Teen Spirit' is the only good song from the nineties." I nodded to my dad's laptop. "Google it."

"Et tu, Miranda?" He gripped his chest dramatically. Nick laughed. I rolled my eyes. My dad was looking at me like I'd earned all A's, like he was just so stinking proud of me. It made me squirm. Had Nick told him what I'd said to his parents? Had he told him I was his hero? Did I want to be Nick's hero?

"Dinner's ready," my dad said, moving to the oven and opening it. The enchiladas smelled amazing. I had to admit that. And I was starving. He placed the bubbling casserole on the stovetop and stood for a moment, as he often did, admiring his work. "We were waiting for you."

"Waiting to wake me up with your noise." My dad gave me a sharp, perplexed look. I was embarrassed by my bad mood, but I couldn't help it. How long would Nick be staying here? Had his parents called? What was going to happen next? Weren't these questions that needed to be answered sooner rather than later?

"What's wrong, kiddo?" my father asked.

"Nothing," I said, chastened.

My dad served us in the kitchen and we sat down at the table. Nick bumped the side of my foot with his and I gave him a meager smile. I actively tried to cheer up, to shrug off the weary bad mood I was in, to clear the clouds in my mind and rally. I reached over and took a swig of his root beer. The enchiladas helped. But when Nick and my dad returned to their banter, I felt the quick sizzle of annoyance again. When had Nick ever even mentioned Nirvana, about whom he was now speaking with such enthusiasm? A few weeks ago, when my dad asked Nick what he thought was the greatest rock band of all time, Nick, obviously out of his element, came up with Van Halen. The worst band ever. My father had frowned and said, "We have to fix that."

"This song came out in 1987. It's not even from the nineties." I poked my enchiladas and pouted. The music blared.

"What?" my dad asked, confused.

"This song isn't even from the nineties."

I hated myself.

"How do you know that?"

And then I hated him. "I don't know. Because Wikipedia," I said. "Because you've been talking about it since I was two and I looked it up. And you're wrong."

I looked at my dad. He looked at me. Then he turned to Nick. "Well, if you weren't so damn grumpy, I might be impressed by that." I saw Nick smile a little when my dad said this. How different things were for the two of us. In Nick's house, there was no teasing, no joking. It was a different planet. A cold, weird, lonely planet. Why should I begrudge Nick his share of my father's corniness?

"I'm in a bad mood. Sorry." I let my eyes go from my dad's face to Nick's and back again to my dad's. Though it seemed impossible, "It's the End of the World as We Know It" was still playing. How long was this damn song? Every verse seemed like the last, but then another would start. "Oh my god." I slapped the table. "This song is endless. Maybe what happened is it came out in 1987, but then it took until the nineties to finish playing." I'd caught my dad off guard and he laughed. For once I'd out-teased him.

My dad shook his head. "You two are fools. I feel very bad for you both."

"Whatever, old man," I said. I glanced at Nick. He was enjoying our banter.

"You're both so stupid, you probably don't know this song actually has amazing musical roots." He turned to Nick. "You know Bob Dylan's 'Subterranean Homesick Blues'?"

Nick and I looked at each other, stunned, and then Nick looked down at his enchiladas and began turning completely red.

"What?" My dad looked from Nick to me. "What?"

"Nothing." I actively tried to suppress a smile, but it wasn't working.

"Don't tell me you don't like Dylan." My dad looked to Nick, dismayed.

"No, no," I said, kicking Nick's foot hard under the

table. "Nick's a huge Bob Dylan fan. He did research on him. On the internet." I looked over to see Nick's shoulders shaking with suppressed laughter. It looked painful, and yet it was so good. "He's actually the one who taught me all about him." Nick shot me a desperate look, then looked back at his plate. I relented. "No, we were just talking about him yesterday. That's why it's funny. That you should mention him."

"I don't get what's so funny." My dad turned to Nick. "You know Dylan, or no?"

Nick nodded silently, mortified.

"He knows him!" I said. I tried to stop smiling but couldn't. "I mean yes. Of course. Everyone knows him."

"Dylan's a genius," my dad said. "Bob Dylan changed everything."

"Oh my god!" I said. Nick looked like he was going to die. "Please stop saying Bob Dylan's name!" I cried out.

"What?" My dad looked at me, truly confused. Then he turned to Nick. "What?!"

"Nothing," I said. I breathed. "We all know and respect him. Yes. End of story."

"Well." My dad took a long swig of his beer. "All is not lost then."

Finally "It's the End of the World" ended. "Oh, here," my dad said, hopping up from the table and heading to the stereo. "I'm going to find that Dylan song."

Nick looked at me. "Oh my god," he whispered. Even on his worst day, Nick was still the most adorable person I'd ever know.

"Try to control yourself," I replied.

"Subterranean Homesick Blues" was jangly and mild. No jackhammers.

"I like this song," I said to my dad. He gave me a disbelieving look. "Really."

After dinner, Nick and I did the dishes, then walked back to the living room where my dad was watching a basketball game.

"It's the playoffs," he said as we plopped down on the couch. What he meant by this was the channel was not up for changing. It was basketball or nothing at all.

I tried to care about the game, but I was so uninterested that it was hopeless. By ten o'clock, I was done, even before halftime. I peeled myself from the couch.

"I'm going to bed," I announced. "You guys mind?"

"Get Nick a towel and a washcloth," my dad said, eyes still on the game.

"Okay," I answered. "Hey," I said to Nick. "I'm excited. About tomorrow."

"Yeah, me too." He grinned.

"What's tomorrow?" my dad asked.

"Oh my god," I said to the floor. "Prom. I didn't tell you. We decided to go yesterday."

"It's tomorrow?" My dad peeled his eyes from the TV and looked up at me. "What're you going to wear?"

"I have my dress. From last year." Even mentioning the dress made my stomach squeeze tight. It was possible I'd developed a full-blown phobia. I still hadn't laid eyes on it since I took it off my sad body that night and hung it in the back of my closet.

"Oh," my father said. He looked at Nick, then at me. "That's great."

"Yeah, I can't wait." Nick rubbed his palms self-consciously on his jeans.

"You have a tux?" my dad asked Nick. "Do boys wear tuxes now?"

Nick smiled at me. "I left it in my closet."

"He does have three pairs of swimming trunks, though," I said.

"We can figure it out," my dad said. "I can loan you a suit," he said.

"No," I said emphatically. "I'm sorry, but you are not wearing my father's suit to prom. We'll figure something else out." I didn't know what else there was to figure out, but I didn't want to think about it. "Tomorrow," I said.

"Tomorrow," Nick said. I felt bad for having been so grumpy before, and for crapping out now, at ten o'clock.

"All right," I said. "See you guys in the morning."

"Night," my dad said.

"Good night," Nick said.

I moved Nick's stuff into the guest room and put sheets on the futon in there. I left a neatly folded towel and wash-cloth next to his giant backpack, along with a Beanie Baby elephant I found on one of the shelves. How strange, I thought, that Nick would be sleeping down the hall from my bed tonight, surrounded by the detritus of my child-hood. There was a photo of my dad and me hiking in the Organ Mountains. There was one of Letty and Luciana and me sitting on the plaza in Santa Fe, looking exhausted and happy after a day of shopping. Luciana was three. She was sitting on my lap, looking up at my face rather than at the camera. We looked like we could be sisters. Next to that was a school photo of me from the third grade. I don't know why my father had framed it. It made me think of the terrible time after my mom left. For a while my dad said she might come back. But there came a point—I didn't know what happened or what changed, probably something I didn't know about—when he started telling me the truth. She wasn't coming back. She'd stopped responding to the efforts Benny and he made to communicate with her. The Garden was really good at being a cult. Everyone on the inside was protected from everyone on the outside. All of us who wanted our people back. I stood looking at that school photo for a long time. Then I grabbed it, put it facedown on the shelf, and moved the one of Letty and Luciana and me in front of it.

I washed my face and brushed my teeth. I cleaned the sink before I went to my room. Before I put on my pajamas, I opened my closet and reached back and pulled forth the zipped garment bag. I grasped the zipper and opened it a little. I saw the green dress peeking out from inside. I put my hand in and touched the soft fabric. I remembered trying it on. I'd turned to look at myself in the three-way mirror at Dillard's while Syd sat on the floor, her back against the wall. *Your boobies are defying gravity,* she'd said. Then she'd gone back to looking at her phone. Was she texting HIM then? Was she congratulating herself for having cut me off at the pass, setting me up with Quinn Johnson before I could ask Nick?

I heard Nick and my dad in the kitchen. They'd moved on to the Beastie Boys, and my dad was now extoling the virtues of each individual Beastie. "You know all three of them came to be real feminists," he said while the song "Girls" was playing.

"That's cool," Nick replied eagerly.

I zipped the bag up and put it back in my closet. I

couldn't do it. Not tonight. I hung it front and center and considered that progress. I found the strappy gold heels I'd bought to go with it and laid them on the floor of the closet directly beneath the garment bag.

I promised myself I'd try the dress on in the morning. First thing, before I could talk myself out of it.

I got in bed and tried to sleep, but something wasn't right.

I got out of bed and closed the closet door.

That was better.

17

I woke to the front door creaking open and then closing quietly. It was my dad heading out for a Saturday morning run. Most Saturdays I'd accompany him—we'd argue about whether we should do five or six miles, and we'd end up doing seven because we were both too proud and stubborn. I guess he decided to let me sleep this morning. I sat up, groggy, and stared at the closed closet door. I promised myself I'd try on the dress first thing in the morning. And it was, undeniably, the morning.

I slipped out of my pajamas, opened the closet, took out the garment bag, and tossed it onto the bed. In one quick motion, I unzipped it and then reached down and lifted the dress carefully off the hanger. Boom. Done. I was holding it. And god. It was gorgeous. It was even more gorgeous than I remembered it being. I unzipped the side zipper and stepped in. I held the top up with one hand while I zipped the side with the other. Then I leaned forward and adjusted my boobs.

It fit perfectly.

I stepped in front of the mirror.

My boobies were defying gravity.

I looked at myself from one side, then the other. I grabbed the gold shoes and slipped them on. I looked kind of awesome. I had to admit. In the space between my shoes and the dress's hem I could see the scar on my ankle from the night I snuck out my window to meet Nick in the orchard. It was astounding how much had changed since the last time I'd worn this dress and since Syd had gone. Just a few months ago my favorite occupation was sitting in a graveyard, watching traffic on the highway, and crushing on a boy I thought hated me, who wouldn't even look at me when we passed in the hall. I was content to observe him from afar, obsessively gauging whether it was allergies or a cold that was making him sneeze, putting together theories about where he'd gotten the hair tie he was wearing the morning he walked into French with his hair pulled back in a ponytail. That was my whole life back then. My whole life was watching things from afar. It was so small, so insignificant, a thing to be seen out of the corner of a stranger's eye from a car going eighty. How could it be that that boy was here now, in my house, asleep down the hall with a backpack full of underpants?

I had to admit, he was right. Nick was right. We had won. Against great odds, we'd fallen in love. We'd changed everything, and we'd both been changed. I felt light and floaty standing there in my dress. I tried to identify the feeling and was shocked to realize it was happiness.

I grabbed my phone from the windowsill and texted Nick. *Awake?*

Sniffing ur stuffed animals.

Wanna see something cool?

Y.

I flung open my door and click-clacked down the tile in my heels, but before I even knocked, he called out, "What's that sound?" I heard him grab the doorknob.

"What sound?" I said.

"You're wearing your dress, aren't you? That's what you want to show me?"

"Yes." I stood back so he could get the full view. "Open."

"No." He turned the lock on the door. "Not until tonight."

"What? That's so dumb."

"It's not. Where's your dad?"

"Running," I said to the door. "Hey, what are you wearing in there?" I tapped my fingertips gently against the wood.

"Jeans."

"That's all?" My breath quickened.

"Saint George, too," he said. "You can't come in. No girls allowed. George and I are very serious about this." I could hear he'd gotten closer to the door too. I imagined his heart was only about a half a foot from mine.

"This is really dumb." I leaned against the doorjamb. "But okay."

"Hey, my mom called," he said.

"Really?" I'd been so caught up in the dress and winning and love and happiness, I'd almost forgotten that everything was still total shit. And that Nick didn't even know the whole story. The weight of it returned. "When? What'd she say?"

"She wants to talk. She said she was sorry."

"For what?"

"I dunno. My dad, I guess."

"Hey, Nick." It was a singularly bad idea—I knew it was—but I had the sudden notion that I might be able to tell Nick about Syd like this. From behind a closed door, without having to look into his eyes and see the Boy Scout in the picture. And wouldn't it be better that way? If we could go forward with no secrets between us?

"I need to tell you something." I swallowed. "I've been trying to tell you for two days." I summoned courage. I put my forehead on the door. "It's about your dad." I took one gigantic breath, made fists of my hands. But before I could get it out, Nick spoke.

"About Syd?" His voice was very loud through the door.

"What?" I said.

"I know," he said. "I've known."

"Your dad told you?"

"No. I saw a document, something from my dad's lawyer, something my dad was submitting for the investigation. Evidence or something. Saying the complainant made threatening phone calls to our house from a number in Colorado. It was Syd's name. It said she'd—"

"When?" I barked at the door.

"What?"

"When did she call?" My focus tightened frighteningly. The world became tiny.

"I don't know. Three months ago."

"When did you find it?"

There was a long pause. "About a month ago."

My heart dropped. I took a step back, repulsed. Then I stepped forward again and did the first and only thing I could think of doing. I kicked the door, hard. It hurt.

"What the hell?" he said. I did it again, only harder. "What the hell, Miranda?" He was lucky we weren't face-to-face. I might've punched him.

"You've known for a month where Syd is?" My voice echoed in the hallway.

"I don't know where she is."

"A number in Colorado. Really, Nick? I thought you were supposed to be so fucking smart. You don't know where Colorado is?"

"They came from a Wendy's. She was probably just passing through."

"What town?"

"What?" That he didn't seem willing or able to keep up infuriated me.

"Jesus! Where in Colorado?"

"I don't know. I can't remember. It started with—"

"Alamosa?"

"Yeah," he said. "That's it."

I felt like I was moving underwater. Everything was happening so slowly, and my foot ached, and I was wearing a prom dress, and Nick was on the other side of a locked door, saying the most insane things and breaking my heart. "You lied to me, Nick."

"I didn't lie."

"Yesterday!" I yelled it loud and furious. It filled up the whole house. "I asked you who the girl was and you said you didn't know."

"But you knew too. Didn't you?" He was angry. And he had a point. I did know yesterday. But it wasn't a good enough point. I heard the doorknob turn. "I'm opening the door. This is stupid."

I grabbed it. "No," I said, pulling it shut again. "You've

known for a month! I've known for—two days. And I had
to find out by catfishing your stupid fucking dad. I went
to his office, Nick!"

"What?"

I plowed ahead. "And I'm telling you this right now
because I couldn't look at you one more second knowing
I was keeping it from you. But I guess you don't have the
same problem."

Nick was silent. "I didn't want to know. I didn't want
it to be happening. I didn't tell you because I thought if
you knew about my dad—"

"Stop." I tried to cool my head but couldn't. "God.
Nick. I believed in you. I believed you were good. And
brave. And honest. When I told you that you weren't like
anyone I'd ever met, I meant it." Tears tried to come.
I willed them to stop. "Was I wrong?"

There was nothing. Only silence.

"Nick?"

I heard him take his hand off the doorknob. He'd answered me. He'd answered me in silence. And I didn't
have time for silence.

"Do you know anything else that you haven't told
me?"

"No." He sounded defeated. Again, there was a long
silence. "Can we just talk without this door between us?"

"We'll talk later." It was a lie, of course. I already knew
later I'd be gone.

"I thought I was doing the right thing. Please. Can we
just talk? Now?"

I stood back and took a snapshot in my mind of the
morning sunlight on the tile in the hallway and the closed

door and the new scuff marks I'd made when I'd kicked the door with my gold shoe. I needed to remember this moment—to keep it. Because the chances were very high I'd look back and remember this as the very last moment I spent in love with Nick Allison, maybe the last time I'd ever even speak to him.

"Let me just go change my clothes," I said. "I'll be right back."

I turned and clicked down the hall and into my bedroom. I opened the bedside drawer, grabbed Syd's phone and her letter from Stanford, a coin purse I knew contained at least a hundred dollars, and the letter Patience had sent me with her address on it. I grabbed the first two articles of clothing I saw—a pair of running pants slung over a chair and my R.E.M. T-shirt off the floor—and shoved them into my bag. Then I reached into the drawer again and grabbed *Lives of the Saints* and threw it in, along with the phone and the letter and the cash. I worked fast. There was no thinking. All my decisions had been made. There were no decisions. I was on autopilot. It was so easy.

I found my keys in my purse. I walked out of my bedroom and down the hall to the front door and then out to my car. I swung open the door and got in and turned it on and backed out of the gravel and onto the road.

And I just started driving.

Before I even knew what I was doing, I was a mile away. Then two. Then I was getting on the highway. And then I was gone. I took out the letter with Patience's address and typed it into the map on my phone. I glanced at the distance and the time it'd take to get there. Six and a half hours. I didn't know if that was near or far or a long time or a short time. I only knew that I would be there, at Patience's doorstep, in six and a half hours.

I put my phone and Syd's in the console under the radio. I wouldn't need the map until I got to Albuquerque in a few hours. I'd never driven to Albuquerque by myself. I'd never driven anywhere outside Las Cruces, really. But I knew how to get there: you went north on I-25. There wasn't even another direction. I-25 ended in Las Cruces. You could only go up.

My one regret was that I hadn't left a note or anything for my dad. He wouldn't know where I was until I texted to let him know. And I didn't want to text him, not yet. All I wanted to do was drive. So that was what I did.

At 8:15 A.M. I passed Hatch and by 9:00 P.M. I was approaching Truth or Consequences. My dad should've come home from his run by now. But he hadn't called or texted. Maybe he'd seen someone while he was out running and got caught up in a conversation. My father couldn't pass up a chat with one of the little old ladies who walked the ditches in the morning. His *viejitas*. Or maybe he hadn't noticed my car was gone. Maybe Nick hadn't told him I went to change my clothes and never came back. It didn't matter. I considered it lucky and I pushed him out of mind, along with everything else—Nick and the hallway and my freshly broken heart. I pushed it all out and focused solely on the highway and the little towns hanging off the side of it, down in the river valley, so peaceful from this distance.

But the farther away I got, the more difficult it became to deny Nick could've been right. Syd had been in Alamosa three months ago. There was no way of knowing if she was still there. She could've just been passing through. She could've stopped to see her mom on the way to somewhere else. She hadn't been there a week after she disappeared, when Patience wrote me back. She'd been somewhere else then, and she could have gone on to somewhere else in the last three months. But I wouldn't let that stop me either. In fact, every time the thought occurred, I pressed harder on the accelerator in protest. It was too late to turn around now. I was nearly to Socorro. I was probably only an hour and a half away from Albuquerque. I reached for my phone to check the distance and the damn thing rang in my hand.

My heart splattered on the windshield like a bug.

It was my dad.

I knew there were patches of I-25 with no cell phone reception. Lots. I could theoretically be going through one of those right now. *NO SERVICE.* Sorry, missed your call. But I'd made one bad choice in leaving without telling him. I allowed myself that one bad choice. From here on out, I only had good ones left.

"Hi." I tried to sound calm and sorry.

"What the hell's going on, Miranda? Where are you?" His voice was a freight train busting into the side of my quiet morning, blowing it to bits.

"I'm pulled over on the side of the road. Outside of Socorro. Did Nick tell you I left?"

"Of course he did. Jesus Christ. Socorro? And why are you pulled over? What's wrong?"

"I'm just—I pulled over to talk to you." I hadn't actually pulled over, but now I felt guilty for lying and began easing my car to the shoulder. I went over the very loud rumble strips and was sure my dad could hear it.

"I honestly don't know what to say to you, Miranda."

"I know. I'm sorry, Dad. I'm sorry. But I know where she is."

"No." He was silent for three seconds. "I'm getting in the car. Stay where you are. You stay right there."

I'd expected my father to be upset, but I hadn't expected him to stop me now. "No," I said plainly. "I'm going to find Syd. I'm not a kid, Dad."

"You are a kid! You're my kid, and I'm telling you to sit your ass in that car and wait for me."

"This is why I didn't tell you I was leaving."

"Oh, don't give me that horseshit. Don't turn this into a referendum on my parenting. You snuck out and you lied. And now you're god knows where and—and where are you planning on sleeping tonight, by the way?"

"I'm coming home. After."

"Don't be stupid, Miranda! You can't drive to Colorado and back in a day."

"Yes, I can."

"Oh Christ. And if you can't? You're not thinking."

"I'll get a hotel. I have cash."

"You can't rent a hotel room! You're seventeen years old!"

I didn't know you needed to be a certain age to rent a hotel room. But I wasn't going to let this detail stop me. "I'm coming home tonight. Or I'll stay with Syd." I rolled my eyes at my own foolishness while I said it.

"Oh, now that's fucking brilliant." I heard his heavy footsteps on the gravel. I heard the *beep-beep* his truck made when he unlocked the doors. He was on his way.

"What are you doing?" I tried to keep calm.

"I'm getting in the goddamn car and I'm coming to get you."

"Please don't."

"No, sorry, Miranda. You lost the privilege of suggesting what I should and shouldn't do when you left the house this morning."

"Listen. Will you just listen to me for a second?"

"No. I won't. That's how angry I am right now. I will not listen to you. Hold on two seconds." I heard the sounds of the inside of his car. It was much longer than two seconds. In that time I tried to come up with a good argument, but I couldn't. I'd lost.

"Are you there?" He was back, speaking a little more calmly.

"Yes," I answered.

"There's a rest stop before Socorro—it's that big wooden one; we've stopped there. The one with the rattlesnake signs. Drive there. Lock your doors and wait for me. This is what is happening. I'll be there in less than two hours. Do you understand me?"

I couldn't find any other protest, sitting there in the car in my prom dress as the semis sped past me. I was burning with anger at my dad, at Nick, at Syd. "Fine." I didn't care if he could hear me crying. He'd won. I'd lost. It didn't matter anymore.

"All right." My dad was silent. "I love you, Miranda. You know I love you more than anything in this world. But goddamn, this is the stupidest thing you've ever done."

"Okay, thanks. Great. Thanks so much," I said. "That's just wonderful."

"I'm sorry. I didn't mean that. Just get to the rest stop. I'm checking my phone. It's exit one fourteen. What mile marker are you at?"

I could see the next mile marker in the distance. "One oh three."

"Great. Good. You're close. Drive eleven miles and you'll be there."

I can do math, I thought to myself. "Bye," I said heavily.

"See you in a while."

I felt like I'd sprung four flat tires. How had that conversation gone so badly? I'd been blown away by my father like a leaf in a strong wind. *See you in a while.* If Syd had been with me, she'd have face-palmed. *Nice,* she'd say. *You should be a lawyer.* There was nothing to do but drive the eleven miles. I waited for a semi to pass, then I eased back over the rumble strips and onto the highway.

I found as I passed each mile marker, my anger increased and my fear decreased. It was a formula, an equation, a natural law being proven inside my body. When the big wooden rest stop appeared in the far distance at the side of the road, looming like a great monument to failure, with its giant signs warning in many languages about the lurking danger of rattlesnakes, I put on my blinker.

But as I approached the exit, I couldn't do it. I couldn't stop. I reached into my bag and took out *Lives of the Saints* and let the book open to where the spine was broken on Saint Jude. I looked at my mother's writing, the stars she'd written around the words *Patron saint of the IMPOSSIBLE!*

I laid the open book on the passenger seat. The little flame over Jude's head flickered. I reached the exit. I pressed my golden toe to the pedal.

18

As soon as I passed the rest stop, I freaked. I didn't know what to do. I pulled over and grabbed my phone. I looked at it for a long time. It felt like a weapon now, evidence I'd need to get rid of. I knew I needed to call my dad. I needed to say, *No. I'm going. Turn around and go home.* But talking to my dad hadn't worked out well a few minutes ago. I considered turning my phone off and not turning it back on again until after I'd seen Syd—if I did see Syd. My dad could just wait. But I couldn't do that, either. He'd lose his mind.

I texted Nick instead. *Will you call my dad?* 575-555-6552. *Tell him I'll be home tonight. I'm turning my phone off. Tell him that, too.* I pressed send. I considered sending another text saying something to Nick. But I couldn't think of anything to say to Nick. I tapped on the map and noted the next highway exchange happened outside of Santa Fe. I could remember that. I turned my phone off and put it in the glove box to keep it out of sight. Then I chucked Syd's phone in there too. I looked down at the book. Ryan Gosling Saint Jude looked serene and thoughtful.

I flipped the page and went to the last paragraph and I drove, my eye moving from the highway to the book and back again. I couldn't remember how Jude had been martyred. It suddenly seemed like very important information. *In Beirut . . . along with Simon the Zealot . . . by ax.*

I flipped the page back.

Hey, girl, it's gonna be all right, Jude seemed to say.

I noted I wasn't crying; I wasn't even close.

I gripped the steering wheel and got back on the highway.

I kept reminding myself to loosen my grip on the steering wheel. I was giving myself blisters. By the time I reached Albuquerque, I'd left reality. I was living in a sci-fi novel, driving into some postapocalyptic dust bowl city, searching for signs of life. And I was wearing my prom dress. This detail hadn't been lost on me over the last three hours. I kept rolling down the windows and lifting my arms to keep the flop sweat from ruining the fabric. I hadn't brushed my teeth or washed my face before I drove off. I guess part of me believed there was no way I'd actually go through with what I was doing right now. Part of me thought I'd drive around the block, cool down, and go home, change clothes, and talk to Nick. But that was not what happened. This was what happened. And now I needed to pee. Bad. I'd passed loads of gas stations, but the fear that somehow my father would catch up to me if I stopped for three minutes kept me from pulling off the interstate. Now I had to *piss like a racehorse*, as Syd would say.

When I reached Albuquerque, I took the exit toward Central Avenue and followed it until I came to a gas station directly across from the UNM campus. I'd been to this gas station before, just earlier this year, when my dad dragged me to see Neil deGrasse Tyson speak on campus at Popejoy Hall. We filled up here before we headed home. I was relatively certain this wasn't the one and only gas station in the city of Albuquerque, but it was the only one I knew, and so I went out of my way to find it.

"Fill up on pump three." I slapped the bills down. The guy behind the counter looked me up and down with apprehension. He was a man who didn't like funny business and wanted to know whether or not I was up to it. Before he could come to any conclusions, I turned and headed back outside, my dress billowing behind me. "Pump three," I repeated as I pushed through the door and the bells jingled.

Outside, no one gave me a glance. Granted, there was no one else getting gas. But there were plenty of passersby. And not a single one of them gave me a look. It felt good to be anonymous. If I'd gone to any gas station in Las Cruces in a prom dress at noon, everyone would know about it by one. By two the old lady at La Cocina would be genuflecting at the sound of my name. Here in the big city, I felt like an adult. I was free. Across the street, at the entrance to the university, there was a big bronze statue of a wolf perched on a boulder, her head down as if about to pounce. UNIVERSITY OF NEW MEXICO LOBOS, the sign beneath it read. The wolf was eyeing me, fierce and unafraid. I tried to internalize her gaze, to own it for myself, and for Syd.

I grabbed my running pants and T-shirt from the passenger seat and swished back inside to collect my change and use the bathroom. I asked the guy behind the counter if he had a map of Colorado. He laughed. He didn't carry maps. No one carried maps anymore. "Don't you have GPS?"

I sauntered to the bathroom. It was revolting and closet-sized and the walls were covered in graffiti and yuck. There were no hooks, and there was no way I was putting anything down on the disgusting floor. So I put my purse on my shoulder, hitched up my dress and slung it over my head, and squatted there, peeing for so long, it became comical. If Syd could've seen me now, she'd have loved it. I watched myself in the filthy mirror as I washed my hands. Then I commenced taking off my prom dress, trying to keep it from touching the floor while at the same time wearing my purse and putting on running pants over my high heels. (Though I'd intuited a need for *Lives of the Saints* on the way out, I hadn't thought to grab shoes.) All in all, it was a circus act. It took at least ten minutes. When I walked back into the store with my dress over my arm, wearing running pants, a T-shirt, and heels, the man gave me a disapproving look. My status as a fishy person had been confirmed.

I kept my head up and grabbed two bottles of water, a bag of almonds, and a troubled-looking banana. I took my items to the counter and made sure to look directly at the man while he rang me up so he'd know I was in charge. I was a lobo. I was fierce.

When I got back to my car, I carefully draped my dress

over the passenger seat. I opened my glove box and rooted around for the map of New Mexico my dad insisted I keep in there (just in case), the one Syd had made fun of me for having. Thankfully, the map's detail extended into the southernmost part of Colorado. I found the route I'd need to take to get as far as Alamosa. Once I got there, I'd worry about how to get to Patience's.

I eased back onto Central and then back onto the highway. The traffic was heavier and there was a snarl of interstate exchanges to get through. Then I nearly missed the exit to get on Route 84 at Santa Fe. But once I made it through Santa Fe, I relaxed a little. I was doing a good job keeping my father, and Nick, off my mind, though every once in a while I saw the closed door, or the rest stop receding in my rearview mirror, and felt awful. When I thought of what I'd said to Nick this morning, I felt worse. I hadn't even heard him out. I hadn't even begun to imagine what I'd have done if I were in his position. *I didn't want to know. I didn't want it to be happening.* And then I'd done exactly what I'd accused him of doing. I lied. I said I was going to change my clothes so we could talk things over. And I left. Now I was four hours from home. I might not even make it back to Las Cruces until morning. I was standing him up for prom. Again. For real this time.

I had to push him out of my mind. If there was anything that would make me stop and turn around, it was Nick. I could surrender, for him.

And I couldn't surrender. Not now. I just had to keep driving.

———

After Santa Fe, the landscape changed. The stark, sun-blanched desert became red earth dotted with lush piñon. I rolled down my windows and let the cool air in. Only when I heard it whipping through my car did I notice I'd driven the entire time in silence. No music. Nothing.

It felt right. Silence was right. The world was gigantic here: mesas upon mesas, stretching across the entire horizon. They went on forever. I looked down at Saint Jude, his impassive face. He was unimpressed. But not me.

Eternity, I thought.

I'd driven to eternity in gold heels.

It was so perfect, it was miserable.

19

Alamosa was small and flat. For some reason, I had the idea I'd cross the state line into Colorado and immediately run into a Rocky Mountain. But Alamosa was in a great valley. Like Las Cruces, it was all agriculture. In the far distance the Rockies sloped, green and huge and glorious. I pulled off the highway into a Walmart parking lot. The Walmart was hopping on a Saturday afternoon. For a moment I sat watching people come and go. It felt good to be in the land of the living, even if it was just Walmart.

I knew the only real way to find Patience's trailer was using my phone, so I set a rule: when I turned it on, I wouldn't check to see how many phone calls I'd missed, how many voice mails, how many texts. I'd use the map and nothing else.

But, of course, the second my phone came back to life, I couldn't resist checking. I saw I had seven missed calls and twenty-two texts. Ugh. That was all I could think. *Ugh.* I resisted looking to see who'd called and written. I assumed all the messages were from my dad and Nick.

Maybe Letty, if my dad had told her what I'd done. I felt heavy again with guilt.

The road to Patience's trailer turned out to be less than a mile from the Walmart. I pulled back onto the road and followed the electronic lady's directions very carefully, listening for each one with a solitary focus. My stomach was one big cramp. All I'd eaten all day was a few almonds and a bottle of water. The banana languished on the seat next to Saint Jude. In the last few hours, it'd died.

Far too soon, I was turning off the paved road and onto a thin dirt one. A sign made of plywood stuck on a telephone pole read LEO LANE in black paint. This was it, the address from the birthday cards. I steeled myself. But then, as I started going down the road, there didn't seem to be anything on it. Not a thing. Just crops. It was a road to nowhere. I was certain I should turn around, but the road curved and I could see in the distance a yellowish trailer with a dirt lot in front. Behind it, a field of onions. Alfalfa on all the other sides. As I approached, I saw the trailer had no yard. It was just overgrown weeds and then the onions, ready to be picked, the golden skins pushing up out of the dirt. Three dangerous-looking steps led to a warped front door. There was no railing, no porch, no mailbox, and there were no cars in the driveway.

The trailer looked abandoned.

"Shit," I said to my car. I parked on the side of the road. When I turned my car off, everything went silent. I told myself the absence of a car and a few weeds didn't mean no one lived here. I got out and walked to the trailer. My dumb, high-heeled footsteps in the dirt were the only sounds happening on Earth. I climbed the three rickety steps and knocked. The door was thin, made of aluminum. I probably could've pulled the whole thing off the hinges if I wanted to. My knocks were sucked back into the silence of the day. There was no answer. I checked: it was locked. The blinds were down in the windows. I had no idea what to do.

I walked to my car and grabbed my phone and tapped it to see the time. The alfalfa across the road waved in the breeze. It seemed the alfalfa went on forever down the road, all the way to the mountains. I tossed the phone back to the seat.

My father was right. This was a monumentally stupid plan. In fact, it wasn't a plan at all. It was just me, driving off, leaving a scorched path in my wake. I looked at the sky and thought of Nick. *I thought I was doing the right thing.* I pressed my eyes shut to keep the tears from coming. The sky was huge and blue and the few balloony clouds against it looked out of place. They were stupid too. I wished I could travel back in time. Maybe I could've talked Nick into opening the door before everything had been ruined. I could've gone in, pressed my cheek to his chest bone, felt his warm skin and his smell—all salt and forest and boy. *We won,* I could've said.

What was I doing here?

I looked in at the clock again: 1:50. The next time I looked up, a jet had sliced the sky cleanly in two with a sharp white contrail. I watched the jet disappear into the blue, then watched the contrail widen slowly, then dissipate, then vanish, until the sky was one whole thing again. My feet hurt. I opened the door to my car and got back inside. It was two o'clock. It was decision time. I was either staying here as long as it took on the off chance Syd would show up, or I was driving home right now and begging the forgiveness of my father and Nick.

If I left right now, I might even make it back in time for part of prom. If I left right now, there was still a very small chance everything might be okay. Saveable.

I looked over at Ryan Gosling Saint Jude. He had no advice.

Hey, girl, his serene eyes said. *Don't ask me.*

I didn't need advice, anyway.

I was staying. I needed to talk to Syd. I needed to see her, to know that she was alive, that she had existed.

I folded my arms and waited. I didn't think a single thought or have a single emotion. I must've dozed off. I woke when I suddenly heard car tires on gravel and turned to see a car coming down the road. I was sure it hadn't been more than fifteen minutes, but when I looked at the clock, it was 3:03.

There, I thought. *It's official.* I'd stood Nick up. Again. I'd treated him like crap the morning after the worst day of his life. He'd never forgive me, and he'd have every reason not to. Inside me, something broke cleanly. *Snap.* Done.

But I had to put that aside. Because holy crap. It was Syd's car pulling into the dirt space in front of the trailer. I could see the top of her head over the seat back, her wild curls pulled back.

Syd was alive. She was real. She existed.

I opened my door and walked to the car and looked in. She was sitting stone-faced, staring out the windshield. She was wearing a Wendy's uniform. She turned to look at me. She looked down at my shoes. She looked at my face. Then she swung the door open and got out of the car and stood there. She looked so tired. Her hair was barely contained in a thick ponytail. Her name tag read WELCOME TO WENDY'S. I'M SYDNEY.

"Hi," I said. I resisted an urge to throw my arms around her.

She stood with her mouth shut and her arms crossed. She looked at me as if I were a door-to-door salesperson. She was being polite, waiting for me to talk for thirty seconds so she could say she wasn't interested and then go inside. "What are you doing here?" she asked.

Though I'd been hurling myself toward this conversation at eighty-five miles per hour all day, pursuing it at the expense of all the good things in my life, now that it was actually happening, I found I had no idea what I was doing here.

"I have your phone," I came up with finally.

When she didn't say anything, I walked to my car and opened the door and grabbed her phone and the Stanford letter. She watched me walk back in my heels. Without expending a single facial expression, she made it clear she believed I was the single most ridiculous person alive.

I held the phone and the letter out to her. She glanced at the Stanford letter and then folded it in three and shoved it into the pocket of her khakis. She slipped the phone into the other pocket. "Okay," she said, as if everything were taken care of.

"Okay." I tried to find something else to say. I didn't want to start with Stanford or Dr. Allison or the fact that she disappeared four months ago without a trace and how I'd like some answers as to why she'd done that. "How's your mom?"

She snorted in disbelief, as if I'd asked a really insen-

sitive question. "She's a mess." She made a gesture toward the dilapidated trailer. "She's not here." Her mouth
shut and she commenced looking at me with the same
deep lack of interest.

I wanted so badly to feel sympathy for Syd. I'd found
sympathy for her even after I found out she'd lied to me
for months about Nick. But standing here in front of her,
feeling her indifference pouring onto me like smoke, I felt
a gigantic anger well up inside me. I'd risked everything—
Nick would never forgive me, and my father would never
trust me again—and she'd be happy ending our conversation right now and never seeing me again as long as she
lived.

"I think Ray reported your car stolen," I said. "FYI."

"Okay," she answered sternly. "I'll figure it out."

I waited to see if she'd say anything else, but she didn't.

"I'm glad you're okay." I swallowed.

She snorted again. I noticed that each time she'd made
the little snort, I felt like punching her. "Thanks," she said
flatly.

"I guess I'll go then."

"Okay." She straightened. Her gaze went past me,
following the alfalfa to the distant mountains.

"Wow." I looked at my shoes. "That's it? Just *see ya,
wouldn't wanna be ya*? After everything?"

"Everything?" I saw her face redden. "You don't even
know what you're talking about, Miranda. Just get back
in your car and drive home. To your dad."

A few months ago I'd have died from the look she was
giving me. *Died.* But not now. Not today. I took a step forward. Then another. Then, unbelievably, I took another,

until I was standing inches away from her. I could hear her breathing.

"I came here to help you." It came out sounding like a threat.

She puffed up. "I don't need your help."

"Well, good," I said. I wanted to push her—that was what my body wanted to do. I straightened my arms at my sides to keep it from happening. "Great."

I turned and walked to my car, my legs shaking beneath me, my brain on fire. I flung the door open. My phone was lit up on the seat. My dad was calling. Of course. Perfect. I grabbed it and turned it to silent.

"Wait." Her voice was like a slap in the face.

"What?" I yelled. "You wanna insult me some more? No, thanks."

"Just wait a minute." She took a step.

I stood there with the car door open.

"Last year. The prom thing. I had to do that. It was the only thing I could do."

"No, Syd. It wasn't. You could've just told me the truth."

"Yeah." She looked exhausted. "But I didn't. Because I know you. And you'd have acted like a lunatic."

It was that word: *lunatic*. It made me think of my mother.

"No. You don't say shit like that, Syd." I was surprised by my calmness. "I am not a lunatic. I'm a person. And don't act like you had to take care of me. That's bullshit and you know it. I'm sorry about whatever went down between you and—" Hard as I tried, I found I couldn't say his name. "Whatever. I'm sorry. About everything. But I drove here to see you. I've been looking for you for months.

I've been dying worrying about you. And you can tell me to go home to my daddy. Whatever. You can go inside and close the door and we can never speak to each other again. I can live with that. Totally. But I won't stand here and let you call me names. That time is over." I didn't want to stop. I felt righteous. Correct. Now I could get in my car and drive away. I was the winner. Of what? Who cared? "Oh—and by the way, Sydney, I believe the words you forgot were: *I'm sorry*. There they are, in case you want them."

Syd shook her head quickly. She scrunched her nose. She brought her fingers up to her temples. I thought for a moment she was going to have a sneezing fit.

But she didn't sneeze.

She started to cry.

I realized after it'd started happening that I'd never seen Syd cry. Not once.

"God," she said. Her face contorted. "This is so stupid." The feeling of correctness drained out of me. There was no winner. There wasn't going to be a winner. Had I driven all this way to be the winner of an argument? To make Syd cry?

"I am sorry," she said. "Miranda. I'm sorry."

"You just left," I said after a long silence.

"I know."

"And then I find out you lied. And the phone in my glove box. Very dramatic, by the way. And you never even called or wrote a single email or anything."

"I know." It was so weird to see Syd cry. "I'm sorry."

"Well, okay. It's okay. I know." I would've preferred staying angry. That was easy. Watching Syd crying was possibly the most difficult thing I'd ever done.

"You wanna come inside?" she said.

"Yes," I said. I grabbed my phone and closed the door to my car. She nodded and walked up the stairs and put her key in the lock. I followed her, careful on the stairs in my shoes.

"Why are you wearing those fucking shoes?" she said, turning from the top step and looking down. There were still tears on her cheeks. "Oh my fucking god. Is it fucking prom? Please tell me it's not prom."

"Yes. It's prom. I don't want to talk about it. I don't want to talk about Nick."

"Does Nick know?" she asked. I could tell it hurt her even just asking.

"Yes," I said. "He knows."

She nodded.

It was dark and stale inside the trailer. To the left was a tiny kitchen. Syd opened the blinds over the sink and the afternoon light poured in. There was hardly any furniture, just a beat-up sofa and a TV in the corner sitting on a chair, a bookshelf, a folding chair, and a TV tray. Syd opened the blinds in the window over the sofa and revealed the field of onions, the road far beyond it. I could see one bedroom down the dark hall. That was it.

"Where do you sleep?" I asked. She nodded at the sofa then plopped down on it. She let down her mass of hair and shook it out. She smacked the cushion and I walked over and sat down beside her.

"Pretty glam, huh? You should've seen it when I came. It was disgusting." I noticed the kitchen was spic-and-span.

"She's bad?"

She nodded.

"I wrote her. She wrote me back. She said you weren't here."

"That was me," she said. "I wrote it with my left hand. I was sure you'd know."

"No way," I said.

"Yeah," she said. "I'm sorry about that, too."

"I guess I couldn't believe you'd come here."

"Yeah." She didn't offer anything more and I didn't press her.

We sat in silence for a while. It was cold in the trailer. There was nothing on the walls. The longer I sat there, the more questions I had. Could she go back to school and graduate? Was there any chance she could still go to Stanford? I didn't want to ask.

My phone rang again. "Crap," I said. "I'm sorry."

I answered it. "Dad," I launched in. "I'm with Syd right now. I'll be home—"

He didn't let me finish. "Okay." He was calm. It was unnerving.

"What?" I said.

"Write this down. Get a pen." He sounded exhausted.

"Do you have a pen?" I asked Syd. She got up and went to the kitchen and came back with a pen and handed it to me. "I have a pen." I held up the pen and Syd smiled.

"Write down this address: 14 Camino La Mesilla, Española."

I wrote it on the back of my hand.

"Okay," I said. "Got it. I'll be home tonight. Dad, did you hear me say that?"

"Did you get the address?"

"Yes."

"That's Benny's. We're staying here tonight. It's one

hour and fifty-eight minutes away from where you are. If you're in Alamosa, Colorado."

"I'm in Alamosa." I looked at Syd. I couldn't imagine leaving her. The notion that in a few hours I'd be watching cartoons in a roomful of cousins was preposterous.

"I'll be there," I said. "I'll call when I'm on my way."

"Yes." He was trying to keep his voice steady. "Please call."

"Okay," I said.

"Mir," he said. "I was really pissed at you. I still am. But I love you. Okay?"

"Okay." I didn't want Syd to hear me tell my dad I loved him. "Me too."

"Okay."

"Okay, bye." I hung up.

"You need to go." Syd was so vulnerable. It was weird.

"What if you came with me?" I said.

"That's really sweet." She nodded, holding back tears. "But I can't."

"What are you going to do?"

"I'm going to stay here. Until the fall. I took the GED. I got into NMSU and UNM. I think I'll go to UNM. They offered me a scholarship."

"What about Stanford?" I felt a stab of guilt for asking.

She nodded slowly. "Well. I asked if I could defer my enrollment. Until next year. I explained everything. Well, not everything. But how I had to come here and how I'm sort of taking care of my mom. I thought they'd laugh in my face, but they were actually pretty cool. The request is still under consideration. I guess I'll know sometime soon. But I don't even know if I want to go there. I only applied there because—ugh." She looked down into her lap. "It's so stupid now, I don't want to say it. But I only applied there because Samuel told me—he told me he was trying to get a visiting professorship there." She seemed not to believe what she was saying, how ridiculous it was. She took a sharp breath and held it and shook her head. "I was so stupid."

"It wasn't your fault. That guy is . . ."

"Yeah." She looked up into my eyes. "What about you? You still going to UNM?"

"I got a scholarship to UNM," I said. "A little one."

"That's awesome. Maybe we'll both go there."

It sounded so good right then, going to UNM with Syd. We could go back to the way things were before. We could be together. I could even take up again my practice of avoiding Nick Allison on campus. Everything could go back to how it was.

"I also got into Brown," I said.

Her mouth was a giant O. "Oh my god. Mir. That's amazing."

"I'm going there." I must've just been waiting to say it to Syd, because when it came out of my mouth, I knew it was true. "It's so screwed up. Nick got into Harvard. But he's going to UNM."

"Nick." She shoved my knee. "You in love? Or whatever?"

I nodded and choked up. "I screwed it up. He'll never speak to me again."

A car pulled up. "Ah shit," Syd said, sitting up. "That's her." She was suddenly nervous.

"It's okay." I reached out for her hand. "I want to see her."

"Okay." She nodded. "Yeah." We sat there on the couch, watching the door.

I heard the car door slam outside.

I turned to her. "Why did you come here, Syd?"

"I dunno," she said, staring at the door. She turned to me. "I needed my mom."

We heard the three steps. The door opened. Then she saw me. "Miranda! I wondered whose car that was!"

Patience looked old. That was the first thing I noticed. But she was the same. She opened her arms and I got up and went to her and we hugged. She was skin and bones and smelled like wine and cigarettes.

It was exactly how I remembered her smelling.

"Hi," I said.

She wasn't going to end the hug anytime soon. "Oh my goodness," she said. "I can't believe it's you. I've been telling Syd to call you. She finally called you."

"Not exactly," I said.

"Leave it alone, Mom," Syd said from the sofa.

"Oh, Syd," Patience said as she looked me up and down. Her eyes rested on my feet. "Look at those shoes." She took my hand and stepped back as if to get a better look, taking me in as if I were wearing a ball gown or a wedding dress instead of running pants and an unwashed twenty-year-old T-shirt. "My goodness gracious." She sighed. "You're grown-up, Miranda. You're an absolute beauty."

Now. My father loved me. He went out of his way to show it. But he'd never have stepped back to look at me this way. He wouldn't even know how. It was a pure mom move.

A sudden, strong wave of grief came over me as I stood

there in the middle of Patience's dark, empty living room. For the first time in so long, I missed my mother.

I didn't just miss having a mother in general. I missed having mine. The one who was not standing there in front of me in this moment. The one who'd driven away one morning while I was at school, taking the universe with her.

"You okay, sweetie?" Patience said, looking concerned.

I nodded and turned to Syd and she stood up and came over and seemed to understand why I suddenly had tears in my eyes. She put her arms around me. "They're all right shoes," she said, and I laughed through my tears. Then Syd reached over and slipped the purse off Patience's shoulder and hung it on a hook behind the door. She pointed to the couch and Patience obeyed, walking across the room and sitting down.

"How long are you staying?" Patience's face was lit up like a child's.

"I can't stay." I looked at Syd. "But maybe I can come back? For a visit. Maybe this summer, after graduation. Before I go to college."

Syd frowned and nodded. "That'd be awesome."

"You're welcome any damn time, my girl," Patience said. She sat back against the couch cushions and crossed her legs and looked at us in seeming awe. "Look at you two."

Syd and I looked at each other. "Here," Syd said, linking her arm with mine. "I'll walk you to your car." She turned back to Patience. "Did you eat the sandwich I left for you?"

"I don't believe I did, no." Patience hopped up.

"Eat it," Syd said.

Patience ignored Syd. "Oh, Miranda." She came over again and edged Syd out of the way and gave me another big, bony hug and a kiss on the cheek. "It's so good to see you."

"You too," I said. "I'll see you again soon."

"Okay," she said. Then she leaned in and whispered, "Thank you. For everything you've done for Syd. She's lucky to have you."

Syd looked down at the carpet. "Okay, come on," she said. "Wrap it up." She swung open the front door and the late afternoon sunlight poured in. "And turn on the lights," she said to Patience as she walked out and I followed.

"Okay," Patience said, watching us go.

It wasn't much of a walk to my car. I turned and hugged Syd and by the time we separated, I was crying again. "Okay," I said, trying to get my shit together.

But then we just stood there. I didn't know what was supposed to happen next. The idea that Syd could turn and walk back into that trailer was more painful than anything I could imagine.

"You should go," she said. "I've gotta force that woman to eat a sandwich."

"Yeah. My dad's having a coronary in Española."

"He came with you?"

"No. He told me to stop at a rest stop outside of So-corro this morning. And I told him I would. But then I kept going. So I guess he drove to my uncle Benny's. And now he's praying the rosary, waiting for me."

Her eyes filled with tears. "You kept driving. That's really cool. That took a lot of balls."

I grabbed her hand again. "I need to know that we're going to stay in touch. I can't not know how you are."

She nodded. "Yeah. I know. I'll call you. I promise. I'll get a phone. You'll be the first to know."

I took a deep, shaky breath. "Can I come back? For real? To see you?"

"Yeah," she said. "That'd be—" She teared up again and nodded. She stepped in and gave me a strong, fast hug, then pulled away. Then she turned back to the trailer and I watched her walk across the road and climb the rickety stairs. She looked back at me and waved. Then she opened the door and disappeared inside.

I saw the lights go on in the kitchen and I stood staring at the window for a moment, immobilized.

Then I got in the car and turned around and drove back down the weird, empty road, through the town and on toward the highway, toward my dad, who I missed right then as much as I'd ever missed anyone ever.

Before I got onto Route 84, I pulled off the road and looked at my phone. My dad and Letty had been texting all day, multiple times an hour. But Nick had only texted once, this morning, a few minutes after I'd driven away.

What's going on?

After that, nothing.

I'd screwed up irreparably. I knew now for sure.

I sat in my car and tried to think of what I could do, what I could say. It felt like something someone else had done, kicking the door and walking away and driving off without a word. But it wasn't someone else. It was me. There was no getting around that.

I'm sorry.
I tried to think of something else to say, but I couldn't.

When I pulled onto the highway, the sun was low in the western sky, and blinding. It was like the universe had exploded against my windshield and I was driving into the huge, shimmery mess it'd left behind. It was perfect, really. It felt like I was driving into a golden convergence of all my crap, a swirling accumulation of unanswered questions and bad ideas, lost causes and mysteries and desires with no end, all those wounds, healed and unhealed and unhealable, the big griefs and the little griefs, the great truths lying just outside the reach of my understanding, all those planets out there bursting with life my father would likely not live long enough to know for himself, and in the hot center of it all, the endlessly greedy heart inside my chest, consuming everything, the good and the bad, so dumb in this way, and yet so beautiful.

Nick and his tuxedo with the hole in the pocket and the father he wanted to keep secret. *I didn't want it to be happening.*

And Syd, the most brilliant person I'd ever know, scrubbing the linoleum countertops in the tiny kitchen of her mother's trailer, looking out onto a sea of onions.

The sick smell of wine and cigarettes that followed Patience everywhere, and would likely follow her right up until the end, until it consumed her entirely.

And my mother, the great blank space at the center of my life, forever leaning on a pew with her long black hair fallen into her face, somehow obscuring my own view of everything.

What was she like now? Allowing myself to wonder, even for a second, hurt like hell. My mother was a person in the world. She was real. And she was gone. My dad was right. There would never be a *someday*. Waiting for *someday* wasn't an option for us. I suddenly understood why people used the word *heartbreak*. That was just how it felt: a deep fissure, opening, cracking open. And not just for me. For all of us. For Nick, for Syd, for my dad. It was just so heavy, all this crap we'd have to carry forward into our own lives. It was cumbersome and expensive. And yet still, we'd have to find a place for it. There was no other way.

You come to a point.

My dad.

I thought of my dad. His heart—his actual heart. It was a real thing, beating right now inside his chest, two hours away from me, totally the most normal thing in my life, the most reliable.

I'd promised to call him from the road.

I called.

It rang once, and he was there.

"Mir?"

I tried to sound like I wasn't crying. "It's me."

"Are you all right?"

"Yes," I said.

The tears and the bright sun made it nearly impossible to see anything in front of me through the thick haze reflecting off my dirty windshield. I squinted through it until my eyes found the white lines on the highway.

"I'm on my way."

20

It was sunset when I pulled up to Benny's. The sky was a hard blue cut through by stacks of pink and orange clouds. Stepping out of the car, I had the feeling that if I could only get quiet enough, I'd be able to hear it.

I checked my phone again. Nick hadn't written back. I thought of all those *next times*. I'd squandered them. I tried to find a place for this new pain, this brand-new baby grief, but there was nowhere to put it.

I'd just have to carry it.

The house looked exactly the same as it had the last time we'd been here a few Christmases ago, like a house in the middle of a major renovation. Only the goat population in the side yard had grown. When I closed my car door, the goats looked up, curious. Two had escaped their enclosure and threatened to approach, but after a moment they went back to eating the tall grass at the edge of the dirt road. I was glad to be out of the car. My feet were killing me.

My dad appeared, a tall, dark figure against the light pouring out of the front door. The screen door clapped shut behind him. He stood there with his hands on his hips. He looked tired and his hair was wet. He must've just taken a shower, which meant he hadn't taken one this morning, when he got home from his run to find me gone. "Why are you wearing those shoes?" he asked.

I looked down at them. "It's prom," I said, as if that were a good enough answer. "You see this sunset?"

I didn't know if my dad was planning on launching into a lecture about responsibility right then or if he intended to wait until later, when he had more time and perhaps access to a whiteboard.

He stood on the porch a moment, then came down the steps and walked over and stood beside me. We leaned against my car and looked at the sky. I'd been dreading having to face him, to explain myself, but now I was so glad to be standing with him. So relieved.

"You okay?" he asked after a while, still looking at the sky. His voice was tired.

"Yeah." I swallowed hard and tried to keep the monsoon of tears inside my face. "I'm sorry."

"I know," he said. "I know you are." Remarkably, he didn't say any more.

"Did you talk to Nick?" I asked.

"Yes."

"He hasn't called or texted or anything."

"He went and talked to his mom. He didn't know where you'd gone, Mir."

"I screwed up," I said. "But I needed to see her."

"I know," my dad said. He looked down. "Nick told me."

"Everything? About Syd? What happened?"

My dad closed his eyes heavily. "He told me everything. Yes." He scooted over and put his arm around my shoulders. "He told me last night after you'd gone to bed. We talked. He's been struggling with this for a very long time. You know? Nick is— He's been handed a lot, Miranda."

I nodded.

"Did you see Syd's mom?"

"Yeah," I said. "She looked awful, but she was the same."

"God. Poor Syd." He shook his head. "It's so hard to see someone you love hurting." I didn't know if he meant me seeing Syd, or Syd seeing Patience, but both applied, really. I guessed it applied to him seeing me, too. In fact, it probably just went on like that forever, until all the hurting people had been seen by all the other hurting people and everyone had been accounted for.

"I want to see Mom, Dad." I was surprised I'd said it, and surprised it'd come out sounding true.

"Yeah?" He tried to smile away the threat of tears. It didn't work.

"Yeah," I answered. "I'd need you to be there. You know? But yes. I would."

"Ah, baby." He squeezed my shoulder. "You know that might not be possible."

"Oh, I know. Yeah. I know that. But I just wanted to tell you. I want to. Even if it's impossible." I leaned into him. "Because I never wanted to. Before."

"Well. Wanting is good. I've found it's sometimes almost just good enough." He swiped his tears away. "It's worked for me a lot of years." He kissed the top of my head.

"You loved her, too," I said.

"Yes. I did. Very much."

We watched the sky for a minute. "Why do you think she left?"

My dad pinned his eyes on the sky. He wasn't angry I'd asked. He drew a great breath and then let it go. "Your mom was a seeker. She was always looking for something. I don't know what. I think she got lost. She lost herself. We lost her."

"It sucks so bad," I said.

"Yes, it does."

"Hey." I looked up at him. "Did I ever tell you how Luciana told me we reminded her of Curious George and the Man with the Yellow Hat? You and me."

He laughed. "No. But damn. That's pretty good."

"Kinda. I guess. I mean, I have to be George. Who's a monkey."

"And the Man with the Yellow Hat is an imbecile."

"And your point is?"

He laughed again. "Hey, well, now can I tell you something?"

"What?"

"I know 'It's the End of the World as We Know It' came out in 1987."

"Oh god," I said. "Not again."

"I don't want you to go through life thinking your father is anything less than a walking compendium of useless music facts."

"Okay," I said.

"My catalog is complete."

"Dude. I get it."

"No. That song—it was, like, our song. Your mom's and mine. When we were really young, in middle school.

Her folks said it was the devil's music. We must've listened to it a million times. Until we knew all the words and we could sing it straight through."

I looked at him.

"What? There are a lot of words in that song."

"You're telling me your song was 'It's the End of the World as We Know It'?"

"Well. Okay. When you say it like that."

"That is so screwed up. And actually that is the devil's music, now that you mention it." He laughed. "No wonder she joined a cult." I blurted it, and then felt bad. He smacked the back of my head, but I think he did it lovingly.

The sky had changed. It was getting dark. Warm light poured out of the screen door. "We should get in," my dad said. "Letty's got enough food on for an army, and the kids are bouncing off the walls, waiting for you."

"I should take my dress in and hang it up."

"You have your dress, too?" my dad asked as I opened the door to the car and grabbed it.

"Don't ask." I hung the dress over my arm. While I was in there, I gave Jude one last look, then closed the *Lives of the Saints* and tossed it into my purse.

"What's that?" my dad said.

"Oh." Part of me didn't want to show him. It was my book—it was my only connection to my mother. It was all I had, and I feared that if I showed it to him, he'd take it away. It'd disappear, like everything else. "It's a book."

"*Lives of the Saints,*" he said. He put out his hand.

"Yeah," I said. I took the book from my purse and held it out to him.

"Damn it," he said, taking it. "I've looked everywhere for this."

"I want to keep it, okay?" I said. "It's mine."

"Of course." He flipped through the pages. He turned the book sideways and read something my mother had scribbled in a margin. He shook his head and laughed. "Damn. Your mom was funny. She was . . . something else."

He closed the book and handed it back to me. "It's yours."

I put it back in my purse.

We climbed the stairs up to the porch. "Oh, and hey. I googled your thingies."

"You did?" He stopped and turned.

"You're kind of a big shot."

"Right?" he said. "That's what I've been telling you."

"And . . . you're a blessing to me too, Dad."

His face screwed up like he might cry again, but he didn't.

"Go on in," he said as he opened the screen door. The door smacked shut behind us.

Five seconds later I was sitting in the kitchen on a child-size plastic stool while Luciana brushed my hair with a doll brush. Being five, she was very bad at it. It was painful. But with each wince of pain, I was gladder to be here. I'd hung my dress in Luciana's closet and left my shoes in there too. My heart still ached, but at least my feet were happy.

"Please sit very still," Luciana said in her sternest voice when I fidgeted. Her older brothers sat on the couch, pretending they weren't as interested in the hairstyling as they were. The oldest, Paul, was playing a video game on his phone, and the younger, Gus, was watching him.

My dad leaned against the kitchen counter next to Benny, the two of them holding beers. "Your girl's grown-up." Benny flung an arm over my father's shoulder. All of a sudden, they looked just like the photo on the mirror in our hallway.

"She still knows how to screw up pretty bad."

"Let's call her our I-25 bandita," Benny roared.

The boys laughed. Luciana flung all my hair in front of my face. "Let's not," I said from beneath it. The boys laughed again.

"Where's Letty?" I asked.

"Picking up a few things," Benny said. "We're glad you absconded this morning, bandita. We needed a family dinner. Jacob and his crew are coming up from Los Alamos." He gave my dad a sympathetic nod. "Only one missing is Maria."

Maria? It took me a moment to recognize my mother's name.

Silence fell upon the house, which had, to that moment, been very loud. The only sound was the *pew-pew-pew* of video game guns coming from Paul's phone. "Pa-blo!" Benny said in his loud, friendly voice. "Turn that shit off."

Paul simply got up and wandered into the next room and Gus wandered after him.

Benny's house was big and old. I always felt like there were rooms I'd never seen, as if the place just went on and on endlessly, little rooms leading into big ones and big ones into little ones. Letty had impeccable taste. The house had an effortless desert bohemian feel, with lamps sitting on stacks of books and solitary tiny cactuses sitting on heavy old tables. Aside from Benny's one thousand unfinished projects, the place could be on the cover of a design magazine, though Letty would never even think to thumb through one herself. Benny was slow at renovating. In the kitchen, for example, the tile above the counter had been ripped out along one wall and hadn't been replaced. I thought it'd been like that the last time we'd been here, but I couldn't be sure.

Luciana suddenly got very still. I wondered what she was doing back there. "You don't have scissors, do you?" I asked.

"No, but I can get some," she responded without missing a beat. Everyone erupted in laughter. Every time there was laughter, I felt myself on the verge of tears. It was Nick. I couldn't stop thinking of him.

"Hey, Lulu, can I take a little break?"

"Just a little one," she said, reluctantly letting go of my hair. I flipped it back and could see again.

"I'm gonna call him," I said to my dad. I grabbed my phone and walked out onto the porch before I could change my mind.

"You sure?" my dad called as I walked out.

I didn't answer.

I pressed the number and the phone rang. My throat went dry. I had no idea what I'd even say. But after three rings I knew he wasn't picking up. I waited for his voice mail. *"Hey. It's Nick. Leave a message."*

I figured I'd done a lot of missing in my life, maybe more than average. I was pretty good at it. Still, I'd never felt this before. I guessed it was that sharp feeling of love. Without Nick there to receive it, it felt more dangerous than ever, more terrible and fearsome and huge. "Hey. Hi. I just wanted to say I'm sorry. I'm so sorry. I hope we can talk. Someday. Maybe. I totally understand. If you don't want to—" Things were going downhill fast. So I hung up. I stood on the porch and stared up at the silent stars.

My dad was right. I should have just let it be.

I walked back in and gave my dad a sad little frown and he gave me one in return. I plopped back down on the too-small stool, even though Luciana had lost interest in doing my hair and was now inhaling Ruffles from a giant bowl. The stool felt like what I deserved. Punishment. I deserved to sit in the naughty chair the rest of my life.

The screen door swung open and Letty walked in carrying a bag of groceries. "Oh my god, Miranda!" she called out when she saw me. "You idiot!"

I was always shocked by how pretty Letty was in real life. Her hair was perfectly messy and she was wearing one of Benny's worn-out button-downs. Its hugeness made her seem even more tiny than usual. She made a beeline for me and bent down and flung her free arm around my neck. "I'm so glad you're here," she said. "I was praying for you all the way home from the Albertsons." She smelled perfect too. She was so good at wearing perfume, she made it seem like her natural scent.

When Letty made her way into the kitchen, Luciana looked up from where she was scarfing chips. "Lu!" Letty called when she walked over and looked into the nearly empty bowl. "You need to stop eating these chips! They're for everyone." Luciana gave me a big smile.

"I love Ruffles," she said unapologetically, her eyes

wide and her mouth covered in grease. As soon as Letty turned her back to attend to dinner, Luciana started chowing down again.

"What can I do to help?" I stood up and tried actively not to be a lump of sadness.

"Set the table?" Letty said, taking the lid off the most giant pot I'd ever seen. Steam billowed, covering her face.

"Sure," I said. "Oh my gosh, what is that?" I wandered over to her.

"Pozole," she said. "This'll fix you up." She smacked my butt and put the lid back on and then turned and gave me another big hug, this time with both arms. "We're proud of you, Miranda. You did such a good job of pissing off Pete." She turned and my dad and Benny chuckled. Then she turned back to me and put her palms on my face. "You did the right thing, *mi'jita*. You're a good friend."

I loved Letty. She and my mom had been best friends growing up. My mom had introduced Letty and Benny in college. Letty had known my mom longer than my dad had, and her memory of my mother's sanity and goodness was long and strong and her faith that my mother would return remained unshakeable. That she continued to love my mom and pray for her fiercely, as if battling the devil for her soul, meant a lot to me. For all these years, Letty had done a good enough job loving my mom for both of us. It only occurred to me right then, standing in her kitchen, that all the time Letty had been giving me advice about how to deal with Syd's disappearance, she was speaking from her own experience. Her best friend had been *gone, not missing* too.

I went to the cabinet that seemed most logical for keeping dishes, but inside I found an assortment of different sized Crock-Pots. I continued to open and close cabinets until Benny, obviously amused, finally spoke up. "Dishes are over here, bandita."

"Oh." The dishes were in fact in a cabinet by the stove most people would reserve for pots and pans. I wondered what my father, who was so fussy about his own kitchen, thought of the way Benny and Letty lived. I think he loved it. He watched everything going on with what looked to me like longing. Maybe Benny and Letty and their kids made him imagine a future with my mom that had never come to be. Or maybe Benny's face screwed him up. Because there was something of the person he'd loved in there.

I set the dining table for eight and the kids' table for five.

"When's Jacob's family coming?" I asked.

The evening had taken on the feeling of a holiday dinner. I'd located ten mismatched napkins and was hot on the trail of another three. I tried to muster up some cheerfulness even though I knew prom had started in Cruces and Nick hadn't called or texted.

I was sitting on the sofa, spaced-out. Luciana had commandeered my phone and was sitting in my lap playing a Barbie game with the volume turned all the way up when the screen door opened and my uncle Jacob's family came through. Jacob was bald and quiet, an insurance agent with a passion for fly-fishing, and his twin sons, my cousins Marco and Tony, were eleven and extraordinarily

well behaved. His wife, Vanessa, was a real estate agent—
the third-highest grossing one in the Los Alamos area,
she had once found a savvy way to tell us. If Syd were
here, she'd have attacked her with fake friendliness, trying to draw out the dumb motivational sayings a person
like Vanessa was likely to live by.

"Miranda," she said in her overly professional way,
waving to me with a few fingers. Her sons stared at me
like I was a freak. God only knows what they'd heard
about my waywardness on the drive over.

"Hey, Tony, hey Marco," I said as they scurried past me.

After many arrangements and rearrangements and
one epic negotiation on the part of Paul, who ended up
squeezing in and eating with the grown-ups, we were
ready to sit down. As soon as we'd gathered at the table,
though, it became clear that, after all that searching, I'd
set the wrong dishes. I'd put down plates. You ate pozole
from a bowl, of course. I hopped up to collect the plates
and help Letty gather bowls of all sizes from various cabinets. When everyone finally had one (my dad ended up
with something that looked suspiciously like it'd been designed for use by an animal), we lined up at the stove and
served ourselves from the giant pot.

Cilantro, lime, and onion were piled high on plates on
the table, along with stacks of warm tortillas wrapped in
dishcloths. With all our mismatched bowls of steaming
pozole, Letty's old farm table looked perfect, like something a rich Santa Fean would pay good money to achieve.
At the center, an unwieldy bunch of wildflowers sprung
from a pickle jar. Beside it, I noticed, was a little santo. It
was facing the other way, and when I reached over and
turned it around, I saw that it was Saint Jude. Of course.

This one wasn't like any other. It'd been hand-carved from wood. It resembled no celebrity.

I was so hungry when finally everyone had sat down, I dug my spoon in and took a glorious first bite before I realized I was the only one who'd started eating. My father, seated to my left, knocked my knee under the table hard.

There was to be a prayer before the meal.

It would've been more awkward to remove the spoon from my bowl, so instead I lay the handle against the side and put my hands in my lap.

Benny looked around the table. He was such a sentimental guy. That was one reason my father loved him. Benny was never shy to tell the people he loved how much he cared about them. "Well," he began solemnly. "We're here tonight because of our bandita, Miranda. Our sister Maria's girl—and our brother Pete's—who's all grown-up and ready to rebel."

I could feel my face turn red. My dad was smiling. I stared into my bowl.

"Who'd like to lead us in prayer tonight? Anyone can. Paul, you're sitting at the big table, you want to do it? Peter? How about you?"

"Hard pass," my dad said quietly. Benny and Letty chuckled.

"I'll do it." Everyone turned and looked at me. I nodded tentatively at the stunned faces. "I'd like to. If that's all right?"

"Sure," Benny said, giving my dad a quick glance. *"Vámanos."*

My father looked at me, worried I was making a disastrous joke.

But it wasn't a joke. I nodded to reassure my dad.

Everyone got silent. The little lick of flame carved above Saint Jude's head was painted a bright orange. I focused on it, trying to forget that I couldn't pray. I remembered how I'd told Nick it was stupid not to consider going to Harvard simply out of a fear of becoming like his dad. But wasn't that exactly what I was doing? Had my mother taken God away from me? Or was I just scared to have a God of my own, a God without her? It was my crap. I was sick of not having anywhere to put it. So maybe I'd just own it. I'd take care of it. It was mine now. And it'd always been mine.

I closed my eyes and reached for my father's hand on my one side and Letty's on the other. I heard the rest of the hands at the table find the ones beside them. I noted how good it felt to hold hands like that, to be together in this room. My father had kept in touch with Benny and Jacob, the brothers of the woman who'd broken his heart. He liked them—he loved them, of course—but I also knew he'd done that for me. This family of people who looked like me was one more gift from my father.

I swallowed hard. *Four score and seven years ago.* I pushed it gently aside. "God?" I said cautiously, as if he might answer back. "Lord," I continued, steadier. "Whoever you are. Whatever. Thank you." My father squeezed my hand and I took that as encouragement. "Thank you for this wonderful food we're about to enjoy, and for the family here tonight, and for those who couldn't be here." My voice shook, but I drove through it. "We ask that you guide us and help us to do the right thing. Help us to love one another." I took a giant breath. "And we ask that you protect my mother, Maria Black. That you help her." I felt the tears come down my face. I paused. My father tightened his grip on my hand. "Oh. And if you could help my dad find his Goldilocks planet—and maybe do a NASA press conference—that'd be super-cool too." I heard a few laughs. "Amen?" I asked, tentative.

"Amen," the room said.

I opened my eyes. I wiped my tears. When I turned to Letty, she nodded. She approved of my prayer. Letty was definitely the most religious person I knew, so I took that as a solid win.

It was done. I'd done it. I'd prayed. It was so stupid. All this time, I'd been waiting for something to come back to me, something that had been taken away. My *zero*. But instead it felt like something had escaped. It'd been inside me this whole time. I just needed to let it out.

"Good prayer, bandita," Benny said. He, too, had tears in his eyes. He lifted his beer bottle. "To Maria," he said. Everyone picked up their glasses.

"To Maria," we all said. My father and I looked at each other. He nodded the nod that had for so long meant the same thing: we were going to be okay. Things were going to be fine. We'd get through.

"It's the end of the world as we know it," I whispered.

"And I feel fine." He shook his head. "I can't believe you don't like that song."

I shrugged and he kissed my head. "Good job," he whispered.

The pozole tasted so good, I emptied my first bowl in a matter of minutes. When I got up from the table to serve myself another, the clock on the stove taunted me. *It's too late,* it said with its blocky red digits. *Get over it.*

I stood in front on the giant pot of pozole and let the steam hit my face. I ladled another bowlful and headed back to my seat. There were conversations happening all over the table, but I was content to be alone with my soup. Luciana was sitting with my phone hidden beneath the kids' table, still transfixed by her Barbie game. It was probably for the best she had my phone. That way I couldn't check every five seconds to see if Nick had replied. I'd told her to tell me if I got any calls or texts while she was playing, and she claimed to know what I was talking about, but I couldn't be sure. I was just considering going over and taking a peek to check for myself when Paul suddenly rose from the end of the table and walked tentatively to the front door.

He peered out the screen door.

Everyone got quiet. I could hear that the goats were bleating in the side yard. Benny looked like he might stand up, but then he didn't.

"Hi." I heard a voice come from the darkness. Someone was out there. I glanced down at Saint Jude and had a moment of total heart-thumping bewilderment, thinking I'd called up an actual miracle and when Paul opened the door my mother would be standing on the porch, her dark hair pouring over her shoulders. *THE IMPOSSIBLE!* It'd happened. She'd come home.

My father looked at me.

"What is it?" I asked him, frightened. "What's going on?"

But before he could answer, the voice spoke a little louder. "Is Miranda here?"

"What's going on, Dad?"

He smiled and shrugged.

"Yeah." Paul put his hand on the door handle then hesitated. He turned to Benny. Benny nodded. The room couldn't have been quieter as he opened the door. And then it was like a dream. Total unreality on every level. It was Nick. He was standing in the living room, looking shocked to have so many faces staring at him. He turned red instantly, of course. But when his eyes finally found mine, his face relaxed and he smiled. The only sound in the universe was the jangly music emanating from the Barbie game on my phone in Luciana's hand. She was holding it, dumbstruck, staring at Nick. *"That's not it. Try again!"* Barbie said in her syrupy voice. *"Keep trying. You can do it!"*

I stood up, stunned, and for what seemed like a very long time, the two of us just stood there in the silence, staring at each other.

"Hi." It was all I could think to say.

He smiled self-consciously. "Hi." I was so astonished to see him that it took me a moment to recognize that something about him was weird. But then I saw it. Of course. He was wearing his Eagle Scout uniform, complete with a red-and-blue-striped neckerchief and a very dumb beret, which he snatched off his head and clutched in his hands politely as soon as I laid my eyes on it.

Paul let go of the door and it smacked loudly into the silent room.

"Come on!" Barbie said from under the table. *"Girl, you got this!"*

"Wow," I said, my eyes steady on him. "This is definitely the weirdest, most embarrassing thing that's ever happened to me."

Nick smiled wide. "I'm so embarrassed for you."

"May I be excused?" I asked the silence. I didn't know if I was asking my dad or Letty or God or anyone at all. Really, I was only making it clear to everyone that I was going to walk outside with the boy I loved and no one on Earth or any other planet was going to stop me.

"Yes," a few adult voices and Luciana said at once.

I walked over to Nick and stared up at him, then took his hand and pushed open the screen door. "Wait." I stopped suddenly and turned around. Nick looked confused. "Yes," I said to him. "Here. Lulu, come here. Show Nick that rad Barbie game." Luciana stood and walked over dutifully. "Here." I pushed Nick back inside. "Lulu, this is Nick." Nick bent down and put his hand out and she shook it. "Actually, everyone: this is Nick." I looked to Luciana. "He's a real Eagle Scout, Lu." Luciana looked way too impressed.

"Two seconds," I said to Nick. I gestured to the sofa and he sat down reluctantly. Luciana climbed up and sat next to him and shoved the Barbie game into his face.

I bolted to Luciana's room, threw open her closet, and found my dress hanging there limply on the tiny hanger, the fabric pooled on the floor. It was still gorgeous. I slipped out of my clothes and put it on. I yanked out the ponytail holder and let my hair fall onto my shoulders. I searched Luciana's room for a mirror but could only find the tiny one inside her dollhouse. It was so small, I couldn't even see my whole face in it. I spotted some Hello Kitty lip balm on the dresser and dabbed some on my lips. It was sticky, like glue, and smelled like overripe strawberries. I wiped it off with the back of my hand.

I put on my gold shoes. I stepped out of Luciana's room.

Everyone at the table turned and looked at me. I died. I walked through the dining room and into the living room.

"Get the glitter bombs! They give you the power!" Luciana was standing up on her knees and shouting directly into Nick's face. I noticed she'd put on her Daisy Scout sash. "Why do you keep missing the glitter bombs?!"

"Oh well—they're bombs." He was concentrating so hard. "I thought I was supposed to avoid them."

"No!" she yelled. "You have to get them!"

He glanced up and saw me. "Oh," he said. He placed the phone gently down on the couch. Barbie jingled. Luciana looked at me, then at Nick, then back at the phone.

"You're going to lose!" she said urgently.

"Here," Nick said. He handed her the phone without taking his eyes off me.

He stood up. He glanced over to the tableful of people staring at us. I grabbed his hand and led him out the door, down the steps, and into the dark night. The goats bleated a welcome. I turned back to see Luciana's face at the window, pressed there like a fly squashed on a windshield, my phone glowing with pink Barbieness in her hand. A hand grabbed her shoulder and her face was removed from the glass.

I turned back to Nick. I had no idea what to say to him. I looked into his face.

Thankfully, he spoke first. "Okay," he said. He shoved the beret into his back pocket and slipped his phone from out of his front pocket. "Three things." He swiped it on. "Thing one." He handed it to me. I stared at it, puzzled.

"It's an empty room?" I said. The small room had beige carpeting vacuumed in meticulous stripes, a twin bed without sheets, and a window with the blinds closed.

"My empty room."

"You moved out?" I asked, alarmed.

"We moved out. My mom, too." I didn't know if it was good news or bad news or both. "He's accepting a job at a lab in Phoenix."

"Whoa," I said. "Is that good?"

"Yeah," he said. "I think so. I mean, it sucks, of course. But yeah."

I handed the phone back to him.

"And then." He looked at me and smiled and swiped. "Thing two." He handed me the phone again. It was a screenshot of an email from the Boy Scouts of America, thanking him for accepting the summer internship in the Jemez Mountains. My heart fell a little. If he'd taken the internship, it meant he'd accepted the offer from UNM. We'd be living across the country from each other.

"Awesome," I said, and I tried to feel it. "That's awesome. You're going. You're doing it."

"But wait." He took his phone back and swiped again. "I had to sort of negotiate that one. Because it was part of the offer from UNM." He handed the phone back to me, but I couldn't take my eyes off his face. I still couldn't believe he was standing in front of me. He nodded at the phone. "Look at it," he said firmly.

I looked at it. It was another screenshot of another email.

This one began, *Dear Nicholas, I'm delighted you've accepted your place in the next freshman class at Harvard.*

"What?" My eyes shot up to his. He was smiling. "Nick!"

"Yeppers." He shrugged.

I threw my arms around his neck. "I'm so happy—I'm so happy for you."

"Thanks," he said. "I just hope I can get a job with a degree from that place."

"This is what you want?"

"It is," he said. "I talked to your dad a lot about it last night. And today I talked to my mom—I was all ready to fight. But the first thing she said, and I'm quoting her here: 'I don't give a shit where you go to college.'"

"What? Your mom's awesome."

"Yeah. And I just sort of realized you were right. I can't live my life that way. Being scared. All of a sudden, it just was like: yeah. This is it."

"I'm sorry, Nick." I pulled back. "I'm sorry for what I said this morning. I didn't mean it. And I'm sorry for leaving. I honestly didn't even know I was leaving. I just—left."

"I'm sorry too," he said. "I should've told you everything." He looked down at my dress. "You look amazing, by the way." He seemed suddenly nervous.

"You look amazing too," I said. He laughed. "So this is it? This is the uniform."

"I figured it was a go-big-or-go-home sort of deal, you know. Driving all the way up here. The only way this'll work is if we're honest with each other. And so, you know. I'm just going tell you the truth. And the truth is I have achieved the highest advancement ranking attainable within the Boy Scouts of America." He smiled.

"Oh my god, I'm so glad you're here," I said.

"I didn't have anything better to do. It's prom night, but my date stood me up."

"That's cold," I said. "What a bitch."

"Nah, she's cool."

"Oh. Good," I said. "Here, come here." I reached up and adjusted his neckerchief.

"Here." He leaned down and kissed me so sweetly.

"Hey, you wanna see something?" I asked.

"You know I love seeing things."

"Wait here for two seconds?" I took off back up the stairs.

"This didn't end well for me last time," he called.

I turned and gave him a Scout's salute. "I promise. I'll be right back."

I ran into the house. Everyone had resumed eating and talking but got silent again when the door slapped. Vanessa was clearly getting annoyed with my shenanigans. She shot her boys a look to indicate I was an example of one very particular way they should never even consider behaving.

"Uncle B, can I drive your truck? Just over the hill and down into the valley?"

Without hesitation, he reached into his pocket and tossed me his keys.

I couldn't believe it. "Oh my god, really? Thank you!" I turned to run back out.

"Bandita." He stopped me with his big voice.

"Yes, sir," I said, turning back to him, breathless.

"Don't mess up my truck."

"I won't," I said. "I promise."

"Bandita," he said again.

"Yes," I said.

"Don't mess up my truck."

"I swear," I said. "I won't even change the radio station."

He furrowed his brow. "Okay, *ándale*, then. Go get your boy."

"I love you!" I shouted into the room.

I ran back out and around the side of the house where Benny's giant silver Ford F-150 was parked under the carport, gleaming. It was daunting. I hiked up my dress and climbed up into the cab. I pushed the seat way up and started the truck. The engine rumbled on. I felt like I was sitting behind the wheel of a semi. I backed out carefully, inch by inch, then turned around and pulled out of the driveway, stopping where Nick was standing by the side of the dirt road, looking at the goats, his hands in his pockets and a big smile on his face. When, after many trials, I finally figured out which button did what, I rolled down the passenger-side window.

"Hey, you," I called down to him. "Get in my truck."

He got in and closed the door. "This is a freakin' truck," he said.

"I know a place," I said.

I pulled forward and turned down the rough dirt road adjacent to Benny's. The goats in the side yard stopped what they were doing to watch us rumble past. The two who'd been out earlier must've found their way back into the enclosure. One goat was standing on top of the little house at the center of the pen and looked confused and unhappy about it.

A little ways down, the road got steep and took us up onto a tall mesa. On the other side, there was nothing.

Glorious nothing. Just high desert and the little road going off into the pure darkness.

I drove slowly. "I feel like a boss," I said. I turned on the radio and country music started blaring. "Nope," I said, and switched it off.

We went about a mile farther, the darkness becoming more and more profound. Then I stopped and turned off the truck.

"Watch." I turned off the headlights. It was pitch-black. "Look." I pointed up, out the windshield.

And there it was. The Milky Way. My old God. My *zero*. Just the same as I remember seeing it for the first time on the hood of my dad's car, still so close that it felt like I could reach up and touch it.

"Whoa," Nick said, looking out the windshield.

"Right?" I said. "My dad used to bring us out here. But come on. *Ándale, pues.*"

We climbed out of the truck and walked to the back and I pulled down the tailgate. "Little help, Eagle Scout?" I said, and Nick put his hands around my waist and helped me up. Then he hopped onto the tailgate himself.

Because my uncle Benny was a self-respecting person, he kept his truck spotless, even the bed. There wasn't even a stray leaf in there. "Check it," I said. I tried to maintain as much dignity as I could as I hiked up my skirt and climbed on my knees into the bed and lay back. Nick lay back beside me. I loved the feeling of his body—his being—next to mine.

"Wow," he said again, quietly.

We let it be silent for a long time. I still couldn't quite believe Nick was here. He'd driven all the way here—to eternity—for me. I reached for his hand.

"Is Syd going to be all right?" he asked.

"I don't know," I answered. "I think so."

The silence returned. It felt like the silence wanted to be part of our conversation. It was that huge, and that insistent. It was the only thing that was certain—right there, all around us.

The silence wasn't going anywhere.

"I've had a crush on you since freshman year." I offered this truth to Nick and the sky and the big, silent night.

He turned to me then turned back to the stars. "The single biggest fight my mom and I ever had was after freshman year. Because she wanted me to switch from French to Spanish. She thought Spanish would be more useful. And there was no way in hell."

"For reals?" I smiled.

"I hate French, Mir."

"And you're so terrible at it too." I laughed and looked at the stars. They were so bright and so close, I could feel them inside me, inside my eyes, inside my brain. For a moment I had that same weird feeling I'd be able to hear them, if only I could get quiet enough. They were ready to talk. They were going to answer all the big questions. They were going to account for all the longing and not knowing and wanting and wanting and wanting.

But, no. It was only silence. It was only our breathing, and the rest of our lives out there, waiting for us. Unknown. Unknowable.

"I'm going to Brown," I said.

"I figured that," he said. "I mean, I hoped."

"I decided before you. Just so you know."

"Okay," he said.

"Because. You know Brown is, like, an hour away from Harvard."

"It's actually one hour and twenty-one minutes by train," he said. "Then there's a nineteen-minute walk from the station to the Brown campus. So, me to you, it's one hour and forty minutes all together. Give or take a few minutes, depending on which dorm you end up in."

I felt my heart rise up in my chest. It felt like it was floating there above me. "Nah." The stars got all smeary through my tears. "Your math's off, nerd."

"What?" He sounded actually offended.

"Do you really think I wouldn't meet you? At the station?"

"Oh," he said. "God. I hadn't even thought of that."

"We walk together," I said.

"Yeah," he answered. "We walk together."

We looked back to the stars. Somewhere deep in my memory I could hear my dad slapping the hood of his car, saying, *The Milky Way is right here!*

"Oh my god." I turned to him. "This is it."

"This is what?" He turned to me.

"The do-over."

His smile came slowly. "The do-over," he said.

"We won." I offered up my fist and he bumped it.

"We won!" he yelled into the giant, silent night.

"Suck it, haters!" I called out.

The silence vanished our words.

We stayed out there a long time, looking up.

ACKNOWLEDGMENTS

My thanks to those who read this book and, with their light, helped it grow: Kimberly Belflower, Carra Martinez, Steve Moore, Jenna Jaco, Sherry Kramer, Naomi Shihab Nye, Rachel Feferman, Susannah Benson, Beth Eakman, Dalia Azim, Quetta Carpenter, Graham Reynolds (whose catalog is complete), Abe Young, Travis Riddle, Clair Homan, and James Magnuson. Kirk Lynn, always and forever my favorite reader, thank you.

I'm grateful to Reed Elliot at NASA for his insights, and to Rolfe Shmidt who explained pure mathematics to me in one pristine email. My friend David Modigliani went to Harvard and he seems to have turned out fine. I appreciate his thoughtfulness on the subject. Tennessee, Jensen, and Ophelia: my NM teen squad, thanks for answering so many weird questions. Without the support of St. Edward's University, especially Dean Sharon Nell, I wouldn't have written this book. Thank you.

I'm indebted most of all to Sarah Barley at Flatiron Books, and to my agent, Emily Forland. You two have given this book so much—so much time and attention and smarts and care. I simply can't give enough *thank-yous* for all you've given me.